Beneath The Scars

A. M. Carroll

ISBN: 0999235702
ISBN 13: 9780999235706
Library of Congress Control Number: 2017950128
Shalimar Press, Jamesville, NY

Prologue

*H*e follows her down the stairs, into the subway station, and then onto the northbound 6 train. It is a busy night on the train—Friday night from downtown Manhattan—and no doubt, she is now on her way home to the Upper East Side. He didn't intentionally run into her this time, although he does know where she frequents and lives. Anytime he wants to see her, he can. She is a creature of habit if nothing else. He has kept tabs on her from the first night they crossed paths, approximately twenty years ago, when she was just a child.

He considers himself a social scientist, and she is one of his social experiments. But unlike most scientists, who sit in labs all day long, he is out in the field, working, inflicting pain and trauma on his subjects and then studying how they respond. And so far, she has exceeded all his expectations, far more than that of his other subjects to whom he has caused trauma. Humans can be so predictable. Usually, when a person experiences a horrifying event, the person will take one of two roads: use the event to increase his or her sense of purpose and meaning, or succumb to drugs as a means of self-medication and coping.

Lacey Burke has taken the former road, becoming a superstar cop among New York's finest. She had graduated first in the police academy and then skyrocketed to the level of detective, racking up numerous service awards along the way. He was at her podium ceremony when the mayor thanked her for her stellar service record. He always takes care to blend into the crowd, wearing various disguises so his subjects don't recognize him. But tonight, it is an accident that he is on the same subway train as she, so he is not wearing any disguise. He wants to get close to her, to see if she will remember him and all that he did to shape the outcome of her life so far.

If she knew how much I have helped her, she would probably thank me, he thinks to himself as he is standing in the subway train, watching her play on her phone. She looks up and makes eye contact with him and then looks away, as though she didn't see him, as though he doesn't exist.

Bitch, he thought, if you only knew how much influence I have had on your life, then maybe you wouldn't look right through me.

Not taking any chances that she will look up again and remember him, he takes a step back and mixes in with the crowd.

Chapter 1

I come up, gasping for air.

"Help! I can't swim!" I scream.

I am struggling to breathe. For every mouthful of air I take in, I also take in a mouthful of water.

Out of nowhere, a man's arm grabs me and yanks me out of the water. I lay on the cold, wet cement surrounding the pool, fighting to breathe, gasping for air.

"Help me, Lacey!" she screams. I look at the other little girl, still in the water. She is drowning. Flailing her arms, she is screaming, "Help me!"

I reach out my arm, but she is too far away to grab it.

"Grab my arm!" I yell anyway, because I don't know how else to help her.

I look over to the man who just pulled me out of the water.

"Help her!" I shout at him. "Help her!" I shout again. Why is he just standing there watching her drown?

The man looks at me and slowly backs away into the shadows from where he came. I can no longer see his face, but I can feel him still there. He is watching her drown.

I frantically scream for help as I watch her little head go under the water, bobbing up and down. My arm is not long enough to reach her. And I cannot swim myself; otherwise, I would jump back in the water.

I wake up screaming. The nightmare is always the same. I do not know what it means. I am about five or six in the nightmare, the same as the other little girl who is drowning. The man who pulls me from the water is always the same. I don't know who he is. Who is he? Who is the other little girl drowning? Where are we?

The nightmares started approximately six months ago. I was riding the subway home after meeting a friend for dinner in downtown Manhattan. Sitting in my seat, distracted by my phone, I happened to look up and made eye contact with a man who was standing in front of me. He was holding onto a pole to keep his balance, and when I looked up, our eyes met for a brief second. He was not a particularly attractive man, very plain and nondescript. If we hadn't made eye contact, I probably would never have noticed him on the train. I went back to looking at my phone, not thinking anything of the incident or of who the man was. The next time I looked up from my phone, he was gone. That night was the first night I had the nightmare of the little girl and me drowning. The man who pulled me out of the water but watched the other little girl drown was the same man I had seen on the subway.

Chapter 2

I lace up my sneakers and take off toward the park. Running always energizes me. Some days I run two miles; some days I run six miles. Whatever I feel like at the moment and however much time I have dictates the distance. It is a beautiful spring day in New York City. Warm enough not to need a jacket but cool enough to keep the sweat at bay. Up ahead Jason is jogging. Jason Reed is my partner at work. We are undercover police detectives for the New York City Police Department. Jason is more of a push-up and pull-up kind of guy who feels obligated to do some cardio here and there, mainly because I harass him about not being able to keep up with me when running down suspects.

"Hey," I say as I approach him from behind. "Early night?"

Last time I saw Jason was at Manny's Bar, when I had decided to head home around midnight. I know he was trying to score with some random girl at the bar, so I am surprised to see him in the morning hours, let alone working out.

"Had a great night, thanks for asking, Lacey. I just needed some fresh air," he says with a wink.

"Ugh. No details, please," I request with an eyeball roll.

I've known Jason for about two years. We met when we became partners in the NYPD's Major Crimes Unit. He certainly is one of

NY's finest, which is why he always has a plethora of girls falling all over him. We instantly clicked, and he became one of my good friends, but sometimes it's tough to stomach what a womanizer he is—especially since, over this past year, I think I have fallen in love with Jason. I have been fighting those feelings by reminding myself what a player he is or how it would be foolish to risk what a great friendship we have. And so I've been keeping myself busy with my current boyfriend, Tyler Hathaway.

"What's the plan for tonight?" he asks, trying to keep up with me.

"Some charity event," I say, slowing down my pace.

"Money?" Jason asks, referencing one of his many nicknames for Tyler.

"Of course. Who else would drag me to such an event?"

"Skip it, and do happy hour with me," Jason offers.

"Oh, please, Jay. I just hold you back from scoring," I tease. "It's easier for you if I'm not around."

"Whatever, Lacey. I don't have a problem scoring either way… just thought you would have a better time tonight without your douche boyfriend."

"You're right; I would. Text me where you end up, and maybe I'll meet you out later," I say with a wave, as I pick up my pace and run ahead of him.

I am used to the negative comments regarding Tyler. Despite my efforts to have Jason and Tyler become friends, or at least *friendly*, the two men do not like each other. Each time the three of us hang out, Tyler inevitably insults Jason. Not on purpose, but the way Tyler talks to people usually ends up being offensive to the person on the receiving end. And then I have to interfere as peace-keeper and beg Jason not to take it personally and refrain from killing Tyler.

Tyler is incredibly wealthy and, considering his age, seen by many as an overachiever on Wall Street. He's twenty-seven years old but has accomplished more in the world of finance than most people accomplish in a lifetime. He founded his own investment bank a few years ago and uses the profits to buy real estate all over the world. He is frequently traveling around the globe to manage his investments and buy new ones. After initially meeting Tyler, I wanted nothing to do with him. I found him to be pompous and arrogant and still do. After reluctantly agreeing to a date, I found that I loved the experiences that one is exposed to when money is no object. Where Jason gives me his time, Tyler gives me jewelry, clothing, and trips to places to which I never would have gone otherwise.

At seven fifteen in the evening, the intercom to my apartment buzzes, informing me of Tyler's arrival in the lobby—well, it is Tyler's driver, informing me that Tyler is here and waiting for me in his car. One of my biggest annoyances regarding Tyler is that he never comes up to my apartment. It is always someone, usually his driver, informing me of his arrival downstairs. I do one last mirror check, grab my purse, and head out the door.

In front of my building sits Tyler's stretch, some German-made import. The driver opens my door, and I slide in.

"You look beautiful as always, Lacey," Tyler acknowledges me, barely looking up from his cell phone.

Tyler normally keeps his light-brown hair very short, but he has let it grow out a little bit; tonight he has it slicked back. He is sexy in a sophisticated, mature sort of way. Most people who meet him think he is older than twenty-seven. He's not going to stop traffic, but once you notice him, he garners a second look. And he reeks of money, which is why most women do notice him. All his clothes are designer, expensive, and tailored to fit perfectly. His wire-framed glasses nicely accentuate his face and give him the look of being smart as well as handsome.

I lean over and kiss him on the cheek, hoping to distract him from his phone. He turns his head so that our lips meet and gently returns a kiss on my mouth. After a few seconds, he pulls away and turns back to his phone. I sigh and sit back in my seat. There have been times where we skipped whatever function we were going to and instead had sex in the back of his limo while riding around the city.

"I can't miss tonight's events, Lacey," Tyler says, reading my mind.

"That's fine. And thank you for the dress and shoes," I answer, tilting my head and giving him a shy smile.

I'm normally not a shy person, but for some reason this man reduces me to feeling like an eight-year-old. It might have something to do with the fact that he has a habit of talking to me as though I were a child. We are very different because of social status and upbringing, which causes Tyler to talk down to me sometimes. But unlike Jason I don't take it personally since he is condescending to most people. He has lived a very polished life, whereas I spent most of my childhood bouncing from foster home to foster home in some of New York's worst neighborhoods. I am what most of Tyler's inner circle would refer to as "white trash," and so it has become Tyler's goal to force a more sophisticated way of living upon me.

Earlier that day Barneys department store had delivered a red, form-fitting cocktail dress that fit me like a dream. I swept my long blond hair into a half up-do to show off the diamond-stud earrings Tyler had previously given me. He does have impeccable taste when it comes to clothes and jewelry. For events such as this one, Tyler calls one of his favorite stores, usually Barneys, and tells them the event details and what he would like to see me wearing. The store's personal shopper then locates an item based on his specifications and delivers it to my door, complete with matching shoes and any applicable jewelry or hosiery that would also work with the ensemble. Most of the pricier stores on Fifth Avenue know Tyler and have my measurements on file, so there are no unknowns when it comes to my size and what would work with my body type. Between Tyler and the store's personal shopper, my attire always manages to be perfect for the event at hand.

"So, what is the deal for tonight?" I ask.

"The deal, my dear, is a charity event for the Met and then dinner and drinks at Lombardi's," Tyler replies, peering over his Lauren eyeglasses at me. He is really looking at me for the first time tonight and casually lets his dark-brown eyes move down the length of me.

"You really do look beautiful, Lacey," Tyler says, causing me to blush, which in turn causes him to sigh. He goes back to looking at his cell phone. "You should try not to blush so much. It's very childish and rudimentary."

"Right, I'll work on that," I reply half-jokingly but know he wouldn't catch the sarcasm.

Does he really think it's something I enjoy doing and can control? I know Tyler is Mr. Good-for-Right-Now. He is excessively stiff and too serious to deal with long term. This relationship has been going on for a little over two years, and I can feel the end approaching fast, even though he has been trying to move it to the next level. He keeps suggesting we move in together. As tempting as that is—because he has a beautiful town house overlooking Central Park—I know I don't want to marry him. I have been avoiding any move that would bring us closer to matrimony.

We pull up to an indiscreet building that has a long, black carpet thrown in front of it with photographers hanging around on both sides. That's one thing about rich people. They love to have their picture taken while they give away money. There's no such thing as anonymous donors with these guys. I slip my arm through Tyler's as we make our way into the building. Wearing high heels, my five-seven frame equals Tyler, who stands about five-nine. I have told him before how uncomfortable I am in heels, but it's a moot point; he buys them for me anyway. I think he feels taller when I look taller.

Once inside Tyler immediately starts the whole meet-and-greet façade. I recognize Laura Steinberg, a pretty brunette whom I've met at other functions, and I quietly slip away from Tyler and gravitate toward her. Laura's dad is business partners with Tyler at the investment bank that Tyler established, and we have become friendly after seeing each other at many of the same functions.

"Lacey Burke! I'm so happy to see you here. Aren't these functions so dreadful?"

Laura leans in to give me the fake hug and air kiss on the cheek. Laura is about my age, maybe twenty-four or twenty-five. She has shoulder-length brown hair that is blown out straight every time I see her. And her skin always has a flawless Coppertone glow, as though she just returned from a spa in St. Bart's. But most noticeable about Laura are her big brown eyes, which are almost too large for her face and appear out of proportion with the rest of her facial features. But for some reason they work for her and make her pretty in a sultry sort of way.

"How are you?" I ask as I reciprocate the fake air kiss.

"Follow me. I need a drink," Laura declares.

"Tony, I would love a beer. But my dad would stroke out to see me drinking a beer at this dump, so make it champagne, please," Laura barks as she approaches an elderly gentleman in a tuxedo working the bar.

"Coming right up, Miss Steinberg," Tony replies with a smile.

"I'll also have the same, Tony, thank you," I say as I watch Tyler across the room mingling, not even noticing where I am.

"Why does he bother to bring me?" I ask Laura as we lean up against the bar and survey the crowd. "He doesn't even realize that I left his side."

"Probably because most people think he's gay. That's why he brings you. I mean, I know he's not, but there have been rumors," Laura informs me.

"Oh, so that's why he likes me on his arm," I say as I gulp the drink Tony has just handed me. "For the record, he's not. He's actually insatiable in the sack, just doesn't like showing much affection in public."

"Yeah, I know he's not gay. But he spends most of his life working, never really having time for a relationship. And then he has impeccable taste when it comes to clothing. I guess most people just assumed he had a man at home who he wasn't willing to parade around town with," Laura says. "So anyway, Lacey, what's it like being a cop in this city? I would be scared shitless having to deal with some of the people I see walking around."

"It's not so bad," I say, taking another drink from Tony. "Most days are actually pretty boring. It's not like in the movies. We are usually sitting around doing surveillance and waiting for something to happen."

As if on cue, my cell phone notifies me of a text message from Jason:

We are at Brandy's if you can escape. Rachel is here.

Brandy's is a bar on the Upper East Side of Manhattan, not far from where I live. It's a casual neighborhood bar that Jason and I frequently go to. Rachel is Jason's younger sister, who is in her senior year at New York University. Because of her studies at NYU, she doesn't get out much, and I'm not able to hang out with her as often as I would like. Now I just have to figure out how to get out of here.

"Are you here with a date, Laura?" I ask, trying to make small talk while I plan my exit.

"No, I'm not currently seeing anyone. I'm here with my dad and trophy stepmom. What a money-hungry pig she is. She is five years older than me and can't decide if she should try to be motherly to me or act more like my friend. I'm like, don't bother me, and hands off my inheritance."

"Everyone here must look at me the same way for dating Tyler?" I ask, not really caring what anyone else in this room thinks of me but still making small talk.

"No. You didn't break up a marriage, and Tyler doesn't have anyone to leave his money to, so what does it matter? Besides, I think most people still think he's gay and you're just a cover."

Um…okay. This girl is brutally honest. "Yes, I'm not a tramp— just a cover," I mutter sarcastically.

"Yeah, that's all. It could be worse. You could be a cover for a poor man," Laura stammers out as a coughing fit overtakes her from trying to gulp too much champagne.

"Laura, get a hold of yourself. No more drinks for these two," Laura's dad, who is standing within earshot of us, hisses at Tony.

I'm about to remind Mr. Steinberg that I'm old enough to drink as I please when I look around the room and catch Tyler's eye. I think he has just noticed that I'm not by his side. He gives me a wink and slight smile.

"He really is crazy about you, you know," Laura says when she sees me staring at Tyler.

"Right. We are just very different people, Laura. I couldn't be more awkward in this setting, and look at him—he loves being here."

"You'll be more at ease with time," Laura tries to reassure me.

"No, I don't think I ever will. It's just not me."

After a few more cocktails and no attempt by Tyler to check in with me to see how I am doing, I decide it's time to make a break for it. I'm bored out of my mind, and the longer Tyler busies himself with other people, the more annoyed and neglected I am feeling.

"I have to get of here, Laura," I say. I put my empty glass on the bar and look around for an exit.

"Sure, follow me. But you're taking me with you," she replies. She casually heads toward a side door. As if reading my mind, she says, "I've been to enough of these functions to know where all the escape exits are."

We slowly make our way to a side door, very quietly open it, and sneak out.

"Where to, honey?" Laura asks when we are outside on the street. She leads me to a town car with tinted windows that's parked around the corner.

"How about Brandy's on the Upper East Side?"

"We need a ride," Laura tells the driver, and hops in as though it were her car.

And any doubts I had about the owner of the car are gone when I read the license plate: STEINBERG.

Chapter 3

Walking into Brandy's I remember how overdressed Laura and I are for this neighborhood watering hole. This bar is one of my local haunts that's very casual and low-key. Two girls in cocktail dresses aren't the normal clientele at this bar. Luckily it is still early in the night, so the bar isn't too crowded.

"Lacey!" Rachel beams at me and greets me with a great bear hug.

"Rachel, this is Laura," I say, making introductions while pulling away and nodding toward Laura.

Rachel also gives her a bear hug. That's Rachel—one of the warmest, sweetest persons I have ever met, who is also very touchy-feely. No fake air-cheek kisses for her. She will just about knock you to the ground with her enveloping hugs.

"You look so beautiful, Lacey. What I would kill for that body," Rachel says, taking my hand and trying to make me twirl, but I stand my ground, not willing to further flaunt my overdressed outfit.

Rachel is slightly overweight with shoulder-length dark-brown hair. Because of her warm personality, she exudes cuteness.

"Who's your friend?" Jason says, sauntering over and eyeing Laura as a lion watches its prey. His dark-blue eyes twinkle as he sums up a new, potential victim. Oh boy, he'll eat her alive.

"Jason, this is Laura. Laura, this is Jason," I say, slightly exasperated.

I should have warned her about him in the car ride over. Jason smirks at me, as he knows exactly how to push my buttons.

Jason takes Laura's hand and gives it a kiss as though she were the first woman he had ever laid eyes on. God, he did have a way. Laura just stands there with her mouth agape, looking dazed and confused, trying to take in this perfect-looking, six-foot-two specimen standing before her. His black hair is cut short on the sides but still long enough on the top to tell that there would be a slight curl if he ever grew it longer. And for some reason he is never clean-shaven. He always manages to have carefully groomed stubble on his face. The black shirt he is wearing is just tight enough to outline his biceps without being cheesy, and the short sleeves give a glimpse of the armband tattoo circling his left bicep. On the inside of his left forearm is a tattoo of a Gaelic sun. On the inside of his right forearm starts a tribal dragon tattoo that wraps around his lower arm. Everything about him is alpha male, exuding testosterone and man-ified to a T.

"Ugh," I state loudly and snatch her hand away from his. "She's off-limits." I glare at him.

"What can I get you to drink, sweetheart?" Jason asks Laura, ignoring me.

"Um, I'll…um…" Laura stammers.

"Two beers, please," I answer for Laura, who has suddenly become mute.

I grab Laura's hand and lead her and Rachel to an empty booth near the back. I strategically place Laura on the inside with Rachel sitting next to her so she isn't easily accessible to predators.

"Who is that?" Laura asks, finally remembering that she could speak.

"That's my partner, Jason. And Rachel's brother. But I will warn you, he goes through women like a public ladies' room goes through toilet paper. Do not fall for his shit, Laura," I caution.

"Wow, he is *stunningly* good-looking," she says, ignoring me and watching Jason as he walks toward us with drinks.

"Ladies and Lacey," Jason says as he places our drinks on the table and slides into the booth next to me. He leans back and gives me a once-over. "You clean up well, Laces. Speaking of which, where is Money?"

"Oh, that reminds me." I pull out my cell phone. "I have to let Tyler know I left since he probably would never notice otherwise."

"You're still going to Paris with him next month, aren't you?" Laura asks.

"Paris? Why are you going to Paris?" Jason asks.

Oh yeah, I forgot to tell him.

"No, I think I'm going to bail on him. How did you know we are going?" I ask Laura.

"You can't bail, Lacey. You need to go," Laura says. She looks like she has more to say, but closes her mouth and leans back in her seat.

"Why? I hate Paris. Last time I was there with Tyler, I did all the tourist traps and then twiddled my thumbs. He gave me his credit card to go shopping, and I honestly was bored out of my mind. It's just not my thing." I say. "And what's it to you if I bail anyway?"

"I just think he's put a lot of trouble into this trip, that's all," Laura says. She takes a sip of her beer.

"Who cares? We've been there before. It's not like it's for a special occasion or anything," I say nonchalantly.

Laura leans forward as though she is about to reveal a huge secret and says, "Well, he told my dad he was going to propose in Paris. So you *have* to go."

I burst out laughing. "I am so *not* going now. I can't marry him. I was just thinking earlier today how I need to break up with him."

"Lacey, think about it. You'll be set for life if you marry him. You can quit your job and hang out in spas all day and go shopping. It will be great," Laura says.

If she'd known anything about me, I think she would have had trouble saying all that with a straight face. I sit back in my seat and pretend to think about it.

"You're not seriously thinking about it, are you?" Jason asks. "You can't marry him. He's such a douchebag. You would be miserable."

"Why not, Jay? This way I can stop working, and you can get a new partner. It's a win-win for us both," I say, smirking at him.

Jason just shakes his head and takes a sip of his beer.

I pick up my cell phone and send another text to Tyler. "I'm letting him know that we need to meet tomorrow. I'll tell him then that I am not going to Paris with him. Jason's right. He is a douchebag, and I would be miserable. I don't love him and can't marry someone for money. It's just not me. Time to end it for good, something that should have been done months ago."

"You know, he's only been inside my apartment once in over a year because he thinks it is too dumpy to hang out in. He always sends his driver in to get me. It drives me crazy. He's not exactly

Mr. Warm-and-Fuzzy," I say, continuing to defend my decision to break up with Tyler.

"Well, I'm glad you're getting rid of him, Lacey. I never really liked him anyway," Rachel chimes in.

Jason rolls his eyes and nudges me with his elbow. "Since your social calendar will free up after tomorrow, come to Atlantic City with me this weekend. I'm in a poker tournament with Chris, and he's bringing his wife."

I wrinkle my nose thinking about how much I dislike Jason's friend Chris Curtis. Chris is one of Jason's best friends and is an undercover narcotics detective in Brooklyn who is notorious for turning a blind eye if the drug dealers set him up with blow jobs from the local skanks. "No, I don't want to go. Gambling's a waste of time and money."

"We're staying at the Borgata. It has a very nice gym and pool you can work out in," Jason says.

"Take one of your bimbo girlfriends," I say, shaking my head.

"No, it will be more fun with you. Last time we went was a riot. What do you say?" Jason asks, twirling a piece of my hair with his fingers.

I think about it for a minute. Our long weekend in Atlantic City a couple of months ago had been fun.

"All right, I'll go," I say, shrugging, still not convinced that I want to go. But Jason is right. What else do I have to do?

We spend the next few hours getting to know Laura and catching up on the latest happenings in Rachel's world. The bar has been getting more crowded, but I don't notice right away. I love hanging out with Rachel and Jason and have been enjoying Laura's company. For a spoiled rich girl, she handles herself well in a dive bar.

"Excuse me, Jay, but I have to use the ladies' room." I nudge him out of the booth.

As I make my way weaving in and out of the crowd, I feel someone groping my ass as I walk. I turn around to slug the asshole and come face-to-face with Kellan Walker. Aw, fuck. How did I not see he was here?

"Hello, Kellan, how are you?" I ask, dripping with politeness and removing his hand from my ass.

"You look amazing, Lacey. I would have told you earlier, but you were being closely guarded." Kellan nods in Jason's direction.

I give him a dramatic eyeball role. Kellan is a NYC firefighter, and for some reason, he and Jason cannot stand each other. No one can ever really remember how the dislike started, but the two cannot and should not be in the same room together. Both are incredibly good-looking, and both play the field. I'm sure the feud started over a woman many years ago, but it didn't matter anymore. Basically, they just try to stay out of each other's way whenever possible.

"He's not my bodyguard, Kellan. We just work together and happen to hang out a lot," I say, feeling the need to explain my relationship with Jason.

"Really? Maybe if you spent a little less time with him, then you and I could get to know each other better. What do you say, Lacey?" He puts his arm around my waist and pulls me closer to him.

"No thanks, Kellan. You're not my type. Now please remove your hands, and get out of my way." I use my elbow to jab him aside. I can already see Jason getting up from the table and don't want to be in the middle of their shit.

When I get back to the table, Jason and Kellan are nowhere to be seen, which is fine with me.

"He felt the need to tell Kellan exactly what he thought of him. As if it wasn't already known," Rachel says, explaining Jason's absence from the table. "I think they are outside."

"Whatever," I say. "Don't care."

"My brother has a temper and never shies away from a fight," Rachel continues, feeling the need to justify his behavior to Laura. "He's very protective over the people he cares about, and the whole bar could see Kellan pawing you."

"Well, I think it's sweet. He's so chivalrous," Laura adds with a dreamy look on her face.

"He's a jackass. I can take care of myself," I tell Laura. "Really? He's thirty, not thirteen," I direct back at Rachel.

"He's always been that way, Lacey. You can't change it. He really cares about you, you know."

"Yep, I know," I say curtly. "And I can take care of myself." I am eager to end this conversation. Rachel and I have already discussed it many times before, and nothing new is being said.

"So, Laura, where do you usually hang out?" I make a stab at meaningless conversation to change the subject.

While Laura is going on and on about bars and clubs she likes going to, Jason slides back into the booth next to me. I give him a dirty look and turn back to listening to Laura.

After a while, the crowd begins to disperse, including Rachel, who has a paper to write in the morning. When Laura decides to call it quits for the night, I walk out with her and wait with her on the sidewalk until her car and driver show up. We exchange cell phone numbers and promise to hang out again.

I am a few blocks from my apartment, so I begin the walk back home.

"Wait up, Laces," I hear behind me. I keep walking and pretend not to hear Jason.

Man, these heels are killing me. Maybe I should have let Laura's driver take me home. I start to take the shoes off when Jason catches up next to me.

"My feet are killing me," I say, leaning on his arm to maintain my balance and get these shoes off. "You don't have to walk me home. I'm fine."

"Yeah, okay. You can't even walk," Jason says. With one swoop he picks me up and throws me over his shoulder.

"Jason Reed, put me down *now*." I wiggle to get off his shoulder and give up after a few tries. We have played this game before, and I am too tired tonight to fight him. Besides, my feet *are* killing me. "You are so annoying."

"Why do you always fight me, Laces? You know I'm just looking out for you."

"Because you always go about it in such a jackass sort of way. I can take care of myself, you know," I say as I dangle over his back.

"I know you can, but sometimes it's just easier for me to do it."

"Jay, would you ever marry someone for money?" I am still questioning if I'm making the right decision about Tyler.

Jason stops and puts me down on the sidewalk. "He's an asshole, Lacey. After you informed him that you left the party, he should have gotten in his limo to come find you and see what was wrong. Instead he kept schmoozing with the people he really cares about. And, no, I wouldn't marry for money. Unless, of course, she was really hot as well."

"Thanks for your input," I say sarcastically, and start walking in my bare feet.

"You deserve better, Lacey." Jason scoops me up in arms again. "Most guys would carry you to the moon and back. You certainly shouldn't be with someone who won't even get out of his car for you."

"You're a total cheese," I say, smiling at Jason's moon comment.

Chapter 4

I bob out of the water gasping for air. I can't breathe. For every mouthful of air I take in, I also take in a mouthful of water.

An arm from somewhere pulls me out of the water.

"Help me, Lacey!" she is screaming. She is still drowning.

I reach out my arm to her, but she is too far away to grab.

The man backs away into the shadows from where he came. I can no longer see his face, but I can feel him still there. Watching her drown.

I can't swim.

I look at the clock. It is about four in the morning. Jason had just carried me home a couple of hours earlier. It is too early to get up, but I know I won't be able to go back to sleep. I lay there staring at the ceiling wondering what it all means. I get out of bed and walk to the kitchen to make some tea. I am disappointed not to see Jason sleeping on my couch. Sometimes he crashes if he is too tired to walk home. His apartment is on the Upper West Side, across Central Park.

I think about what it would be like if Jason and I were more than just friends. The thought has crossed my mind more and more frequently lately, especially with the demise of my relationship with Tyler. I wonder if my breakup with Tyler will affect my friendship with Jason at all. I remember a night three months ago when Jason kissed me. We were in a bar near Wall Street where Jason was meeting up with a few of his noncop friends for happy hour. He asked me to tag along because Rachel was also meeting him out for a drink and he thought she would have a better time if I was there as well. The bar we were at became very busy as the Wall Street suits filtered in, leaving their workweek behind. I was perched on a barstool when Jason moved closer to me to let someone in to order a drink at the bar. In the process, he ended up standing between my legs.

"Sorry, Lace," he whispered in my ear.

But his apology was futile as it wasn't his fault and he didn't have anywhere to go until the guy next to him got his drink. And then without any warning, he pulled on my ponytail so my face tilted up toward his and planted a kiss on me. At first I was shocked, but then my body went completely limp as it turned into the softest, sweetest kiss I had ever experienced. It was like a warm tidal wave had washed over my body, and all I wanted was him never to stop kissing me. But then he did stop. And when he did, I immediately gathered my composure and told him to cut the shit. I gave him a dirty look as I wiggled my legs around him so he was no longer standing in between them and turned to Rachel, who was sitting on the barstool next to me with her jaw dropped. I continued a conversation with Rachel as though the kiss never happened, and Jason and I never talked about it after that. But I have thought about it a lot. And I have wondered what it be like to have someone kiss me like that again. Or *if* someone will ever kiss me like that again.

I pick up and cradle my cat, James Bond. He looks as though he is wearing a tuxedo—mostly black with a white undercarriage. But then he has a black marking near his neck that is in the shape of a bow tie.

I was living on the streets, in between foster homes, when I first met James Bond as a stray in a park. He would sleep on top of me at night for warmth. Some nights he would wake me up with his hissing at something in the dark that only he could see. I would lie there with my eyes open but couldn't see anything in the black night. I would wonder what was there that was so awful to cause him to hiss. His markings, protective nature, and toughness had earned him the name James Bond.

I look out the window at the city that never sleeps while holding James Bond. It feels like tonight, I am the only one awake.

I start to pack for our overnight trip to Atlantic City. Maybe I should just cancel. No, Jason will just pester me until I agree to go.

It doesn't take long to fill up a carryall bag with what I need. I pack a nice outfit in case we go clubbing and casual clothes for the rest of our time there. When daylight starts to break, I head to the park and go for a run. I had made arrangements to meet Tyler for breakfast where I plan to end our relationship. Running and plenty of caffeine will energize me enough to get through the day.

After my shower, I head to the coffee shop for my breakup breakfast with Tyler. I'm not really looking forward to doing it, but I realize it is long overdue and needs to be done.

I am there before him and take a seat at a booth near the door. I am surprised when Tyler arrives on time. He is never on time and usually keeps me waiting.

"Lacey, what is going on? You ditch me last night, and then I get a strange text from you about wanting to meet for breakfast this morning?" Tyler slides into the booth seat across from me.

"Tyler, we can't see each other anymore." I do not want to squander any time with small chitchat. I look at this man with whom I have spent the last few years of my life and realize I feel nothing for him. I'm not upset or happy at ending this relationship, but I am completely indifferent, as though I'm having breakfast with a coworker.

"This relationship hasn't worked for me in a while, and I don't want to waste more of our time," I continue.

"*What?* Get over it, Lacey. Whatever isn't working can be fixed," Tyler says nonchalantly and then orders two coffees and two bagels from the waitress, who has come to our table.

"No. That's part of the problem," I say once the waitress leaves. "I don't drink coffee in the morning. Or *ever*. Tea. I drink tea. But you wouldn't know that because you are only concerned with yourself and what you think I should be doing and wearing or how I should be acting."

"Lacey, *honey*. I will work harder to pay more attention to you and your wants." Tyler is clearly placating me at this point. "And I will order you a tea when the waitress comes back, okay?"

"No. It is more than coffee versus tea. We are just too different, Tyler. I am uncomfortable in your world, and you have no interest in mine," I say.

I am somewhat confused at his pushback. I honestly didn't think he would really care that this relationship is over. After all it wouldn't take him long to find a replacement for me, one who would be more suitable at his stuffy events.

"Why would I be interested in your blue-collar world, Lacey? You deserve better, and eventually you will be able to leave all that behind." Tyler reaches across the table and grabs my hand. "I can and *will* give you anything you want."

"Whatever," I say, pushing his hand away. "You know it's the blue-collar workers who make *your* world run smoothly."

"Right. I apologize. I didn't mean for it to sound that way. What I meant was I'm not real interested in always talking cop talk."

"You never want to talk cop talk. You never ask me how my day has been or how work is going, you realize that?"

"I just don't want to hear about you in dangerous situations or dealing with unlawful people. You deserve better, and I want to give you that better life."

"Sorry, Tyler. I just can't be in this relationship anymore. It's not working for me." I stand up. "I wish you well, but it is over for us."

"Lacey, wait," Tyler says. He throws a twenty-dollar bill on the table to cover the food and follows me out of the coffee shop.

"Lacey, please," Tyler says, grabbing my arm.

I turn around and face him.

"What do I need to do to make this work? Tell me, and I'll do it," Tyler says, and for a moment my heart actually softens for him.

"We are *so* different. Doesn't that bother you? Or did you just assume I would conform to your world and standards?" I ask. We are standing out on the sidewalk, and he is still holding onto my arm.

"If conforming to my world and standards means living a life most women can only dream about, then I don't understand what your problem is."

"You just don't get it. Conforming means losing myself and what makes me who I am. And being someone I'm not would make me miserable. Is that what you want?"

"No, of course not, Lacey. I love you for who you are."

"I think you love me for who I can potentially become, Tyler. Spoiled arm candy to have your picture taken with. But I don't think you love me for who I am *now*." I gently remove his hand from my arm.

"Please think about this, Lacey," Tyler says, lowering his head and looking at the sidewalk. "I think we can work it out. *Please*."

"Good-bye, Tyler," I lean over, kiss him on the cheek, and walk home.

Chapter 5

*B*y the time Jason knocks on my door later that morning, I am more than ready to go. My date with Tyler ended more quickly than I thought it would. I thought we could at least have had a nice breakfast together. With the extra time I had this morning, I took care to style my hair down and put on some makeup.

"You look nice today. You should put yourself together more often," Jason says when he sees me.

"Whatever. You know I can't at work, Jay. My hair is too long and gets in the way. Where are we meeting Chris?" I ask as I put down extra food and water for James Bond to eat today and tomorrow.

"I told him to pick us up here."

"All right, let's head down and wait on the street, then." I grab my carryall bag, pet James Bond good-bye, and lock up as we head out.

"How did it go with Money?" Jason asks as we walk outside.

"It went fine," I reply. "And I don't want to discuss it with you, so don't ask me any more about it."

"Okay." Jason tilts his head and looks to be trying to read my vibe. "He was an asshole, Lacey. You really do deserve better."

"Yeah, yeah," I respond, not really listening because I've heard it before.

We don't have to wait long before Chris pulls up to the curb in his ten-year-old Cadillac. He and his wife, Marie, get out and greet us. Marie is an attractive woman with shoulder-length brown hair that has blond highlights around her face. She's about twenty-nine years old but looks forty because of her smoking and the heavy makeup that she piles on. Chris is about thirty. He has shoulder-length curly brown hair that he always wears in a ponytail and today is sporting a goatee and extra-long sideburns that could almost pass for an ungroomed beard. If I had never met him before, I would think he was sexy in a bad-boy sort of way. But because I do know him, I think he looks like one of the dirt bags he is trained to arrest.

"Lacey, I'm so glad you decided to come. It will be much more fun to have someone to hang out with other than these guys," Marie says as she kisses me on the cheek.

"Marie, it's nice to see you again," I say, returning the greeting.

I climb into the back seat with Jason, who thankfully insists on riding in the back with me and lets Marie ride up front with Chris.

"So how are the kids?" I ask, referring to Chris and Marie's four children, all of whom are under the age of twelve.

"They are monsters, Lacey. I couldn't wait to get away this weekend. Chris's mom is taking care of them tonight, thank God. That reminds me," she continues, looking at Chris. "Did you tell your mother about the lasagna I made for them to eat tonight?"

Without waiting for an answer, Marie picks up her cell phone and calls Chris's mom.

As we leave New York City and embark on the road toward Atlantic City, Chris, Jason, and I make small talk about work, our latest arrests, and so forth.

"Lacey, how old are you anyway?" Chris asks while Marie is still talking on her cell phone.

"Twenty-five," I answer, handing my phone to Jason to start a game of hangman.

"Where did you go to high school?"

"I graduated from Hillside in Jamaica, Queens," I answer. "Why do you want to know?"

"Really? That's a tough school. Did you know Harry Miller?" Chris asks, referring to a well-known drug dealer who lived in Jamaica, Queens. Harry was found dead, floating in the East River, about two weeks ago.

"Yeah, I knew Harry. He saved my ass many times when I was a kid. I was sorry to hear of his death." I take the phone back from Jason.

"Huh. Why would he save your ass?" Chris asks.

"Harry had a younger sister who was my age. She was jumped and beaten to death when we were about eleven. After that Harry kind of took me under his wing and treated me like his sister. I think he felt bad because he couldn't save his real sister or something. Anyway, I got beat up very bad when I was about twelve. Harry gave me a gun and taught me how to shoot it. We would use the rats in alleys or down by the piers for target practice. After that I was mostly left alone. I probably wouldn't be sitting here today if it wasn't for Harry."

"Wow. I can't imagine having to carry a gun when I was twelve," Marie says. She is done with her cell phone conversation. She turns around from the front seat and looks at me.

I shrug. "I think it's more normal than you realize. Especially in the poor neighborhoods around where I grew up. It's learn how to survive or be killed."

"So how did you ever get out of there?" Chris asks.

"What's with the twenty questions, Chris?" I am bored with talking about myself.

"Just curious as to what makes you tick," Chris says.

"I lived on the basketball court and got a scholarship to NYU. That's how I got out of there," I answer his question.

"And you always wanted to be a cop?"

"No. I never wanted to be a cop. My boyfriend in college was taking the NYPD exam and bet me that I would probably fail it. So I signed up to take the exam when he did and scored higher than him."

"And he didn't make it, but you did?" Chris says, looking amused.

"No, he made it, too. We went through the academy together." I'm immediately sorry that I shared this information when I see how fast Jason turns his head toward me.

"Really? Who?" Jason says, now interested in what I'm saying.

Up until this point he had already known my childhood history. But I've never shared much with him about my ex-boyfriends.

"I'd rather not say." I'm regretting how much I've shared already.

"Who?" Jason persists.

"C'mon, Lacey. What's the big deal?" Chris chirps in.

"Because it's in the past. What does it matter?" I really don't want to go down this road.

"Who, Lacey? Not dropping it until you name him." Jason is staring at me.

"Ethan Fox," I say. I cross my arms and look out the window, knowing it's only going downhill from here.

"I know Ethan," Jason and Chris say almost at the same time.

"Yeah, I know," I say, looking at Jason. "He's a super nice guy."

"He *is* a nice guy," Jason agrees.

"Is he the guy we always see at the Yankees games?" Marie asks Chris.

"Yeah, he goes to a lot of games."

"Oh, he's dreamy." Marie turns around again. She is looking at me and smiling. "Why would you ever kick him out of your bed?"

"He is pretty hot, isn't he?" I say, grinning.

"How long were you with him?" Jason asks, giving me and Marie dirty looks.

"I met him when we were in college. We dated about three years."

"Really? You were pretty serious, huh? Why did you break up?" Chris adds fuel to the fire.

"I don't want to talk about this anymore." I look out the window.

"I want to know. Why did you break up?" Jason repeats the question.

"It just didn't work out. Relationship ran its course. That's all. No big deal." I am still looking out the window.

"Are you still friends?" Chris asks.

"Sure. We go to lunch maybe once a month."

"Why am I just hearing about this?" Jason looks annoyed.

I ignore him and keep looking out the window.

"So how did you make detective so fast? Was it because of the high-profile arrests you made? I heard you were a real superstar in uniform," Chris switches subjects, likely because he sees how agitated Jason has become.

"I wasn't a superstar. I just did my job." I start a new game on my phone with Jason.

Chapter 6

We arrive in Atlantic City and check in at the hotel. Jason flirts with the front-desk girl and talks her into giving him an upgrade. Our room ends up being a suite and on a higher floor than Chris and Marie, much to Marie's chagrin.

"I think she would have given you the penthouse if it wasn't already booked," I say, smiling up at Jason.

"Don't be disappointed, Lacey, but I requested two beds," Jason says, putting his arm around my shoulders as though he is breaking bad news to me.

"Aw, that's too bad," I say in my sweetest, most innocent voice. "I was hoping you could teach more than just table games while we are here."

"Wow, this is nice," I say when we get to our room. "Too bad we are only staying for one night."

"Come here, and look at this bathroom," I yell to Jason. "This tub could fit ten people, and there is even a TV in here. Maybe I'll just hang out in here for the rest of the day."

When I walk out of the bathroom, Jason is talking to someone on the hotel phone.

"We have four hours until the tournament. What do you want to do until then?" Jason asks when he hangs up the phone.

"I think I'm going to take a bath. You should see that bathroom," I say, following Jason into the bathroom.

"Hmm, sounds good," Jason says. He starts unbuttoning his jeans with one hand and tugs at my shirt with his other.

"Alone," I say, swatting him.

"Really? That's no fun." Jason looks truly disappointed as he buttons up his jeans and takes my arm to lead me out of the bathroom. "Let's go eat, then."

"It's amazing how fast you can switch gears," I utter under my breath.

"I know you too well to push it, Lacey. But I at least should try to get you naked, right? I wouldn't be a normal heterosexual male if I didn't," Jason says as we leave the room and wait for the elevator.

"I don't think I agree with that. I have hung out with men where no sex was involved," I say.

"Maybe, but they all thought what it would be like to fuck you," Jason says nonchalantly. "And they wouldn't have said no if you offered."

"You're such a pig, you know that? Just because you are oversexed doesn't mean every guy is," I say as we get on the elevator.

"You think I'm abnormal, huh?" Jason texts Chris that we are getting lunch in the hotel restaurant if they want to join us. Chris lets him know that he and Marie are already in the restaurant. "Every heterosexual male that meets you wonders what it would be like to fuck you."

"I think you're way off. So every girl you meet you want to fuck?"

"I didn't say every girl. I said *you*. You're beautiful, and because you don't know how beautiful you are, it's an even bigger turn-on."

"Whatever. I think you're way off." I feel my face turning red and look down at the floor for an escape hatch that I can crawl through.

"All right, Lace. Let's go eat." Jason grabs my hand as we get off the elevator and leads me to a restaurant located in the lobby.

We join Chris and Marie, who are already seated at a table when we walk into the restaurant. They are both sipping draft beers. I order water, and Jason does the same. The silence at the table is palpable and awkward. It feels as though we walked into an argument between Chris and Marie, who are now doing their best not even to look at each other.

"Lacey and I are going to walk the boardwalk and try the other casinos after lunch," Jason says, breaking the silence.

"What do you like to play, Lacey?" Marie asks.

I shrug. "Slots, I guess. I really don't know how to play anything else."

"I'm going to teach her how to play blackjack," Jason says. "Or maybe roulette. Better odds than slots."

I nod. "Just nothing too complicated or expensive, okay?"

"Okay," Jason says. He smirks at me as if he's amused by something.

"And then let's go clubbing tonight, Lacey. There are some great bars around here, and these guys are going to be busy playing poker," Marie says, with a mischievous grin on her face.

"Just be careful. There's also a lot of trouble around here," Jason says.

I can tell he isn't thrilled with the idea of us clubbing without him.

"Sounds good, Marie," I say, ignoring Jason.

After lunch Jason and I stroll down the boardwalk, debating what casinos to venture into. I would rather not venture into any, but I let him lead the way.

"You know, I find Chris incredibly rude," I say.

He had texted on his phone throughout most of lunch and made very little attempt at conversation.

"I know you don't like him. We obviously walked into a fight they were having." Jason opens a casino door for me.

"Why do you always defend him?"

"I've known him since I was fifteen, Lacey. I was in their wedding, for Christ's sake."

"I didn't know that." I follow Jason back to where the table games.

"The problem is Marie got knocked up about a month after they met, and he has felt trapped ever since. I think they got married when he was about eighteen or nineteen. They were both too young."

"It's still no excuse to cheat and fight, and you know it. Get divorced, and move on already."

"What do you know about his cheating?" Jason takes a seat at a blackjack table and indicates for me to sit in the chair next to him. He puts money on the table and then splits his chips with me.

"Everyone knows how he trades favors with drug dealers and users. It's disgusting." I look at the cards I've been given, and Jason explains the game to me.

"Yeah, well, narcotics is a different world, Lacey," Jason says while we wait for the next hand to be dealt.

"There you go, defending him again." I look at Jason in disbelief that he could actually condone Chris's behavior.

Jason shrugs and continues explaining the game to me. I look at him after most hands for his direction as to whether I should hit or stay. The dealer even gives me advice since the floor isn't busy and he is obviously bored. When it's all said and done, I break even, and Jason ends up a little ahead. I give my chips back to Jason so he can cash them in.

We leisurely stroll back to the Borgata, periodically stopping into different places to do some shopping. It's a beautiful day, and the boardwalk is crowded. We decide to sit down on a bench and people watch.

"Why don't you go to the spa tonight instead of out clubbing with Marie? I'll pay for you to get a massage or whatever you want," Jason says, looking at me. His blue eyes dance in the sunshine.

"Why? What does it matter?" I ask, but I know Jason doesn't want me to go out without him.

"Lacey, you're in a strange city. And Marie tends to drink too much."

"She has a lot of reasons to drink too much," I say, looking at Jason, daring him to challenge that statement.

"Fine. Just be careful, and text me wherever you are going."

"Yes, boss," I say, grabbing his knee.

I frequently tease Jason about his bossiness. He is a higher-ranked detective than me at work and has seniority, so I am technically supposed to follow his command during work hours. But his overbearingness often carries over into our personal time, and I tease him about it as a gentle reminder to take a step back.

"I really think you should go to the spa instead," Jason suggests again for the hundredth time when he sees what I'm wearing out.

I've changed into a black miniskirt and a silver metallic tank top.

"Hey, I'm a single girl now, remember? Maybe I'll get lucky." I wink at Jason as I pull down my V-neck shirt to expose more cleavage. "What do you think?"

"I think we shouldn't leave this room, and then we'll both get lucky." He picks me up and carries me toward the bed.

"Put me down, Jason." I pretend to fight him, but I'm too busy laughing at the same time. "And don't you have to get going?"

I start to usher him toward the door when he finally puts me down, even though if he seriously didn't want to leave the room, I wouldn't fight him about it.

"Yeah, I do." Jason looks at his watch. "You are going to Caesars for dinner and then where?"

"Probably back here. But I promise to text you and let you know for sure, boss." I open the door for him and give him a gentle push out. I quickly close the door before he has a chance to come back in or before I do something to make him stay.

I finish doing my hair and makeup and then head to the lobby, where I am meeting Marie.

"Marie, you look beautiful," I say, surprised and not lying. She has changed into a black dress and redone her hair and makeup.

"Thanks, Lacey. You look beautiful as always. Love your shoes," she says, pointing to my strappy-heeled, silver sandals.

"Thanks. Let's get the hell out of here before Jason changes his mind about doing the tournament and tracks me down." I grab Marie's hand and lead her out the door.

At Caesars, we decide to eat at an Italian restaurant. We opt to eat at the bar since we don't have reservations and want to avoid the wait time.

"So, Marie, how are you and Chris? It was a little chilly at lunch today. Everything okay?" I ask. I have decided to skip over the small talk and jump right in.

"Don't get me started on that prick." Marie waves her hand like she doesn't want to talk about it, but she keeps talking. "Before we went to lunch, I saw a text message come in on his phone. It was from one of his little hooch girlfriends. He wouldn't let me read it. And you know what? I no longer give a shit. I can't deal with his cheating anymore."

"Oh, Marie," I say, shocked she is aware of his indiscretions. "I am so sorry."

"Please. I'm so done with him. He cheats and then promises me he won't do it again. He gets all nice and lovey-dovey. But then he turns around and cheats again. I give up." Marie dives into her risotto and orders another glass of wine. She then proceeds to take off her wedding ring and throws it in her purse. Uh-oh.

"Let me know if I can do anything for you." I don't really know what else to say at this point. I'm still surprised she knows about Chris's cheating and has remained married to him.

"You know what you can do for me? Remind me how fun it is to be single. I so need to let off some steam and relax."

"I can do that," I say, clinking her wineglass with mine.

I pull out my cell phone and see I have a text from Jason, asking what we are doing. He is such a control freak.

"Where are we going next?" I ask Marie. "Jason wants to know."

Marie rolls her eyes. "What's it like working with him anyway?"

"What do you mean?" I ask, unsure where she's going with this.

"I was just wondering how you manage to work with someone who is so in love with you. Doesn't it get awkward?" Marie takes another sip of wine.

"You must be joking, Marie."

Marie shrugs. "Chris says Jason is in love with you, but you won't give him the time of day."

"I think you're mistaken, honey. Jason wants to fuck me, but he is in love with himself—that's about it."

"Well, more power to you for not giving in. I don't think any breathing woman could resist him." Marie pauses and thinks for a minute. "But he's cut from the same player's cloth as Chris, so you're smart to stay away."

"Right," I say, still thinking about what she was saying.

It's not true. It can't be true. Jason's actions since I've known him have been loud and clear about loving the single life and not wanting a relationship. I would just be another roll in the hay for him.

"Tell him we're going back to the dance club at the Borgata," Marie says, reminding me why this conversation started in the first place.

"Okay." I let Jason know where we are going next.

We finish our meal and decide to have another glass of wine before heading back to the Borgata. As we are talking, a man walks over to us and offers to buy us drinks.

"Oh, no, thank you. We are set." I smile and nod at him.

"Lacey," Marie hisses at me when he walks away. "What's your problem? He was cute. And I need to forget my asshole husband, remember?"

"Oh, right." I say. "There will be others, I'm sure. I don't hang out in bars to pick up men. And I just got out of a relationship and usually have Jason sitting next to me anyway."

Marie rolls her eyes. "Let's make a game out of this. We don't buy another drink tonight. No matter what it takes, we have to get someone else to buy it for us."

"I don't know, Marie. I'm not very good at flirting." I am not too comfortable with her game. And I don't have the patience to make small talk with men I'm uninterested in.

"Just smile and make eye contact. Most of the men in this bar are staring at you anyway; it will be like taking candy from a baby." Marie looks around the bar. "It will be fun. Just try it."

"Fine. But don't expect me to tolerate someone all night just because he bought me a glass of wine."

Marie rolls her eyes again. "You need to lighten up."

"Game on." I am somewhat annoyed at her for thinking I need to lighten up. I down my glass of wine and look around the bar for someone to buy me a drink.

"Courtesy of the men over there." The bartender nods at three guys across the bar as he fills up our wineglasses.

"That was fast," I say to Marie as she raises her glass and mouths a thank-you across the bar. She is obviously good at this game.

I politely smile and take a sip of the wine.

"Let's go over and say hi," Marie says, standing up.

"Let's not," I say, staying seated.

Marie starts walking to the other side of the bar. I take a few more sips of my drink, in no hurry to join Marie even though she is waving me over. When I finish my drink, I reluctantly get up and drag myself over to where they are standing. Marie makes the introductions as though she is old friends with everyone, even though she just met them herself. I smile and say hello.

"Lacey and I are headed over to the Borgata to check out the bars there. Maybe we'll see you guys later?" Marie says as she finishes her glass of wine.

"Absolutely, we'll swing over later," one of them promises.

"Great." Marie waves good-bye, and I follow suit.

"They were hot, huh?" Marie asks once we get outside.

"Sure," I say. "What's your plan here, Marie? I mean it's not like we can meet someone and bring him back to our hotel room. And we sure as hell are not going back to someone else's room."

"Lacey, most of the people here are from New York. You meet someone, exchange numbers, and meet up sometime in the city. I'm not looking for a fuck tonight, maybe just a fuck in the future," Marie explains as she links her arm through mine as we walk.

Maybe she and Chris are perfect for each other.

Chapter 7

ack at our hotel, Marie pulls me into a dance club, and we make our way to the dance floor. The music is pulsating, and the sound is vibrating through my body. I'm not a great dancer, but I'm also not the worst on the floor. No one will compliment me on my moves, but no one will make fun of me either. The dance floor is crowded, so it's easy to blend in. Almost immediately I have some guy put his hands on my hips and grind behind me. I turn around, and I am pleasantly surprised to find a gorgeous young man pressing his body up against mine. I smile and decide to go with the flow. I see Marie has also found someone to dance with. After a few songs, my dance partner grabs my hand and pulls me toward the bar. I signal Marie to follow.

"You are stunning. What is your name?" he whispers in my ear.

"Lacey. And you are?" I am mesmerized by his green eyes. He has black hair and copper-toned skin, as though he just walked off a yacht in Miami.

"Blake. What are you drinking?"

"Anything," I say, practically wiping the drool off my chin. *Smooth.*

Marie comes over and introduces herself. She also goes limp when she gets a look at him.

"How about shots, ladies?" Blake asks us as the bartender lines up the shot glasses, not waiting for an answer.

He hands us each a shot of Jägermeister, and down it goes. I would have done a shot of goose shit if he had put it in front of me.

"Where are you from, Lacey?" Blake asks as he orders another line of shots.

"Manhattan. I live in Manhattan," I say, staring at him. "Where do you live?"

"Scarsdale," Blake answers, referring to a town in upstate New York. He hands us another shot; which Marie and I happily lick up.

"Let's keep dancing, shall we?" Blake leads me back onto the dance floor.

Marie follows and picks up a new dance partner along the way. Blake is a good dancer. I try to keep up, but after a while, I think he gets bored with my moves and decides we should just slow dance even though the music is still pulsating at a fast beat. Fine with me. He wraps his arms around my waist, and we sway to my heartbeat, which I'm sure he can feel jumping out of my chest. After what feels like an eternity, someone, who I'm assuming is Blake's friend, interrupts us. The man points to his watch, and Blake nods, turning back to me.

"Baby, I have to go. My friend is getting married next week, and we're here to take him out and have a good time. Maybe we could meet up later?"

"Absolutely."

"What's your number? I'll call you later and see where you're at?" Blake punches my number into his cell phone. "All right, Lacey. I'll see you later."

He puts his finger underneath my chin, gently tilts my head back, and kisses me on the mouth. His tongue explores my mouth, and I feel as though my knees are going to buckle. It is a little bit too much tongue, but because I've had too much to drink, I enjoy it anyway. He pulls back, smiles at me, and then kisses me again.

"All right, I really have to go," Blake says. He signals for his friends to wait for him, as they are headed toward the exit. He gives me another long, tongue-filled kiss on the mouth and then follows his friends out the door.

"Wow," Marie says, standing next to me as we wave good-bye to Blake. "He is gorgeous. And I thought he was going to rip your clothes off right here in the bar."

"Yeah, I was kind of hoping he would," I say, still staring at the exit. I look at my phone, hoping he would have called by now even though he has just left, and instead see a text from Jason wanting an update.

"Let's try a more relaxed bar. I feel like I just had a workout," I say to Marie, leading her to a different bar in the hotel. I let Jason know we were switching locations.

"And no more shots. Those hit me hard," I add as we take a seat on barstools. "And the game is over. I don't feel like being social anymore."

"No," Marie whines. "Look, those guys from Caesars are here. Let's talk with them."

"I'm not leaving my seat. If they want to talk to us, they can make the walk over." I keep my butt planted on the barstool.

"Fine," Marie says.

She waves the three men over. I am amazed at her lack of subtlety.

"I'll just have a beer," I say to one of them when he asks what I want to drink. They are not bad looking and are pleasant enough to talk to. Marie could have picked worse, I guess.

My head is getting fuzzier and fuzzier as the night goes on. Our new social circle has expanded, and we are now mingling with about ten people at the bar. One of the guys at the bar feels the need to show off his juggling skills with three lemons. Not to be outdone, I feel the need to show the bar how I can juggle four lemons with two hands. Then I show how I can juggle three lemons with one hand. Out of the corner of my eye, I see Jason leaning against the bar smiling at me. Shit. I stop the juggling and do a little curtsy for the bar to let them know I'm done and walk over to Jason.

"Is this what you do when I'm not around? Perform juggling shows in bars?" Jason asks, still smiling at me.

He looks so hot leaning against the bar, smiling in his black T-shirt and jeans. I put my arms around him and bury my face in his neck.

"I'm exhausted," I whisper.

"And hammered," Jason whispers back, wrapping his arms around me.

I am so comfortable in his arms. I could stay like this forever.

"Where's Chris and Marie?" Jason asks, looking around.

"I haven't seen Chris, and Marie is over there talking with those guys," I say, not moving.

"What do you mean, you haven't seen Chris? He was out of the tournament about three hours ago and was supposed to find you guys."

"I haven't seen him, Jay. He's not with us."

"What the hell," Jason mutters under his breath and pulls out his cell phone. After his text conversation with Chris, Jason puts his phone back in his pocket and mutters, "Asshole."

"Where is he?" I ask, but I don't really care. I'm holding onto him in order to keep myself standing upright.

"He's busy." Jason hugs me tighter.

"I'm going to fall asleep like this, you know," I whisper, and I start giggling.

"Go ahead. I'll carry you back to the room," Jason says, shrugging.

"Why are you so good to me?" I ask with a big sigh.

"Why wouldn't I be, Lacey? And what have you been drinking?" Jason pushes my hair back and tries to see my face, which is still buried in his neck.

"Everything. What do you want to do? Stay out or go back to the room?" I don't really want to move.

"I'm beat, honey. It's four in the morning. And you're ready to pass out," Jason says, propping me up.

"Okay. Let's round up Marie." I break from Jason and look around the bar to try to find Marie. "There she is." I point in her direction and start walking her way. Jason grabs my arm to keep me walking upright.

"Marie, we are leaving," I announce when we reach her and her admirers.

"Give me five minutes, okay?"

"Why?" What is she going to accomplish in five minutes when she has had the whole night to close any deals?

Marie gives me a dirty look.

"We'll be waiting over here." Jason leads me to two empty barstools and helps me up onto one. He orders a beer and water from the bartender.

"Thanks," I say, taking the beer from him and having a sip.

"The water is for you," he says, taking the beer back. "I don't think I've ever seen you this drunk, Lacey."

I wave him off. "I'm fine."

"You can barely walk," Jason says, smirking at me.

I take back his beer and drink it up, maintaining eye contact with him the whole time. It's my way of daring him to take the beer back.

"Go ahead, drink up, Laces. You know I could take total advantage of you tonight, and there's nothing you could do about it," he says, staring into my eyes and wrapping a piece of my hair around his finger.

"Are you promising me a good time later, Jay?" I tilt my head to the side and smile at him sweetly.

"Anything for you, honey," Jason says. His eyes are like lasers, peeling away my layers. I crumble under his scrutiny and look away, blushing. He leans over, kisses me on the cheek, and says, "You're so cute when you blush."

"Let's go," I say, bored with his game, and I try to get off the barstool.

"You stay here. I'll get her." Jason walks over to Marie and gently takes her arm while whispering something in her ear. Marie nods, says good-bye to her new friends, and follows Jason back to me.

Jason grabs my arm and tries to help me off the barstool.

"Paws off. I'm fine," I say, shaking him off.

I hop off, misjudging my footing, and land flat on my ass. I sit on the floor, stunned, while Marie breaks out laughing. Jason helps me up while trying not to laugh.

"You okay, Lace?" he manages to ask while trying to hide his face so I can't see him smiling.

I give him a dirty look. "I'm fine," I hiss, getting up and brushing myself off. "Thanks for asking." I walk out the door and head toward the elevator, trying to hold my head up high as though nothing happened.

"Don't be mad, Lacey." Jason takes my arm again and helps me into the elevator. I let him help me this time.

"I'm not mad. But I think I hurt my ass." I giggle and rub my backside.

"Oh, sweetie, I'll make it feel better." Jason puts his arms around me and pats my ass.

I put my arms around him and nuzzle his neck. My favorite position tonight.

Marie is looking a little wobbly, so Jason takes her arm to steady her while still keeping an arm around me. The elevator doors open on Marie's floor.

"Okay, ladies," Jason says, nudging me. "We need to walk. Walk." He nudges me again.

I reluctantly let go of him and grab his hand as we walk out of the elevator.

"You have your key, Marie?" Jason asks, still holding on to her arm.

"Yeah, it's here somewhere." She digs into her purse and pulls out a plastic key card. She opens her room door and lets us in.

"Where's Chris?" Marie asks for the first time tonight when she sees there is no one in the room.

"I think he was in the lobby getting water or something," Jason says.

He sounds as though he is trying to cover for him. Jason pulls back the sheets on the bed and asks where her pajamas are. He seems anxious to put her to sleep rather than have her wait up for her husband, who is obviously missing in action. I crawl into the bed and make myself comfortable while Marie changes into her pajamas.

"Not you. Get up. You're not sleeping here." Jason pulls me up into a sitting position and then helps Marie into bed and tucks her in. "Marie, you need anything before we leave?" Jason asks Marie, who is now snuggled up in the bed.

"No, I'm good. Thanks for everything, Jason. Good night, Lacey."

"Good night, honey." Jason bends down and kisses her on the forehead.

"Good night, Marie," I say as Jason helps me stand and leads me out of their room.

Once in the hallway, he pulls out his phone and texts Chris.

"What are you doing?" I ask.

"I'm letting Chris know his wife is in bed and he needs to get back here." He shakes his head in disgust. He takes my hand and leads me back to the elevator so we can go up to our room.

"I am so tired," Jason says, lowering his head.

"I'm sorry you had to babysit us." I'm suddenly ashamed at how much I've drunk and how I am acting.

"I don't mind babysitting you, Lacey, but I shouldn't have to put someone else's wife to bed. That's just wrong what he did."

"You go above and beyond for your friends, you know that?" I say, standing next to him and resting my head on his shoulder.

He doesn't say anything; instead, he just sighs and leads me back to our room. I look in my carryall bag for something to sleep in and realize I forgot my pajamas.

"Hey, Jay, do you have a T-shirt or something I can sleep in?"

"Here." Jason hands me a white T-shirt and boxer shorts.

I go into the bathroom to change, wash my face, and brush my teeth. When I come out, Jason is already in bed, watching TV.

"There's some aspirin and water on that nightstand. You should probably take something before you go to sleep."

"Thanks." I take two aspirin. "Did you at least win your tournament?"

I am standing in between the two beds. I'm debating what bed to get into, the empty one or Jason's. Maybe it is all the alcohol I drank or the men I flirted with tonight, but right now my body is screaming to get laid.

"No, I came in third."

"Well, that's good, right?" I have no idea.

"I won five thousand dollars."

"Wow. That's great."

"Go to bed, Lacey."

"Okay," I say. I crawl into Jason's bed and begin my attack. I move so I'm lying next to him and kiss his cheek and neck area.

He laughs. "This is so not going to happen, sweetie. You're way too drunk." Jason grabs my hands so that I can't touch him and wiggles his way toward the side of the bed.

"Oh, come on, Jay," I say, trying to free myself while at the same time moving so that I can get on top of him. "Let's just have sex already. What are we waiting for?"

"Goddamn it, Lacey," Jason says, still laughing but trying to get me off him. He flips me over so that I'm on my back and my arms are pinned above me. "This is not going to happen tonight. *Behave.*"

After struggling and not being able to get my hands free, I relax. "Fine," I pout.

"I'm going to let you go, and then I'm moving to the other bed," Jason says, still pinning me down. "You stay here, got it?"

"Yup."

"Stay." Jason slowly releases me and gets out of bed, clearly not fully trusting me to stay put.

As I'm watching him pull back the covers and climb into the other bed, I can't help but smile. He really is beautiful.

"What if I were to tell you this will be your only chance *ever*?" I ask, getting out of bed and following him into his. "After tonight it will never happen? Then, would you be willing?"

Jason lets out a big sigh once I've gotten into bed with him again. "We are not negotiating, Lacey. You had too much to drink tonight, and I can't trust you to think clearly. I'm not going to take the chance you'll regret it and kill me in the morning."

He tries to slide out the other side of the bed, but I move to wrap my arms and legs around him so he can't get out.

He laughs again. "You're killing me, honey."

"Then quit fighting me," I whine, getting tired of this game. My body is throbbing for him, and the fact that I keep getting rejected is starting to annoy me.

He grabs my arms and pins them above my head again. Now it's my turn to sigh.

"Relax and close your eyes. I'm going to hold you like this until you fall asleep."

"Whatever," I say, closing my eyes. I *am* really tired and eventually pass out.

Chapter 8

I wake up to someone knocking on the door. I ignore it, hoping the person will go away, but Jason gets up and answers it. It's Chris.

"I've got a problem," Chris says, walking past Jason into our room.

I look at my watch. It's nine in the morning. I put my pillow over my head and groan. My head is going to explode.

Jason shakes the bottle of aspirin near my head, motioning for me to take it. I remove the pillow that's covering my face and take the bottle from him. He has a smirk on his face like he's amused at the pain I'm in. I groan again when I remember what an ass I made of myself last night and swallow two pills with the bottle of water next to my bed. I lay my head back down and close my eyes.

"Can we go somewhere and talk?" Chris asks Jason.

"Why? She won't repeat it." Jason sits on his bed.

Chris thinks for a moment while staring at me and then takes a seat in one of the recliners in the room.

"Okay," Chris says, taking another look at me. "Carrie is pregnant."

"Who is Carrie?'" Jason asks, even though I'm sure he could guess.

"She's a girl I've been banging for a few months." Chris leans forward and rests his elbows on his knees.

Now it's Jason's turn to groan as he covers his face and shakes his head. "You're such a fucking idiot."

I open my eyes now, more interested in the conversation.

"I know. I don't know what to do," Chris says.

"Are you sure? How do you know?" Jason asks.

"She told me last night."

"What, over the phone? Maybe she's lying," Jason says.

"No, she's here. I spent the night with her in another room. She told me this morning."

"You got some fucking nerve, you know that? You left me to babysit your wife while you're in another room fucking your girl-friend?" Jason looks as if he's ready to explode.

"Sorry." Chris looks at his feet.

"If you weren't my ride home, I'd beat the shit out of you, you know that? Maybe I'll do it anyway and just rent a car," Jason says, glaring at Chris.

"C'mon, so I fucking owe you one. I've got a huge problem here." Chris looks as though he may cry.

"What happened to you, man?" Jason has gone from looking angry to looking disgusted. "You transferred into narcotics with a plan to stay there two years to make a few big arrests that would fast-track your career and land you in an office somewhere. And now look at you. Seven years later, and you're a complete scumbag."

"I know," Chris says, still looking at his feet.

After a few minutes of silence, Jason asks, "So what are you going to do with this girl? You plan on leaving Marie with four kids at home?"

"No, of course not. I'm going to try to get her to have an abortion." Chris looks over at me and asks, "Would you ever have an abortion?"

"I don't know what I would do," I answer, feeling somewhat sorry for him, considering his situation. "I've never been pregnant before. Maybe she will."

"Who is this girl anyway?" Jason asks.

"No one. A mistake. A good lay. That's about it. And now I'm going to be tied to her for the next eighteen years."

"Yep. She just got herself an eighteen-year meal plan," Jason says, not attempting to make him feel better.

"What should I do about Marie?" Chris asks, looking at me.

"What can you do? Tell her the truth. She'll find out anyway." I close my eyes. I just want to go back to sleep.

"How is this chick getting back to New York? Are we in for an uncomfortable car ride?" Jason asks.

"No. I'm not that stupid," Chris says, laughing. "You think maybe you could rent that car and drive her back?"

"Get out." Jason stands up and walks him toward the door. "I'm getting an extended checkout and going back to sleep, and we're leaving around three. Don't come back until then."

When Chris leaves, Jason sits on my bed and rubs my belly. "You okay?"

"I guess. Just mortified." I put a pillow back over my face so I don't have to look at him.

"Don't be. It happens," he says, removing the pillow from my face.

"Maybe for you, but not for me." I roll over so I can lie on my side, facing away from him.

"I tried to warn you about Marie. I don't think I could keep up with her drinking, either," Jason says, rubbing my back.

"Yeah, you did warn me. I just got carried away. And I'm so embarrassed at attacking you," I say, still not opening eyes.

"Whatever. We'll hook up one of these days, Lacey. But you'll be sober enough to remember it and enjoy it."

"You promise?" I'm not surprised at his sureness.

"That we'll hook up? Sure, it's inevitable."

"No, that I'll enjoy it." I giggle at how I set him up.

"You're an ass," Jason says. "And just out of curiosity, would you have killed me if I had taken advantage?"

"No, I wouldn't have been mad at you. I would have been more concerned with making sure our friendship wouldn't change."

"Sex changes everything, sweetie," Jason says, still rubbing my back.

"I know. But you are one of my closest friends. Not sure what I would do without you." I roll over on my back to face him.

Jason opens his mouth as though he wants to say something but then decides against it.

"What?" I reach up and stroke his stubbly cheek.

"Nothing." He pushes a piece of my hair back behind my ear. "Let's get some more sleep before we head home."

I sigh. He is holding back on something, but I don't want to press the issue. I close my eyes and eventually fall back asleep.

The ride back to New York is surprisingly pleasant. Either Carrie has agreed to get an abortion, or Marie doesn't know. Or both.

I haul out my phone and pull up the latest edition of *Cosmopolitan* magazine. I love to read the articles to Jason and get his opinion as to whether he agrees or disagrees with what the magazine is say-ing. I show him a list of the articles to see if he has a preference as to what we read first. Jason points to an article, "Ten Things You Don't Know about Sex."

"Really? I find it difficult to believe there would be anything you don't know," I say, smiling at him.

"It'll be a good test of my knowledge." Jason smirks back at me.

I read the list as quietly as I can to avoid disturbing Marie, who has decided to call her kids and let them know she is on her way home. It isn't quiet enough, as Chris immediately becomes inter-ested in the conversation and throws in his two cents. Soon Marie is off the phone and throwing in her comments. And then I move on to the next article. And then the next article. Before I know it, the car ride home has flown by, and I know more about Chris and his sexual preferences than I ever cared to know. But at least it has been an entertaining ride.

Chapter 9

"**Y**ou look like shit, Laces. And you are way off your game. I think that's the first time I've ever beat you in Scrabble," Jason says, handing me back my phone.

We are sitting in an empty house that's been set up for surveillance to watch the house across the street. A judge has issued an arrest warrant for Sal Rizzo, a well-known drug kingpin, who unfortunately cannot be found. The house we are watching belongs to a cousin that Rizzo has frequently visited in the past. We have been watching this house for two days now with zero activity.

"I haven't been sleeping very well," I answer.

"Same nightmare?" Jason asks. He has heard it all before.

"Yes, same nightmare, same faces, same little girl drowning, same everything. I don't know what any of it means. What if it means nothing, and I'm just going insane?"

"It has to mean something. You have blocked out an event when you were younger. Think, and try to remember."

"Don't you think I have already tried to remember?" I snap. "And why are we still watching this house, anyway? What a waste of time. He's obviously not going to show here." I get up and pace. All the caffeine in my system is making me moody and jumpy.

"And there is no one I can ask," I continue venting. "That's the problem. My memory is all I have of my past. No one else knows my past. The foster homes all blend together, you know? I couldn't even tell you what neighborhood I was living in when I was five or six. There were so many."

"Well, maybe if we could at least pinpoint the neighborhood, that could help. I know someone at Social Services; I'll see what he can find." Jason punches some numbers into his cell phone and speaks with someone regarding access to my records. "Great, thanks. E-mail me whatever you find on her. I owe you one. Later."

Twenty minutes later Jason's cell phone buzzes. "Here it is," he says, handing me the phone.

"Well, what does it say?" I nervously ask.

"I'm not going to read it, Laces. That's your information. I'll forward it to your e-mail."

The front door slams, making me jump.

"Nothing new, no visitors, no activity," Jason informs the relief detectives as we get up and leave.

"C'mon, let's eat dinner, and we'll read it together." Jason leads the way into a café near my apartment.

I pull up the forwarded e-mail on my cell phone:

> Jason—Lacey's file attached. No info after she turned fifteen. Out of system. Later, Pete.

"I decided to live on my own when I turned fifteen," I explain while nervously glancing at Jason. What is making me so nervous? I know the gist of my history. A few pieces are missing, but overall there shouldn't be anything surprising.

"Why?" Jason asks.

"I was living with a married couple. They were maybe in their forties. She was real nice, but the husband was kind of sleazy. He began to look at me funny. He started to make creepy, sexual innuendos. I decided it was time to get out of there before something happened." I shrug as though it is no big deal.

"Where did you live?"

I shrug again. "Wherever I could. Sometimes outside. That's when I met James Bond. He was a stray and followed me around." I smile thinking about the nights James Bond and I would cuddle to stay warm.

Jason just stares at me for a minute as though he doesn't know what to say.

The first page in the e-mail's attachment is just a brief written history of me. Full name, DOB, SSN, and so forth. Reason for foster care simply stated: *Child was orphaned at age four when parents killed in car crash. Next of kin could not be found.*

"Why was there no next of kin? Your parents had no relatives? I find that hard to believe," Jason asks after reading the last line.

"I found out a few years ago that my parents were immigrants from Ireland. Social Services was too lazy or underfunded, or they couldn't be bothered with tracking down relatives in a foreign country," I reply.

"You ever think about going there to find relatives?"

I shrug. "Sometimes I think about it. But I also have some resentment too. Why didn't any of my parents' relatives bother to check on me? Someone had to have known that they died and their child was still alive. Did no one care what happened to me?"

"Good point. Or maybe you were already lost in the system by the time anyone was notified of their deaths," Jason says, probably to make me feel better.

The next five pages list the names of foster parents, addresses, dates of occupancy, and comments regarding how I was doing and why the foster care at that address ended. Most of the comments simply state, "Child is uncontrollable and acts out at authority."

"So, you haven't changed much, huh?" Jason asks.

I have to laugh. "You know, Jay, most of these people didn't give a shit about me. They used me to get their foster care or welfare money, and when I no longer served a purpose, they threw me back into the system."

"This one is different," Jason says, pointing to an address in Harlem.

The comment states, "Child is inconsolable. Has stopped speaking and will not eat or sleep."

"Hmm, if you add up the months from my parents' deaths to this address, I was around six. It wasn't my first foster home, so maybe something happened here that made me act differently. I'll start at that address and see if I can get anywhere."

"Don't plan on going alone," Jason orders.

"Whatever," I say, trying to ignore him. "I'm sure you have better things to do."

"Seriously, I'm going with you, so deal with it," Jason says as he walks me back to my apartment.

"Fine, we'll go tomorrow after work."

"You know, there's a movie on tonight I was planning to watch. You mind if I watch it here?" He doesn't wait for an answer and instead makes himself at home on my couch.

"Your TV must be broken, huh?" Did he really think I was going to sneak out to Harlem tonight?

I hand him a beer and get comfortable in the recliner next to the couch. There is no movie, but I don't press the issue.

"I'm glad you're here," I admit, stretching my leg out and poking his arm with my big toe. "I sleep better when you're here."

"I know." Jason grabs my foot and kisses my big toe.

Chapter 10

After work the next day, we hop on the subway and get off at 121st Street. The address is a few blocks away from the subway station. The neighborhood looks familiar, but I don't know if it's because I was here before as a cop or because I used to live in this area.

"There's the apartment." I nod up at a rundown building about ten stories high. Some of the windows are missing, some have bars on them, and some are open to let the cool breeze in.

"What a dump." Jason states the obvious.

"It hasn't changed much."

I walk toward the apartment building. I see a man in front of the building sweeping the sidewalk. He's older, maybe in his sixties, with a bald head, a white beard, and a pronounced belly that lets everyone know he eats well or at least eats what he wants. I know him. Will he remember me?

"Hi, Zo." I walk up to the man with my hand stretched out to greet him.

"Lacey!" Zo takes my arm and instead of shaking it, pulls me in for a bear hug. "It's so good to see you, girl!"

I glance back at Jason, who has uncharacteristically taken a back seat. He's casually observing and letting the situation take its course without jumping in and trying to control everything as he usually does.

"I have to say that I'm surprised you remember me," I say, prying myself out of Zo's bear hug. "It was so long ago. Almost twenty years."

"How could I not remember you? A little blond girl sticks out like a sore thumb in this neighborhood, you know. Heard you was a cop. I'm just glad you got out and were able to do something with yourself."

"Alonzo, this is my partner, Jason," I say, remembering my manners.

The two say their hellos and shake hands.

"Zo, I came back to reminisce and see the old neighborhood. Whatever happened to the people I was living with?" I ask.

Zo lets out a sigh, walks over to the nearest stoop in front of a building, and takes a seat. I sit down next to him. Jason follows us over but remains standing next to the stoop.

"I don't know where they are. Cops showed up a few months after you left and cleared them out. They were dirty…up to something, and it wasn't good." Zo shakes his head. "Never saw or heard from them again."

"Yeah, I remember I tried to stay out of that apartment as much as possible," I add, agreeing that something wasn't right with them.

"Yeah, you were always outside. Sitting on the stoop, playing in the street with the other neighborhood kids. You were a good kid. One of the better ones."

"Zo, do you remember why I was taken from here?"

"No. One day you were gone. And like I said, a few months later the cops showed up and took 'em away."

Zo and I continue talking about the neighborhood and what so-and-so is up to. Some of the people he mentions I remember; some I don't.

After a while I stand up and lean down to give him a kiss on the cheek. "It was great seeing you, Zo. Take care of yourself."

Zo has given me what he information he knows, and I didn't want to keep pressing the issue and ruin our pleasant reunion.

"Don't be a stranger, Miss Lacey." Zo stands up and gives me another hug.

Jason and I walk back toward the subway station.

"Nothing happened here. He's the eyes and ears of this street and would have talked more if he knew anything. I just think my foster parents needed me out of that apartment ASAP and told the social worker whatever to get rid of me."

"I think you're right. What's next, Lace?"

"I don't know. Let's go home and get something to eat."

After returning to my neighborhood, we duck into Shelly's Deli.

"Hey, Jason," Lindsay, the waitress, greets Jason as we sit in a booth by the door.

"Have you slept with her?" I whisper after Lindsay walks away. I'm slightly annoyed that Lindsay has not acknowledged me even though I have eaten at this diner almost as much as Jason has.

"You know I don't sleep where I eat. I prefer my food without spit," Jason says, smiling at me.

"Yeah, I also know you'll screw anything that moves and have zero willpower."

"You got a lot of nerve, sweetheart. I showed my willpower in Atlantic City. Where was yours?" Jason asks with a wink. "And you give me too much credit, Lacey," Jason continues. "I don't sleep around nearly as much as you think I do. And did it ever occur to you that if you had sex with me every day, then maybe I wouldn't have to sleep with others?"

I laugh. "Only you would have the balls to blame me for your promiscuity."

"I'm just saying…you could do more on your part." Jason grabs my hand and strokes my palm with his thumb.

"How about if you go jerk *yourself* off every day," I say jokingly, and I pull my hand away. The touch of his hand has sent an aching for him throughout my body. If he only knew that my insides melt lately whenever I look at him…

"Okay, how about you give me sex five times a week, and I won't sleep around anymore? I mean, until you start doing more, you should be less judgmental of me." Jason is trying his best to remain serious as he makes his case.

"You're impossible. I'll have the chicken club, Lindsay. Thank you," I order as Lindsay approaches the table.

"I'll have the same. Thanks," Jason orders without looking away from me. "Sex four times a week and one oral." He leans forward in his seat, piercing me with his dark-blue eyes.

"Stop it," I say, squirming in my seat and turning pink.

"You're so cute when you're embarrassed." Mission accomplished. Jason has won this control game. He sits smugly back in his seat. "What's the next address we are going to?"

"None. What's the point? Chances are we won't run into another Zo who will remember me. We'll end up just walking around looking like fools."

Jason takes out his cell phone and pulls up the e-mail with the list of addresses.

Shit, I forgot he also has my file.

"How about we hit this one in the Bronx next?" he asks, totally ignoring my previous comments.

"Okay, we will hit a couple more. I just don't want to explore them all. It's too depressing."

Chapter 11

"I'm going to run over to the market around the corner and grab something to eat. You want anything?" I get up and walk around the house we have been doing surveillance in for nearly four days now. There has been no sign of Sal Rizzo. It is a little after two in the afternoon, and I need some air.

"Will you grab me some chips and a Mountain Dew? Thanks." Jason is immersed in a text conversation with someone and barely looks up.

Outside, the warm spring air hits me. I take off my hoodie and tie it around my waist. Underneath, I'm wearing a white tank top. The nice thing about being undercover is that we can wear almost anything as long as our guns and badges remain concealed. The market is about five blocks away, and I take my time walking there. Once inside I grab a couple of bags of chips and head toward the cooler. I'm reaching in for a bottle of water when I see Sal Rizzo and two of his thugs walk in.

Sal Rizzo looks like the typical mobster who has been type-cast in every mob-related movie. His black hair is slicked back, and there's at least a day's worth of unkempt stubble on his face. He's a squatty man, and today he is wearing a black tracksuit that is too long for his stubby frame. There's an unlit cigar dangling from his mouth that he keeps moving from one side of his mouth to the other.

"Get what you need, and let's get the fuck out of this city. I hate being here, and I especially hate this neighborhood," Sal barks at one of his cronies.

I bend down to grab a bottle of water, casually removing the hair tie that's holding my hair in a ponytail and mess up my hair a bit. I see Sal out of the corner of my eye, walking toward the cooler that I'm leaning into. When he gets close enough I spin around and smack right into him. The water and chips go flying.

"Oh, mister, I am *so* sorry," I dramatically say. I drop to the ground and try to pick up the chips and water that have gone everywhere. "I am such a klutz sometimes, and I just wasn't paying attention, you know? I am very sorry." I attempt to clean up the mess I caused while keeping one eye on Sal.

"Hey, sweetheart, it's okay. I'll survive, you know. Here, let me help you up." Sal grabs my elbow and pulls me to my feet. I discreetly pull my tank top down to reveal more cleavage, which does not go unnoticed by Sal.

"I'm sorry. I've just had such a shit day, and now this," I say, flipping my hair to one side and letting out a big sigh.

"Let me take care of this stuff for you." Sal snaps at a crony and tells him to go grab me some more chips and water. "Don't worry about it, honey." He takes me by the elbow and leads me to the cash register. "I'll take care of it."

"Oh, as if my day couldn't get any worse," I whine. "There goes my bus." I watch a bus drive by the window. "My boss is going to kill me if I'm late again."

"Where do you need to go, sweetheart? Maybe we can give you a ride?" Sal asks with the imaginary hook poking out of his mouth.

"Oh, I can't trouble you for a ride. You have been so kind already. I spill shit on you, and then you buy my food."

"Really, it's no bother. Where do you need to go?" Sal says, anxiously looking around.

"You ever been to Lookers on Forty-Second?" I ask, referencing a well-known strip club. Of course, he has been there.

"I thought you looked familiar." Sal smirks and reaches down to brush a piece of hair away from my face.

"Well, I don't normally work Thursdays, but my boss called me in because they are expecting a couple of bachelor parties tonight. And I can always use the money, so why not, you know?"

"We'll get you there. Come." Sal grabs my elbow and leads me to an SUV parked in front of the market.

"We really don't have time for this," one of the goons whispers to Sal.

"Really?" Sal hisses back. "I always have time for drinks and strippers. Let's go."

I slide into the back of the SUV with Sal, and the two goons get in front.

My skin is crawling at having to ride in the same car and be this close to these thugs. I look at my watch. I've been gone about forty-five minutes. Not long enough for Jason to start worrying. And how would he find me if he was worrying anyway? I was in a car on my way to a strip club with Sal Rizzo.

"I'm going to text my boss and let him know I'm on my way. He'll be so relieved. A couple of girls are sick with the flu or something, and we've been a little shorthanded to begin with, and now we have these parties coming in tonight…" I start babbling, hoping to distract him from my cell phone.

I shoot off a quick text to Jason:

Going to Lookers on 42nd with Sal R + 2

I casually silence my cell phone and stick it back into my pocket.

"Thanks again for the ride," I say, trying to fill in the silence.

"What's your name, honey?" Sal's eyes are piercing through me as though I'm wearing see-through clothing. He tugs at the strap on my tank top, pulling on it so it falls off my shoulder.

"Heidi. My name is Heidi."

"Heidi, didn't your mama ever teach you not to get into cars with strangers?" Sal puts his arm around me and keeps playing with my tank top's strap. He continues to move the soggy cigar around his mouth. It must be a nervous twitch or something.

"Well, you seem so nice and really helped me out back there. I really appreciate it." I smile at him.

"We *really* don't have time for this, Sal," stresses one of the goons in the front seat. He turns around and gives me a dirty look.

"Relax." Sal keeps his eyes on me. "We won't stay long. Just long enough to see what Heidi has going on underneath all these clothes. And maybe get a private showing." He tugs at my strap again.

"Oh, you're in for a real treat," I gush at him.

The SUV pulls up to the front of the strip club. Thank God, we're here. Sal gets out of the car first and then turns to help me out. I step out, link my arm through his, and lead him through the front door. I'm assuming we are being watched as long as Jason got my text. I smile and give a wave to the bouncer at the front door as though he should know me. He just nods as if all strippers look the same to him after a while, and he really doesn't care who I am. I lead Sal and his men to a table near the front of the stage. Luckily it's a Thursday afternoon, so the club isn't too busy.

"Wait here, baby. I have to go backstage and get ready. And then I'm going to give you a special show, the show of a lifetime," I whisper with a smile into Sal's ear.

"I'll be waiting." He gives me a wink and rubs his stumpy fingers down my backside.

I turn and head toward a door that is located near the stage. Once out of sight, I pull my cell out of my pocket. A text from Jason lets me know that backup will be waiting. I hear loud voices and open the door that I just went through. Sal and his goons are surrounded. They stand up, get cuffed, and are led away without an incident.

I breathe a sigh of relief and walk around the club to make sure all is well. Jason is talking with two strippers—taking statements, I'm sure.

"Hey, Lacey, good work." I stop to chat with a few other undercover detectives who are still lingering and appear to be in no hurry to exit the club.

"I just got lucky. Happened to be in the right spot," I say, shrugging like it was no big deal.

"Well, you made it very easy for us. He couldn't have been more surprised. Anywhere else, and I think we would have had a standoff. You're okay, right?"

"Oh yeah. I'm fine, thanks for asking," I say, glancing at Jason, who seems totally unconcerned with my well-being. "I have to get out of here. Not really my thing, you know? I'll see you guys later."

Once outside I head for the subway station. I've decided to head to the Bronx and check out another foster home address. The address is in Riverdale, which is an upper-middle-class residential neighborhood in the Bronx. It's a beautiful evening to walk around and explore.

Chapter 12

Absolutely nothing and no one in Riverdale looks familiar to me after walking around a few blocks. I remember Laura saying she lives in this neighborhood, so I shoot her a text letting her know I am in the area. Laura responds back to ask if I would like to catch some dinner at a local Italian restaurant that is nearby. Dinner sounds like a great idea. I was hungry a few hours ago, and now I'm famished. After I get directions to the restaurant from Laura, we plan to meet in fifteen minutes.

"Lacey!" Laura greets me in front of the restaurant as though we haven't seen each other in years.

"Come. I'm famished." I am too hungry for chitchat and lead her into the restaurant. This is clearly Laura's neighborhood. She knows practically everyone in the restaurant, including the hostess and wait staff.

I'm mostly honest with Laura about why I'm in her neighborhood. I tell her how my parents died when I was four and how I spent my life growing up in foster homes. I explain I am now trying to reconnect with my past by visiting areas where I used to live. She doesn't need to know about the nightmare, so I leave it out.

"I can't imagine. No wonder you are so tough," Laura says, looking as though she truly cannot imagine or relate to the life I've had.

"I remember hanging out at a pool in this area. Are there many around here that are open to the public?"

Laura thinks about it for a minute. "Well, the closest public pool to your former foster home is probably the one over on Netherland Avenue. We can take a walk over there after dinner if you want. It's not far from here."

"That would be great. We can walk off some of this food."

I'm really enjoying hanging out with Laura. I have many surface friends but very few close friends. I tend to shut people off before they get to know me. Jason has been the exception. He has gotten closer than anyone. I check my cell phone. No messages.

"What's up with you and Jason?" Laura reads my mind.

"Nothing. He's just a friend, my partner at work. Why?"

"Because he's totally infatuated with you."

I laugh. "You couldn't be more wrong. Right now, Jason is ass deep in strippers. Literally." I relive my day for Laura and how Jason cared more about his fans than me.

"You never slept with him?" Laura asks, surprised.

"No! I'm not going to sleep with someone I work so closely with. It would be too messy," I explain.

"By the way I'm sure you don't care, but my father said Tyler has been a mess since you broke up with him."

"Right. I don't like how it ended. I intended for it to be done more amicably, but it didn't turn out that way." I look at my phone again. "And he has called and sent texts that I haven't read yet. We are just so different, Laura. Neither one of us knew how to relate to the other."

"I understand. You were opposites," Laura says, sipping her wine. "Are you looking to start dating or take a break?"

"If someone comes along who interests me, sure, I'll start dating," I say with a shrug.

"All right, don't look, but there is a guy at the bar who has been eyeing you up. He's in a dark suit at the end, toward the right. He's a divorce lawyer at Meyers and Meyers. Let me know if you want to meet him."

I casually glance toward the man she is referring to. "Sure, he's cute."

"Come then." Laura stands and walks over to the bar. "Hi, Jacob," Laura greets him with an air kiss on the cheek. "Jacob, this is my friend Lacey Burke. Lacey, this is Jacob Meyers."

I shake his hand. He is much better looking up close, with sandy-blond hair and light-blue eyes. Jacob buys us a drink, and we talk for a little while. There are no screaming sparks, but he could have potential. As we are leaving, Jacob grabs my hand and asks if he can call me sometime.

"That would be great." I pick up his cell phone that is sitting on the bar and save my number under his contacts. "There you go."

Outside the restaurant Laura directs me toward the pool to which she suggested we take a walk. As we are walking, I check my cell phone. There's a text message from Jason asking where I am.

> Where are you?
> Dinner with Laura.
> Text me when you get home.

The pool is about two blocks from my former foster home. We approach a white gate that I'm assuming encloses the pool area.

"This should be locked. Pools aren't open yet." Laura tries the handle, and the gate opens. "Nice. They must be cleaning, but it really is dangerous to leave this open with all the kids running around here."

We walk through the gates, and my heart drops. This is the pool in my nightmare. I look around, and it's like my nightmare has become a reality. I see the exact area on the cement where I lay while trying to reach the little girl drowning. I can see how the white walls enclosing the pool are tall enough to cast a shadow during certain parts of the day. Where he stands and watches.

"Look familiar, Lacey?" Laura ventures closer to the pool and bends down to feel the water.

"Yeah, kind of. I should really get going, Laura." I'm feeling queasy and want to get away from this area quickly. My head is spinning. I start backing away toward the gate we came through.

"Yeah, really not that exciting to look at." Laura is looking around and not noticing my panic attack. "You want me to call you a car to take you home?"

"No way. Subway is fine." I can't escape fast enough, and I'm certainly not going to wait around for a car to show up. "Laura, I had such a good time tonight. Let's hang out more often." I give her a quick hug as I practically run to the subway station.

I'm sitting on the subway going home trying to process the night. The train is crowded, and I'm thankful to be surrounded by people even though I feel as though everyone is staring at me. I keep my head down and try not to make eye contact with anyone. I'm freezing cold and trying to control my shaking. It's a warm night, so why am I so cold? It's as if my blood has stopped moving through my body.

Once home I change into my pajamas and crawl into bed. I'm wide awake but trying to get warm.

I check my cell phone. A text from Jason asks if I'm home yet.

> I'm home.
> Do you want me to come over?

I look at the time. It's nine. Do I want to be alone? We don't have to work tomorrow, and I would so love to sleep in, but if I can't sleep then it's going to be a long night and day.

> Yes.

I get up and unlock the door for Jason. I wrap myself in a blanket and pour myself a glass of wine. I'm seriously thinking about turning the thermostat up so that the heat kicks on but decide against it to avoid a thousand questions from Jason.

"It's like seventy degrees outside. Are you all right?" Jason asks when he sees me bundled up like a mummy, standing in the kitchen and drinking a glass of wine.

"I'm not feeling too well. Would you like a glass of wine?"

"Sure. I never got to congratulate you on your work today." He walks over to me and grabs my hand. "Oh my God, your hand is ice." He pulls me in for a hug and rubs my back, trying to warm me up. "What happened?"

"I found the pool," I whisper as tears fall down my face. I bury my face into his chest. He's so warm, like a furnace. "I guess it all really did happen. I was hoping it was just a dream that meant something else, but it really happened," I say, crying.

"Oh, honey, I'm sorry. I wish I had been with you." Jason is rubbing my back.

"Well, you looked a little busy when I left," I say, managing a smirk in between tears.

"Really? I went to high school with those two strippers. It could not have been more awkward. I got out of there as soon as I could and went downtown for drinks with some of the guys I haven't seen in a while. Come." He leads me into the living room and pulls me onto his lap on the couch. I curl up into a ball, trying to soak up his heat, and tell him about my evening.

"Did you notice anyone there who looked familiar?" Jason asks.

"No, I didn't see anyone around," I say. "What do you think it means?"

"I don't know, Lacey, but we'll get to the bottom of it."

I stretch out on the couch. I grab the TV remote and flip through channels. Jason lays down on the couch next to me, mostly on his back with his arm around me so I can rest my head on his shoulder. We have snuggled before, usually during winter nights when I used his body heat to keep warm, so it's not like either one of us takes it as something sexual tonight. Or at least that's what I tell myself whenever we have physical contact. Because of my messy feelings for him, my boundaries have become blurred.

While I'm trying to find something to watch on TV, Jason plays with his cell phone. Out of the corner of my eye, I see a picture of a naked girl pop up.

"Really, Jay? You need to watch porn right now?"

"I met this girl that I was kind of into, but all she does is text me nude pics of herself."

"Aw, poor you. Such quality problems you have," I say sarcastically. I also feel a twinge of jealously at the idea there is a girl that he was into.

"I'm serious, Lacey. Nothing is a relationship killer like sending nude pics so soon after meeting someone. I have to wonder how many other people she sends them to. Why would I want to have anything more than a sexual relationship with her?"

"You're asking the wrong person, honey. I'm not exactly an expert on dating."

"You've never e-mailed or texted nude pics of yourself to someone?"

"No, Jay. I've had two long-term boyfriends. If they wanted to see me naked, then they would arrange to see me in person."

"But you have been on dates with other people and have slept with other people?"

"Unlike you, I don't sleep around. And I've been on a few other dates here and there. No one worth sleeping with."

"You've only slept with two guys?" Jason asks in disbelief, putting his phone down.

"I really don't want to talk about this anymore. Go back to looking at your bimbo."

"Too late. It's already out there." Jason nudges me. "Answer."

"Your bossiness ever take a day off?"

"No. Answer the question."

"Yes, I have only had sex with two guys."

"That explains a lot," Jason says, as though he just realized a medical breakthrough.

"It explains nothing," I say, laughing.

"It explains why you always get embarrassed when I tease you about sex. Christ, I've seen you kick doors in and pummel guys twice your size—but bring up sex, and you suddenly turn timid and meek."

"Whatever. You have no idea what you are talking about," I say. If he only knew I get embarrassed because it is *him* who is teasing me and it isn't about the subject matter.

"Fuck. I just realized that Ethan must have been your first."

"Jason, I really don't want to talk about this anymore. And what do you care anyway?" I ask, pretending to distract myself by scrolling through the TV channels again.

"Wow. That lucky bastard. Remind me to congratulate him the next time we see him."

"Don't you dare mention it." I glare at him and then realize I just confirmed his guess when I see the goofy smirk on his face. "Ugh. I hate you sometimes."

"What's the big deal, Lacey?" Jason asks as he turns onto his side and puts his other arm around me. He takes the TV remote out of my hand and flips through the channels. I close my eyes and go to sleep.

Chapter 13

The sun streaming through my blinds wakes me up the next morning. I'm lying on the couch, and it's about eight o'clock. I'm very relieved to have slept through the night. Jason is sleeping behind me, spooning me with his arms still wrapped around me. I'm in heaven and lay there for a few minutes to soak in his body heat and enjoy having him so close to me.

I reach over and pick up my phone off the table when I hear a text message come in:

Midtown Y offers swim lessons for adults.

"Jason," I say, and I drive my elbow into his side to get him off me.

"Jesus, what the hell?" Jason moves away from me and grabs the area I just elbowed.

"Did you send this text?" I ask.

"What? What are you talking about?"

"You are the only one who knows about that nightmare. How could you send me that text?" I say, pushing him off me and further away.

"You're off your damn rocker, you know that?" Jason snaps, grabbing my cell phone. "I didn't send that. Why would I send that? And you think I text while I sleep?"

"Don't give me that excuse. You can program a text message to be sent at a certain time. You know that." I give him a dirty look. "You're the only one who knows."

"There is no return number," Jason says, looking at the message and then handing my phone back to me.

"You got some nerve thinking I would do that to you," Jason says, still rubbing the area I elbowed.

"Fine. If you didn't send it, then who did?" I ask.

"How should I know?" Jason gets off the couch and walks into the kitchen.

I get up and follow him into the kitchen. He grabs a bottle of water out of the refrigerator and leans against the counter, sipping it, still giving me a dirty look.

"I'm sorry I elbowed you," I say, leaning against the counter next to him. "I just went into panic mode when I saw that text. I've never been good at reining in crazy."

"Fine, I get that," Jason says. He grabs my hand. "At least you're feeling warmer. Still a little chilly, though. I thought I was going to have to drop you off at the morgue last night."

"Thanks for staying here last night."

"You know I would do anything for you, Lacey."

"I know," I say, embarrassed for how I acted earlier.

"I'm going to call Alan Roth and see if he can trace an anonymous text message," Jason says. He is referring to a fellow police officer in NYPD's Computer Crimes department.

"Thanks," I say.

I am feeling like even more of a heel for accusing him of sending the text. I make myself a cup of tea and toast bagels for us while Jason is on the phone.

"He said it's possible but not likely," Jason says when he gets off the phone with Alan. "He said there is a slew of apps that let someone send messages with no return phone number. Most people who don't want to be detected will sign up for the app under a false name while not using their own computer and then use a disposable phone to send the message. If someone was sloppy enough to use his real name or his home or work computer or his real cell phone, then he could be identified. But most people going to the trouble of using these types of apps aren't going to be using a real name. Or own cell phone."

"Well, that sucks." I place Jason's breakfast in front of him.

"Think about anyone else who may know your story. Maybe you told someone else? Laura? Tyler? Tyler has a reason to mess with you now. I doubt he's happy about being dumped."

"I never told Tyler or Laura. And Tyler barely knows how to operate his smart phone. He certainly isn't going to be aware of different apps to send anonymous text messages."

"What about the guy who was in your dream? You went to the pool yesterday, and maybe he saw you."

"It's possible, I guess," I say slowly, chewing my bagel. "I didn't see anyone around, but that doesn't mean he wasn't there. But how would he get my cell phone number? It's a restricted number."

"I don't know, Lace. I guess you can find anything about anyone on the Internet if you try hard enough."

"Nice," I say sarcastically.

"In the meantime, don't plan on doing anything without me."

"Whatever, Jason. I appreciate your concern, but I'm not going to be someone's prisoner. I will live my life the way I always have."

I can see Jason clench his jaw at my defiance, but he apparently decides against arguing with me about it.

"What is your plan for today anyway?"

"No plan." I sit at the table with my leg tucked under my butt and continue chewing my bagel.

"No plan to investigate further into what happened twenty years ago—and now the text message?" Jason asks, likely not believing me.

"How far can I take this? My dream is the only evidence that there was any wrongdoing from someone. So I find out a man probably watched a little girl drown twenty years ago. Chances are, I will never be able to find him anyway or even prove that it happened. I'm kind of hoping I'll wake up one day and go back to forgetting the incident. And hopefully whoever sent the text had their fun for the day and moves on."

"Okay. I just want to make sure you're not going to go off exploring on your own," Jason says, looking at me and studying my face.

"No, I think I'll go for a run and then get my hair cut. It's getting a little frizzy with the warmer air." I look at the ends.

"Let me know if you change your mind. Promise?" Jason gives me that look that dares me to defy him. "I'm very reluctant to leave you alone; you know that, right?"

"I *promise* I won't explore without you." I say, rolling my eyes. "You are way too protective. I'll walk you home since I'm going for a run anyway."

"I will always look out for you, Laces. Deal with it."

"I know." I wrap my arms around his arm and lay my head on his bicep as we walk through the park. "I'm so lucky to have you in my life. You're always there when I need you."

"God, you're a moody thing this morning. One minute you're throwing an elbow at me; the next you're all nicey-nice." Jason reaches over to my forehead and pretends to feel for a fever. "You're still not feeling well, huh, Laces? You usually act like I have a virus or something."

"Well the jury is still out on that one. But I do appreciate everything you do for me."

"I'm as clean as a whistle, honey. It always gets wrapped up."

"Really?" I ask, kind of surprised. "Always?"

"Always. I don't want any pregnancies. Chris has taught me that lesson."

"Hmm. Well, that's a relief to know. I was always worried some pension digger would jam you up."

"Don't worry about me." He pulls me in for a hug and kisses the top of my head. "I'll see you later, okay? And no exploring without me, got it?"

"I promise I won't go anywhere without you." I wave as I break free from his hug and begin my run.

Chapter 14

When I get back to my apartment, I look at my cell phone and see a missed call and voice mail. It's from Jacob Meyers, asking if I would like to have dinner with him on Monday. *Hmmm.* I text Laura to let her know he called. She responds back by asking what I'm doing today and if I want to go shopping. I really don't want to go shopping with Laura, as I have a feeling we don't shop at the same stores. I let her know that I need to get a haircut today and don't need to shop for anything. My phone rings. It's Laura.

"Lacey, please let me take you to my salon for a makeover. *Please.*"

"I'm fine, Laura. I was just going to run over to Quick Cuts and get a trim."

"Lacey, please go to my salon. My hairdresser can do miracles."

"Um, okay. If you think I need a miracle done to me, I'm somewhat insulted." I'm not insulted. I know we have very different tastes. I'm very low maintenance and pay little attention to my appearance.

"Do not be insulted. It's just you are so naturally beautiful; with a little style and a nice haircut, you could really kill it," Laura says, trying to dig herself out of her hole. "Please. I'm going to make an appointment for you. Don't say no."

I relent. It's not as if I have anything else going on today, and it might do me some good to go to a more upscale hair salon. "Okay. Make an appointment. Thanks."

Five minutes later Laura texts me with the appointment time and address of the place. Great. This better not turn into an all-day thing. My idea of a haircut is getting the ends trimmed and then pulling my hair back into a ponytail as I walk out of the hairdresser's.

When I get to the salon, I immediately regret my decision to do this. Laura is already inside, chatting with an Italian man in his forties wearing all black. Laura makes the introductions. His name is Renaldo, and apparently, he is the one who will be performing the miracle today. Renaldo looks slightly annoyed at having to deal with someone as uncouth as myself.

"I just need a trim." I am trying to let him know that this won't be a long appointment and I am not expecting much.

"Well, Miss Lacey, I think you need more than a trim," Renaldo says while picking up a chunk of my hair and quickly dropping it, as though he sees a bug crawling through it.

"Really, I just need a trim. I wear my hair in a ponytail every day for work, so anything other than a trim would be a huge waste of your time." I glare at Laura.

"Lacey, please. Let Renaldo help you. Renaldo, what do you think?"

"Well, I think *some* sort of style would make a *huge* difference. Some layers here and there with highlights. Simple, nothing drastic, and easy to style." Renaldo is likely adding the last sentence for my benefit.

"Don't change the length or the color," I say to Renaldo. "I like my long hair; it's easy to pull up. And my hair is already blond enough. I don't need to look like some dumb, bleached-out bimbo."

"Laura, please," Renaldo says, as though he is no longer willing to deal with me. "There is nothing I can do here."

"Lacey, he won't change the length. Adding layers will make it less heavy. And highlights will brighten up your face and green eyes. Perfect for summer." Laura looks to be desperately trying to appease the situation so that a haircut actually happens today.

"Okay. Nothing drastic, like you said." I direct this at Renaldo.

Two hours later Renaldo is styling my hair. I must admit, it's a huge improvement. The highlights look amazing, and the layers give my hair more volume.

"Thank you," I say, looking at Renaldo.

He nods at me, also happy with the result.

"You were beautiful before, Miss Lacey. All I did was bring it to another level. I hope to see you again." Renaldo puts his hands together and gives me a little bow. Clearly, we have made peace.

"Come, Lacey. We are almost done. Thanks, Renaldo." Laura grabs my hand and leads me upstairs to another level in the salon.

"No, we *are* done here, Laura." I gently pull my hand, but she has a cobra clutch going on and won't release it.

"Lacey, we are getting our nails done. It won't take long, I promise."

"Laura, really? I deal with dirt for a living. Why do I need to have nice-looking nails?"

Laura leads me into a small room with two chairs. We sit down, and two women immediately go to work on my hands and feet. After conceding that I am not going to escape this, I get comfortable; I lay my head back on the headrest and close my eyes. Next thing I know, someone is brushing wax around my eyebrows. The person then takes a piece of paper and rips off some of my eyebrow hair. I look over at Laura, who is trying to keep from laughing.

"If I had my gun, I would shoot you right now, you know that, right?"

"Oh, Lacey, you will thank me later. Especially when you are out with Jacob Meyers and he can't keep his hands off you."

"I haven't called him back yet. I'm not sure I want to go." What I really mean is that I'm not sure I want to expose someone else to my issues right now.

"He's very cute. And a very good divorce lawyer. My father has him on retainer in case the latest gold digger doesn't work out. I guess he's a real shark. That's about all I know about him."

"We'll see. Maybe I'll call him tomorrow." I look over at Laura, who has her head tipped back, enjoying every minute of her manicure. We are so different.

"Thanks for bringing me here, Laura. I guess I needed a little pampering."

"Oh, Lacey, I'm so glad. Promise me you'll come back here every so often and let Renaldo freshen you up."

"Sure." I close my eyes and lay my head back on the headrest.

"Where do you want to go after this?" Laura asks.

"Home," I say, and I am not joking.

"No, I was thinking we would go shopping for some new outfits," Laura says, looking at my jeans.

"There's nothing wrong with my clothes. They are very practical for my work," I say.

"That's my point. You work with a bunch of guys, and you kind of dress like them, too. That's just not right," Laura says, sounding disgusted. "Not with your body anyway. You need to show it more often, honey. Do you know how much I've paid to have tits like yours?"

I roll my eyes at the woman who is painting my toenails.

"You are so dramatic," I say to Laura. "Fine. But we need to go somewhere that is relatively cheap. Keep in mind, I don't have a trust fund."

"Don't worry, I have the perfect store for you. But first I need to stop at my jewelers and check on a piece they are repairing for me."

Once we leave the salon, Laura drags me into an expensive jewelry store that is on the way to wherever we are going for clothes. While she's busy chatting with everyone, I walk around and gaze at the pieces in the showcases.

"That's the engagement ring my ex gave me," Laura says, coming up behind me and pointing to a princess-cut diamond ring on display in a case with several other engagement rings.

"When were you engaged?"

"Last year. It didn't work out, so I returned the ring for store credit. I mean, what was I going to do with it anyway? It's not like I could keep wearing it. And it ended badly, so there was no way I was giving it back to him. I just wanted it out of my home, so I brought it here to sell on consignment."

"Wow. It's beautiful, Laura. They are all beautiful," I say, looking around.

"What kind of ring do you want?" Laura says, also admiring the other rings.

"Oh, I don't know. Not really something I thought about."

"C'mon," she says. "Every girl has an idea what kind of ring she wants. Round? Princess cut? Emerald?"

"Hmm," I say. "Something simple. I'm not really into fancy, as you have learned. They are all beautiful."

After a few minutes of looking everything over, I point to an emerald-cut diamond ring with smaller baguettes on the side. "This one is my favorite. It's simple, yet not boring. But very beautiful."

"Yeah, that is one of my favorites, too," Laura says, gazing at it. "I agree. Very beautiful."

Walking home after shopping with Laura, I must admit that the girl knows her stuff. She hooked me up with clothes that were stylish and flattering yet didn't break my bank.

"Let's go out tonight and show you off," Laura says as she links her arm through mine.

"I told Jason I would meet him at Manny's," I say. Not really a lie. Jason and I hang out every Friday at Manny's Bar.

"Okay," Laura says. She looks somewhat disappointed at having to hang out at another blue-collar pub.

"Hey, it's almost six. How about if we grab a slice of pizza, drop this stuff off at my place, and then head over to Manny's for happy hour?" I've decided my mission tonight is to find Laura a man. It's the least I can do for the girl after she styled me up today.

At my place Laura insists that we (mainly me) change into one of the new outfits that we bought today to wear out. Heading over to Manny's with Laura in tow, I text Jason to let him know that we are going there for happy hour. I also ask if he could bring one of his "nicer" friends to introduce to Laura.

Define nice.

Not you. Someone who won't use and abuse her.

OK. I'll see what I can do.

Once at Manny's Laura and I belly up to the bar and order two beers. There's a decent happy hour crowd but not anyone I know. About an hour later Jason shows up with Rob Bronski, an undercover homicide detective stationed in the Bronx. Rob is perfect for Laura; I'm so pleased with Jason's choice.

"Hi, Rob." I get off my barstool and give him a hug.

"Lacey, it's so good to see you. You look great," Rob says, taking notice of my new look.

I immediately do the introductions, excited for Laura. Rob is a great-looking, super nice guy.

"You look beautiful, Laces," Jason whispers in my ear. He puts his arm around my waist.

"Thanks for bringing Rob. He's perfect. I owe you one," I whisper into Jason's ear.

"Great. How about if we go back to your place, and you can repay me?" Jason whispers back. "You look amazing. What the hell happened today?"

"Laura kidnapped me and tortured me all day," I say. I give Laura a wink and casually remove Jason's tight grip around my waist.

"Doesn't she look great?" Laura asks no one in particular. "All she needed was a little tweaking."

"Yeah, I got tweaked *bad*," I say, rolling my eyes. "Rob, take my seat. I've been sitting all day and feel like standing." I wave to the empty barstool next to Laura.

Rob sits down and orders everyone another round. "So, Lacey, congrats on rounding up Rizzo. Jason tried to take all the credit, but everyone knows it's you who does most of the work," Rob teases with a wink. "I hear Rizzo was on his way upstate when you snagged him. How did you get him to stay in the city?"

I retell the story of how I ran into Rizzo at a neighborhood market and talked him into giving me a ride to "work."

"Weren't you scared, Lacey?" Laura asks.

"No, I wasn't scared. It's part of the job," I say.

"Well, we could use someone like you in Homicide. Why don't you put a transfer in and come on over?" Rob says, smirking at Jason.

"I'm okay for now…until Jason gets tired of dealing with me anyway," I say.

Jason is staring at me with slight smile on his lips, as though he is very entertained by something. I start turning another shade of pink. Ugh, why does he do this to me?

"Lacey, come with me to the bathroom," Laura orders as she gets off her barstool. When we are in the bathroom, she says, "Why don't you two just fuck and get it over with already? I mean, holy shit. The sexual tension is blaring *loudly*."

"I don't know what you mean, Laura." I look in the mirror and reapply my lip gloss. "I can't sleep with him. We work too closely together."

"Oh, give me a break. Sell me a different story. You screw and then move on. Either you remain friends or you don't. If you don't, then you transfer out like Rob suggested."

I admire how directly she just summed everything up. She continues, "I mean, holy shit. I could orgasm just looking at him. How is it that you have held out this long?"

"I know; he is beautiful, isn't he? It's just that he is my closest friend, and I don't want to ruin the friendship."

"Friendship, shmiendship. You'll make another friend." Laura leads the way out of the bathroom and back to our bar spot.

"So, Rob, Laura lives in Riverdale, not far from your station," I say, trying to direct the conversation onto Laura.

"Where in Riverdale?" Rob asks, turning to face Laura.

"What is your issue?" I quietly hiss to Jason as Rob and Laura become more engrossed in their own private conversation. I am so glad they are hitting it off.

"I don't know what you are talking about, Lace," Jason says, taking a sip from his beer, not taking his eyes off me.

"You're making me uncomfortable; quit it," I whisper.

"If you tell me what I'm doing, then I will stop it. But I can't stop if I don't know what it is that's bothering you," Jason whispers in my ear.

And how do you tell someone to turn off his smoldering looks?

"Just forget it. Try to behave, please," I whisper, turning red again.

"Okay, I'll stop. You're just so easy to bother. Here, take a seat." Jason points to a barstool that has opened up.

Laura and Rob are still enjoying their private conversation. I'm so relieved. I sit down on the barstool, and Jason stands next to me, leaning on the bar.

"So, I'm going to work seven to one on Monday and then go to the Yankees game. It's opening day. Why don't you go? Maybe we'll run into Ethan," Jason says, smiling.

"Jay, please don't start. This is why I never told you about him. And I don't want to go. Why don't you just take the whole day off? We have to go to the station and do paperwork regarding Rizzo anyway. I'll write it up if you want, and then you just have to sign off on it." And I may have a hot date with Jacob Meyers, which is another reason I can't go to the game.

"Okay, you talked me into taking the whole day off. Thanks for taking care of the paperwork," Jason says, signaling the bartender for more drinks. "You know, you really do look nice tonight. What happened today?"

"Laura dragged me to her salon. She can be very persuasive sometimes. You think she Rob are getting along?"

Jason looks over my shoulder at the two of them talking. "Yeah, they seem to be all right. It's hard to tell with Rob. He keeps everything close to the chest. She's a good-looking girl though, totally doable. Just have to get past the Daddy's-princess attitude."

"You're so good at summing people up in two sentences or less. Tell me, Jay, how would you describe me to one of your friends?"

"Hmmm," Jason says, while rubbing his stubbly chin. "A moody pain in the ass with a nasty elbow jab. But hot as hell."

"I am *so* sorry for this morning." I pat his rib cage where I jabbed him earlier.

"Hi, Jason." Some pretty blonde walks up to the bar and leans next to Jason, distracting him from my apology. She looks for the bartender as though her real purpose is to get a drink and being able to stand next to Jason is an afterthought.

"Hey, Mary. How are you?" Jason asks.

"Fine, thanks," she responds, moving closer him. The bar is not crowded, but you would think it was three deep, the way she is inching closer to him.

Jason seems amused. "And how's your sister?" he asks the blonde.

"She's good. She'll be out later," the blonde says, batting her eyes at him.

"Well, tell her I said hi." Jason flags down the bartender for the blonde, obviously anxious to get her moving along.

"Have a great night, Mary," Jason says after he gets the bartender's attention and she puts in her order. He then picks up our drinks, grabs my hand, and leads me to an open booth near the back.

"It must be exhausting being you," I say dramatically.

"Not funny. She scares me."

I turn back to the bar. Rob and Laura are still talking, unaware that we have left them. The blonde has moved to the other side of the bar, shooting dirty looks in our direction.

"You think you're capable of having a serious relationship?" I ask Jason.

"Of course I am. And I have had serious relationships before. Just haven't met anyone lately who interests me." Jason leans backs in the booth, looking slightly hurt that I would even question his ability to have a serious relationship.

"Oh right. *Catherine*," I say. Jason had told me about the girl he dated for two years before we met. "The girl who had to move to Seattle to get away from you because she was so heartbroken."

"Right," Jason says, smirking.

"Why didn't you marry her?"

"She was a very nice person, and I did love her on some level. There was just something that didn't feel right. I didn't feel like we were meant to spend the rest of our lives together," Jason explains.

"You ever cheat on her?" I ask.

"No, Lacey, I never cheated on her. I'm capable of being monogamous. I was faithful to Catherine, and I have also had other girlfriends that I never cheated on."

"Since I've known you, you've only had sex flings. I was just wondering if that's all you're looking for."

"Well, you obviously don't know me as well you think you do. I have been in monogamous, long-term relationships. And someday I want a wife and kids. I just didn't want it with Catherine. It didn't feel right with her."

"What are you looking for then?"

"Where are you going with this, Lace?"

"I'm just trying to understand men better. Like, why isn't that blonde relationship material? She's very pretty and obviously would like more from you, so what is it about her that makes you uninterested?"

"Really? You really want to get into this?" Jason asks, sounding amused. "I can't have a relationship with her because she doesn't give me any pushback."

"What does that mean?" I ask.

"If I were to go over there and tell her to get on all fours, she would do it. She bores me after two minutes because I know I can make her do whatever I want. To have that type of imbalance in a relationship doesn't interest me. It's boring."

"Then why are you such a control freak if you think it's boring for someone to do as you say?" I ask, somewhat confused.

"There's a difference between boring and challenging, Laces. I try to control you because you won't let me, so it becomes a challenge. You are far from boring. And ninety-five percent of the time when you think I'm trying to control you, I'm actually trying to protect you. You don't always have the best judgment, you know?"

"My judgment is okay," I say, slightly offended.

"Really? Tyler Moneybags? What a prick he is! And you were with him for how long?"

"Point made."

"And how about getting into a car with Sal Rizzo? I initially wanted to kill you when I heard that."

I gasp. "How dare you!" I say, in a loud whisper across the table and probably a little too dramatically. "That is such double standard. Don't even go there." I cross my arms and glare at him. I am now fuming. "Because I'm a woman it's bad judgment, but if I were a man, it would have been heroic."

"Okay, okay," Jason concedes, holding his hands up. "That was a low blow. You are right. You did what you had to do. It just pissed me off, is all."

"Well, that's your issue, not mine," I hiss.

"You're right. It's my issue. I'm sorry." Jason looks at Laura and Rob, who are now standing up. "Looks like they are leaving."

I turn around and catch Laura's eye. She walks over to our booth and says, "Rob and I are going to share a cab home. We live kind of near each other."

"Okay, are you sure you're fine with that?" I ask. I want to make sure she hasn't had too much to drink and will regret anything in the morning.

"I'm fine, Lacey. I'll call you tomorrow." She leans over and kisses me on the cheek. "See ya, Jason." She waves as she walks back to Rob, who is taking care of the bar tab.

I wave good-bye to Rob from my seat and then turn back to Jason. "I'm going to take off too. I'm suddenly very bored."

"Oh, come on. Don't be like that. I'm walking you home," Jason says, following me out of the bar and onto the street.

"Really, I'm fine. You don't have to walk me home. Go make blondie and her sister get on all fours," I snap at him.

Jason ignores me, grabs my hand, and starts leading the way. "Don't be mad at me, please. I was just being honest. Next time would you rather I lie to you?"

"No, I appreciate the honesty. It's just you hurt my ego a little bit. But I'll survive." After a minute of cooling down, I smile up at him to let him know all is well. "You think it will be a one-nighter or more for Rob and Laura?"

"Oh, I don't think they will hook up tonight. Rob is very slow to close a deal. You said you wanted someone not like me, remember?"

"Well, that's good, I think," I say. I hope Laura will appreciate his moving slowly.

When we get to my door, Jason turns to me and says, "I can't stay tonight." He pulls me in closer and whispers into my ear, "There's no way I'll behave and stay on the couch."

Oh, my. My insides do a backflip.

"Good night, Jason," I say, pulling away from him, pretending to be annoyed with his advances and fumbling with my key.

Once inside I collapse in bed and catch my breath. Wow. That would be a game changer. No, I did the right thing. Sex will change everything between us, and I'm not sure I'm ready for that to happen.

Chapter 15

$\mathcal{I}$ wake up screaming. The same nightmare. It's two in the morning. My neighbors must think I'm a total nutcase. I hear the rain falling outside. Thunder rumbles off in the distance. Sheet lightning lights up my room. Damn, now I'll never get back to sleep. I get up and look out the window. It's like a light show outside. For a brief moment, I think I see someone standing outside across the street. He's standing underneath a tree leading into the park. It looks like he is looking up at me.

I must be losing my mind.

I wait for lightning to light up the sky again so that I can get a better view. Yes, he is definitely looking up at me. I'm sure it's a just a coincidence. He got caught in the rain and is waiting it out underneath a tree. It just so happens that he is looking up at my apartment building. Lightning lights up the sky again. Oh my God! I stumble backward trying to find something, anything, to hide behind. It's the man in my nightmare. The one who watches the little girl drown.

I open the drawer to my nightstand and pull out my gun. I can't believe this is happening to me. I don't know whether to curl up in a ball and cry or run outside shooting. I crawl back to the window, staying low so he can't see me. I peek out the window and wait for the next round of lightning to strike. He's no longer there. Where did he go? I look up and down the street but don't see anyone. Was he ever there? Yes, he *was* there. I saw him, and he saw me. I'm not insane. I change out of my pajamas and throw on a pair of jeans and a hooded sweatshirt. I tuck my gun in my jeans and grab my cell phone. Should I call Jason? No. He would probably tell me to go to hell since I had shot him down. And who could blame him? I throw on my sneakers and head out the door. The street is empty except for a few cabs. I run across the street to the tree where I had seen him standing. No one is there. What am I hoping to accomplish by running around at two in the morning like a madwoman? I don't know. I just want answers and for the nightmares to end.

I hear someone walking about ten feet away from where I'm standing. I turn and walk toward the footsteps. Whoever is there walks faster away from me. I walk faster to try to catch up to him. Next thing I know, I'm running. He also starts running. He's running further into the park, away from the street. What if this is a trap? I'm suddenly reminded of Jason's "bad judgment" comment, but I really don't care at this point. I think I'm gaining on him. Periodically I catch a glimpse of his back whereas before, I was only going by sound. Why didn't I grab a flashlight? Instead I'm relying on lightning, which is happening less frequently. And then there is nothing. I have lost him. He must have gone off a different path or hid behind a tree, and I missed it.

I'm absolutely drenched from the pouring rain. I stand there, looking around, trying to see something, *anything*. Nothing. I backtrack. Maybe he decided to duck down somewhere, and I ran by him. Or maybe there is another path that had allowed him to divert. Anger has taken over any fear I had before. How dare he come to where I live and then hide in the shadows like a coward? Just like before.

I walk around the park for another hour. I can't find him. He's officially gone. I give up and walk back to my apartment. I sit on the couch and fire up my laptop. I had meant to do research yesterday, but Laura kept me busy with the salon and shopping. I start by doing an Internet search of pool drownings in Riverdale. Then I narrow it to drownings that occurred twenty years ago. Nothing stands out. I try more searches with different words and phrases; still nothing comes up that fits. I periodically look out the window to see if he has decided to come back. No one to be seen.

It's a relief when the sun finally comes up. What a long night. I change into my running gear and decide to go for another run. It's amazing how different the park looks in the daylight. It's like Jekyll and Hyde. Even though I know he is long gone, I'm constantly looking for the man from last night. I even extend my run so that I can keep looking, maybe hoping to find a clue as to where he went. It's not surprising that I don't find anything. What did I expect, bread crumbs leaving a trail to somewhere? A big sign saying, "Over here, Lacey"? When I get back to my apartment, I take a shower and then collapse on my couch from exhaustion.

My cell phone buzzing wakes me up a few hours later. It's Jason, asking if he can bring a pizza over. It's noon already. I really passed out. I text back that I'm starving and would love some pizza.

Chapter 16

*J*ason. What would I do without him? Would I ever want to risk our friendship? So then why am I putting on mascara and doing my hair? I have never fixed myself up for him before. My feelings for him are so confusing at this point.

I open the door to let him. "You won't believe the night I had."

"What's the matter, Laces? Did you regret your decision not to let me in last night?" Jason puts the pizza on the table and gets a soda from the refrigerator.

"Yeah, actually I did."

I proceed to tell him about the man under the tree. When I get to the part about me running around the park at two in the morning, I see him tensing up.

"Please don't be mad or lecture me or tell me about my lack of judgment. What was I supposed to do? Go back to bed and hope that he went away?"

"No, but you could have called me. Or, gee, I don't know, you could have called someone at the precinct to do a drive-through of the park." His tone drips with sarcasm, and he tries to keep his voice down.

"Please don't be mad. And how silly would I have looked to call the precinct and ask for a drive-by because I see a man standing underneath a tree during a rainstorm?"

"Fine. Then you should have called me."

"All right, next time, I'll call you. Just please stop lecturing me about it this time." I take a bite of my pizza. "Thanks for bringing the pizza over. I am starving," I say, trying to change the subject and lighten the mood.

"Are you sure it was him, Lacey?"

"Positive. The lightning lit everything up, and I could see his face. It was definitely him. Twenty years later. But definitely him."

"Okay. So how did he find you, and what did he want?"

"I don't know. Maybe he followed me from Riverdale the other day, or maybe he always knew where I lived."

"Well, looks like we need to take a trip to Riverdale," Jason says.

When we are finished eating, I put the leftover pizza in the fridge and grab bottles of water to go.

"You know I can handle this if you have something else to do today," I say. I am trying to give Jason an out as we walk to the subway station.

"Don't start, Laces. Before, it was just a nightmare, and now some guy is stalking you? We need to end this."

Once in Riverdale, Jason leads me to an NYPD station on Webster Avenue. When we walk through the door, a uniformed redhead sitting behind a desk immediately greets him.

"Hey, Jason, what brings you back to these parts?" the redhead asks. I forgot that Jason started his career working in the Bronx and then transferred to Manhattan a few years ago.

"Sara, this is my partner, Lacey," Jason says, signaling to me.

"Nice to meet you, Lacey." Sara shakes my hand and gives me a warm smile.

"I'm hoping you can do a little digging for us, Sara. We need to know about any drownings at a pool over on Netherland Avenue about twenty years ago," Jason says, getting right to the point.

"Sure, that shouldn't be a problem." Sara sits back down at her desk and types into her computer.

"So how are Mike and the kids?" Jason asks, winking at me as if anticipating the "Did you sleep with her?" question.

"Oh, they're good, Jason." Sara turns around and grabs three framed pictures. "That's our oldest, Aiden. Can you believe he is turning seven this year?" she asks proudly.

"Has it really been that long? I remember when you were pregnant with him and the night you went into labor," Jason says, looking at the picture.

"Jason practically carried me to the hospital around the corner. He's such a sweetheart," Sara says to me.

"Well, I was terrified I was going to get stuck delivering him," Jason says, smiling and handing the pictures back. "Excuse me for a minute, ladies." Jason walks away and greets some of the other cops.

"So, Lacey, have you been on the job long?" Sara asks.

"Almost four years. I went through the academy after college. Jason and I have been partners for a few years."

"He's such a nice guy. I was sorry when he was transferred out of here, but I guess it was a better move for him, so he had to do it. My husband and I grew up in this neighborhood, so there was never any reason for me to look at transfers. But the neighborhood is slowly going downhill, you know? I'll be glad when I can retire." Sara turns around and grabs some pages off the printer behind her.

"Here you go, my dear." Sara puts a few pieces of paper in front of me. "There have been two drownings at that pool in twenty years. I'm surprised there's been that many. I sometimes take my kids there. It's not a bad pool. There is always a lifeguard on duty, and they keep it pretty clean. Both drownings happened after hours when it was closed and no lifeguard. Poor kids. Just put a bullet in my head if anything ever happens to my kids while I'm alive, you know? Do you have any kids, Lacey?"

"No, I don't. Maybe someday," I say. I pick up the papers she gave me.

"It's tough to do this job and have a family, but you make it happen if that's what you want," she says, walking around her desk to me.

Seeing that we are wrapping up, Jason makes his way back to us. "Thanks again, Sara. Say hello to your family for me." He takes the papers, folds them, and puts them in his back pocket.

"I will. And come back and visit us more often. Nice meeting you, Lacey," Sara says, shaking my hand again.

"Nice meeting you, Sara," I say.

Jason grabs my arm and leads me toward the door.

"Where is this pool?" he asks once we are outside.

I get my bearings and then start leading the way. "It's a few blocks up here and then a few blocks over to the right."

When the white wall and front gate come into view, Jason takes my arm and pulls me into a coffee shop. "Let's sit for a minute and watch the traffic."

I grab a table in the front with a clear view of the main white gate that opens to the pool area. Jason sits down with a coffee for himself and green tea for me. He pulls out the reports we got from Sara and starts reading.

"This one," he says as he reads one of the reports. "A five-year-old girl drowned twenty years ago. Theresa Brinkley. She was with another five-year-old girl who survived. Unnamed. No witnesses. Ruled accidental. Says the two little girls wandered into the pool area after dark when the gate was accidentally left unlocked. Both fell into the pool. Theresa was unable to pull herself out. A passerby pulled her dead body out of the water after the surviving five-year-old ran into the street screaming for help." Jason sits back in his seat and stares intently at me, as if trying to read my expression.

"I only remember what I told you I saw in my dream," I whisper, still not wanting to believe this happened to me. It was so much simpler when it was just a nightmare and not reality.

"What I don't understand is why you weren't named in the report."

"I don't know. Maybe because I wouldn't give it? Maybe because I was a ward of the state, and the state didn't want to be held liable, so they asked the cops not to use it? Maybe because I was a foster kid, and Social Services didn't want bad press, so they withheld it? Maybe because no one cared what my name was?"

"Well, I guess it could be any number of reasons. And unfortunately, the signing officer who wrote this report died about three years ago, so we can't ask him. I remember his funeral like it was yesterday. Massive heart attack at forty-five."

"It's amazing how you know *everyone*," I say with admiration.

"Well, I've been doing this longer than you have. And I'm a lot friendlier than you are."

"I think I'm pretty friendly," I say, somewhat convincingly.

Jason cocks his head and gives me a look as if to ask if I honestly believe that. "You have a fence built up around you. You're very nice to people, don't get me wrong. But you will allow people to get only so close to you before you shut them down."

"It might have something to do with the fact that I raised myself. By the time I got close to someone, they disappeared from my life. So I stopped trying. And I stopped relying on others for anything."

"Sir, can I get you another coffee?" A buxom brunette walks over to our table and interrupts our conversation.

"Yes, please, and she'll also have another green tea," Jason says, pointing to my mug and giving the brunette a smile as though she just rescued a dozen puppies from a burning house.

Without taking her eyes off Jason, she takes our mugs and walks away.

"Every five minutes we are here, another button comes undone on her blouse," I say, rolling my eyes.

"Hey, there's nothing wrong with that. It is kind of warm in here," Jason says, smirking.

I look back again at the coffee girl. Her breasts are practically popping out of her shirt and are so high up they almost touch her chin. I casually pull my shirt out so I can look at my chest and wonder if maybe the type of bra I have been wearing is all wrong. I shift things around a bit to make my cleavage more pronounced and pull down on my bra to try to make everything lift up.

"As much as I enjoy watching you play with yourself, what are you doing?" Jason asks.

"Just wondering how she got hers to be practically touching her chin," I say, exaggerating somewhat and still admiring what my shifting has accomplished.

"They're fake, Lacey. And you're good in that area, don't worry about it," Jason says, smiling. "But if you want, we can go in the bathroom, take off your shirt, and I'll give you my professional opinion."

"You're impossible. Thank you," I say to the coffee girl when she drops off my tea.

"Here you go," she purrs to Jason as she sets his coffee down.

"Thank you, honey," Jason says to the coffee girl and then waits for her to walk out of earshot before he continues talking. "And what do you care if she hits on me anyway? You had your chance last night and shot me down cold."

I laugh, relieved that we got that elephant out of the room.

"Well, I'm glad you find it funny. Thank God I have a healthy ego that can handle embarrassment," Jason says, laughing.

"You're so full of shit. Embarrassed, my ass. Now you're just trying to make me feel guilty."

Jason shrugs and smiles.

"I haven't seen anyone go in or out of that gate. What about you?" Jason nods toward the pool.

"No, I haven't seen anyone. And I haven't seen anyone walking around who looks familiar either. What do you want to do now?"

Jason waves the coffee girl over. She practically takes her blouse off as she is walking toward us. "Honey, do you know anyone who works over at that pool?"

"Well, the lifeguards change every summer. The only one who is always there is John. I don't know his last name. He's real creepy, though. I never see him talking to anyone. I think he's in charge of cleaning the pool or something."

"Do you know how long he has worked there?" Jason asks his new wealth of information.

"Oh, a long time. As long as I've worked here. At least two years."

"Do you know where he lives?" Jason keeps pressing the issue.

"Uh, no. I wouldn't even want to know that." She looks suddenly insulted.

"Does he ever come in here for anything?" Jason asks.

I see where he is going with this. Maybe we could come back to this coffee shop another time.

"No, I only know about him because sometimes I'll go for a swim after work. If it's real hot out, you know?"

"You've been very helpful. Thank you, miss." Jason lightly touches her arm as he stands up.

"Anytime. Please come back."

I smile at her sympathetically as we walk through the door.

"Let's take a walk over."

Jason grabs my hand and leads me across the street. He tries the white gate that Laura and I walked through the other day. It's locked.

"I thought you said it was unlocked when you and Laura were here," he says.

Without waiting for an answer, he walks around the white fence with me in tow. The white stucco fence is tall enough so that we can't see over it. We keep walking the entire perimeter until we are back around to the gate that leads in. Jason tries the lock again to make sure he wasn't mistaken the first time. Next to the gate is a sign that says the pool is open from Memorial Day through Labor Day.

"It's still over a month to Memorial Day," Jason says. He takes out his cell phone and takes a picture of the sign.

Also on the sign is a management company and phone number; Jason takes a close-up picture.

"Let's take a walk. I don't want to just stand here like idiots. And I don't want to go back to that coffee shop." Jason grabs my hand again, and off we go around the block.

There's a hole-in-the-wall bar that Jason decides to pull me into, and we take a seat at the bar. There are a few patrons already seated at the bar, but other than that, it is basically empty. The other customers look like a hard bunch of drinking locals, and after initial glances at us, they go back to their drinks.

"What will you have?" An overweight, middle-aged man in a dirty white T-shirt asks Jason.

"Two bottles of Bud Light," Jason orders.

I'm kind of miffed at how bossy he is today but let it pass. He does know this neighborhood better than I do, and I don't feel like starting a fight.

Jason pulls out his cell phone and starts writing an e-mail. "I'm going to e-mail this management company's info to a guy I know at the Department of Labor to see if he can pull up a list of employees. It's a huge long shot, but you never know. Last resort would be to call the company directly and ask. But I think that would start questions on their end, which I don't want to deal with."

"Where would I be without you and your resources?" I humbly ask while taking a sip of my beer.

"Right now we are both nowhere, so what does it matter? I doubt this guy will get back to me right away, so we can either keep stalking the pool, stay here and get drunk, or go home."

"My vote is to stay here and get drunk. It's a nice change being someplace where no one is hitting on you," I say, looking around at the other bar patrons, who are all men over forty.

"Yeah, let's go somewhere else with a better view. I know where." When we finish our drinks, Jason leads me out of the bar, and we take a walk to a more upscale bar with a younger clientele. We take seats at the bar and order drinks.

"You think I should text Laura and let her know we are hanging out in her neighborhood?"

"Not now."

"You don't like her, do you?"

"That's not true. I do like her. But we don't know what we're doing yet." Jason leans in and whispers in my ear, "And don't you feel like someone has been tailing us?"

"That feeling periodically comes and goes with me. But I thought it was just me. Did you see someone or something?"

"No. I just got this feeling when we were walking around the pool that someone was watching, and I haven't shaken it yet."

I casually look around the bar. "I don't see anyone who looks familiar."

"Yeah, I know. Let's just hang out here for a while and maybe get something to eat. But I don't want to get Laura involved in this shit."

"Okay," I say.

"That was fast," Jason says, looking at his phone. "My friend at the Department of Labor got back to me with the employees who work at the pool. John Falkner works maintenance at the pool. He was arrested fifteen years ago for selling pot to minors and then again five years ago for DWI."

Jason pulls up John Faulkner's mug shot on his cell phone and shows the picture to me.

"That's not him, Jay," I say, looking at the picture.

"Are you sure?" Jason asks still holding his phone up.

"Positive. That is not the man in my nightmare."

"Fuck," Jason says.

We are now back to square one.

"Hey, Lacey."

I see Jacob Meyers walking my way. *Crap.* Did I ever call him back? It feels like an eternity since I first met him.

"Hey, Jacob." I greet him with a hug and kiss on the cheek. "How are you doing?"

"I'm great. I see you twice in one week. How can one man be so lucky? What are you doing in this area?"

"Oh, we just decided we needed a change of view. Jacob, this is Jason. Jason, this is Jacob. Jason and I work together." Why do I feel the need to explain?

The two men shake hands. "Jacob, why don't you pull up a chair and join us? We were just debating as to whether we should eat here," Jason says, indicating an empty chair near us.

Oh, Jason, why do you love making me uncomfortable?

"You know, the food here is pretty good, but I'm not staying long. I just stopped in for a quick drink. So, Lacey, what about Monday night?" Jacob turns to me, putting me on the spot.

"Yes, I'm free Monday. Just let me know when and where. I look forward to it." I stand up and give Jacob a kiss on the cheek, anxious to keep him moving.

"Great. By the way, you look stunning. Did you do something different to your hair?" Jacob asks, giving my new hairdo a once-over. "It looks lighter or something."

"Oh yeah. I got it highlighted the other day. Thanks. Well, I'll talk to you later." I sit back down, hoping that is the end of our conversation.

"Well, he's obviously not a Yankees fan, huh?" Jason says when Jacob finally walks away.

"Or maybe he just prefers a date with me over a Yankees game. And don't start. You know, I wasn't going to go out with him until you asked him to sit down with us. But the fact you love to watch me squirm pisses me off."

"It had nothing to do with you squirming. I was just trying to be polite."

"You're so full of it, Jay."

Jason sticks a menu in front of my face. "Order something, Laces. I'm hungry and tired of arguing about stupid stuff with you."

I take the menu and order chicken fingers. Jason orders a burger and fries. And then we sit in silence.

"You want a chicken finger?" I ask as a peace offering. He takes one off my plate but doesn't say anything. "Are we still friends?"

He rolls his eyes. "Of course we are still friends. We will always be friends. We just drive each other up a fucking wall. It's absolutely exhausting."

"It is exhausting, isn't it?" I question, thinking about how much time we spend bickering. "We are like an old married couple, aren't we?"

"Yeah, except no sex. It's total bullshit."

Chapter 17

On the subway home from Riverdale, I sit across the aisle from Jason. He is busy on his cell phone and doesn't seem to notice me staring at him. I see a young girl sitting a few seats down, also staring at him. Yes, he is beautiful to look at. He makes my insides melt. I get up from my seat and sit next to him.

"I think you should stay with me tonight," I whisper to him. I'm tired of fighting my aching need for him.

"No shit," he says, not looking up from his phone. "You're not staying by yourself until your stalker is caught."

I think, isn't "stalker" a little dramatic?

"No, I mean I think we should be together tonight," I clumsily try to explain. I put my hand on his thigh and rest my head on his shoulder. "I was thinking about what you said the other day, and maybe I *should* do more to curb your promiscuity."

Jason laughs and puts his phone away.

"That's very sweet of you." Jason pats my hand.

Great. I finally realize I want to be with him, and he doesn't think I'm serious.

"Our stop," Jason says, grabbing my hand and leading me off the subway.

After a while of walking in silence, I tell him I do regret not letting him stay over last night. I no longer care about hiding my feelings. I'm ready to explode.

"I know," he says, and keeps walking.

And then he stops on the street and pulls me toward him. He pulls on my hair in the back so that my face tilts toward his and lays a kiss on my mouth. It's a soft, gentle kiss that makes my knees buckle. He wraps an arm around my waist and puts his other hand on my upper back, pulling me closer to him. I wrap my arms around his neck and kiss him back, smiling.

"You're smiling," Jason says, breaking free and continuing the walk back to my apartment.

"I was just thinking what a great kisser you are," I explain, still unable to wipe the goofy smile off my face. "I'm so glad the first time wasn't a fluke."

"The first time? You mean the time in the bar a few months ago where you almost knocked my head off?" Jason asks.

"Yeah, that time."

Once we are in the hallway leading to my apartment, Jason puts his arm around my waist and pulls my body against his. He gently kisses my lower lip and whispers, "Are you sure you want to do this?"

"Yes, I'm sure. Positive."

I kiss him back, invading his mouth with my tongue in case he has any doubts as to what I want. He smiles and draws me into my apartment. He shuts the door behind me and then presses his body onto mine, pushing me up against the wall. He drives his mouth into mine and begins undoing the buttons on my shirt. His hands are so warm. I start undoing his jeans and pull them off his hips. The anticipation is killing me. I can't get him inside me fast enough.

"Lacey, you drive me up a fucking wall, you know that," Jason whispers, kissing my neck.

He pulls my shirt off and pushes his hand up underneath my bra. I unhook my bra and let it fall to the ground and then wiggle out of my jeans and panties. I'm now standing in front of him, completely naked. I've never been self-conscious of my body before, but after remembering some of the beautiful women I've seen Jason with, I become suddenly aware of my flaws.

"You're perfect, Lace," Jason says, as if reading my mind.

He leads me into the bedroom, keeping his arms around my waist and kissing me. I cup his face in my hands and kiss his mouth, pushing thoughts of insecurities to the back of my mind. He gradually steers me toward the bed and gently lays me down. He lowers himself down onto me. We continue deep kissing, and then he moves lower and softly kisses my neck. His fingers explore my breasts and play with my nipples. I wiggle underneath him so that I'm more comfortable and so that he is now between my legs. Then he moves his hand down my stomach, sliding his fingers between my folds, spreading my wetness.

"I was ready for you two years ago," I whisper gently, taking his penis and rubbing it up and down my wetness.

Pulling a condom from his pocket, Jason sheaths himself and then slides himself into me, filling me completely.

I let out a moan and lean back, arching my back. His hands move around to my backside, and he pushes himself further into me.

"Oh fuck, that feels amazing," I moan, leaning forward so I can kiss his mouth again.

He rocks back and forth inside me. I bring my hips up to grind into him further until we are moving in sync. I can feel him throbbing inside of me. I slide my hands over his back and then settle my hands on his biceps. He thrusts harder and faster. He continues pumping himself into me. Each time he slides into me also brushes against my clitoris. I explode around him and let out a scream as my body spasms. He plunges himself further into me and also lets himself go, each jerk from his penis sending me off again and again until he is finally done. I'm still gasping for air, my heart pounding. He stays inside me as we recover. He strokes my hair and lightly kisses my neck, eventually finding my mouth again. He tastes so good.

"Hmm, now I know what all the fuss is about," I tease, as we kiss gently.

"Lace, you are my end all." Jason rolls off me, trying to catch his breath.

"That was incredible." I lean over and nuzzle his neck.

He puts his arms around me, and I fall asleep in his arms.

Chapter 18

When I wake up the next morning, Jason is spooning me with his arm draped over my waist. He's still sleeping, so I try to sneak out of bed without waking him.

"Where are you going?" Jason asks as he wraps his arm tighter around my waist and pulls me back to him.

"Let me go," I say, trying to slide out of bed.

"Never." Jason tightens his grip.

"I was just going to pee, if that's all right," I say, removing his arm again.

When I return to bed, I crawl back into his arms and snuggle.

"I'm surprised you haven't made a run for it yet," I say, recalling our many conversations about how awkward he finds the morning after to be and how he comes up with excuses to leave as soon as possible.

"I'm lying in bed with my arms wrapped around my favorite person. There is nowhere else I would rather be, Lacey." He kisses my forehead. "Besides I usually use work as an excuse to escape, and that wouldn't fly with you."

I giggle. "Well, maybe there is somewhere *I* have to be."

"I'm still not leaving. You'll have to cancel whatever you had planned to do this morning." Jason rolls on top of me, and we continue where we left off the night before.

He is insatiable. At about noon I wave the white flag.

"Okay, Jay, I cave. You win. You have drained every fluid from my body, and I can barely walk. Plus, I'm starving and need to eat before I pass out." I get out of bed and get dressed.

"It wasn't a contest, Laces," Jason says, laughing and getting dressed. "I just can't get enough of you."

"Well, you have beaten me down," I say, teasing.

When I walk out of the bedroom, James Bond is sitting on my recliner with a disapproving look.

On our way to the pizza shop around the corner, Jason grabs my hand as we walk. I don't fight him this time. We get our slices and drinks to go and find a bench in the park to sit and eat. It is such a beautiful, warm day. As I'm inhaling my pizza, a striking brunette walks toward us. She has a tank top on, and it is cut so low she couldn't possibly be wearing a bra. Her nipples are leading the way.

"Hey, Jason," the brunette cheerfully sings to Jason.

"Hi, Liza. How are you?" Jason politely responds.

"I haven't seen you in a while." Liza is smiling and twirling a piece of hair around her finger. "What have you been up to?"

"Not much really. Liza, this is my girlfriend, Lacey," Jason says, cutting her off—perhaps before she says anything that will make the situation more awkward.

Wait a minute, *what*? Where did *that* come from?

"Oh. Hi, Lacey," Liza says, looking taken aback.

I meekly wave since my mouth is stuffed full of pizza, and I'm just as surprised as she is that Jason has a girlfriend.

"Well, I guess I'll see you around then," Liza says. She and her nipples walk away.

"First of all——" I start talking, still trying to fully chew the pizza in my mouth. "I'm not your girlfriend. We are friends who have started sleeping together. That's it. Second of all, she is absolutely gorgeous. *I* would date her. Don't hold back on my account."

"Really?" Jason asks, somewhat amused, and puts his hand on my thigh. "You know I can set you up with her if that's what you want. Just as long as I also get to participate."

"You're a pig," I say, pushing his hand off my thigh.

"And, Lacey, I don't plan on dating anyone else. So as far as I'm concerned, we are more than just friends. And you aren't allowed to date anyone else either," Jason says half-jokingly.

I roll my eyes. "You will be bored with me after a month. I would be a fool setting myself up for heartbreak to think any differently. So I don't even want to go there with you. I don't even want to pretend it's a possibility when it's not. Let's not make sex into anything more than it is."

"Whatever, Lacey. I would never hurt you," Jason says, looking somewhat wounded at what I just said.

"I know you wouldn't on purpose," I say, backtracking. "But you are who you are, and I would be a chump to try to change you. And I don't want to have to move to Seattle after you break my heart."

"Difference being, I would follow you to Seattle." He smiles and finds a piece of my hair to play with. "It's over for me. I've been in love with you since the day I met you. And we know each other inside and out. We're perfect for each other."

"Oh, please. You have a funny way of showing your love by banging half of New York this past year," I say, not relenting.

"Once again, you give me too much credit. And the girls I did bang were just time fillers until I could have you. You were the one in a relationship all this time, remember?"

"Oh, yeah," I say.

Tyler. I still haven't read any of his texts that he's sent since we broke up. Totally uninterested in anything he would have to say.

"Let's catch a plane to Vegas tonight," Jason says, interrupting my thoughts.

"What? Why?" I ask.

"Let's go to Vegas tonight and get married. What do you say, Laces?" He rubs my hand.

"I say you're crazy. I'm not going to Vegas tonight." I continue eating my pizza as though this is an everyday conversation between us. "Besides, your mother and sister would kill me if we got married without them."

Jason grew up in a middle-class neighborhood in Brooklyn. His father died of cancer when Jason was twenty-two, but his mom still lives in the same house that Jason and Rachel grew up in. I've met her a few times when Jason and I were working and she happened to be in the city for whatever reason. She's a very sweet lady who, of course, thinks the world of her son.

"Then we'll take them with us. We'll spend a couple of nights and fly back Tuesday. What do you say?" Jason persists.

"No, that won't work. Yankees game on Monday, and I have a date Monday night, remember?" I say, grinning at him.

"Wow. You are tough," Jason says, conceding and sitting back on the bench. "Well, don't expect me to ask again. You get one chance, and then you're done."

"That's fine. It's just sex. Don't make it anything more than that, please." I stand up and hold out my hand for him to take and stand up.

"Conversation isn't over, Lace," Jason says, taking my hand and getting up. He pulls me closer to him and gives me a kiss on the lips. "And you're really not going on that date Monday night, are you?"

"No, I was kidding. But we'll discuss it later," I answer.

I have no intention of taking this relationship further. I am in love with him but will avoid at all costs the heartbreak it is destined to bring. I plant another, longer kiss on his lips to keep him from speaking. After a while I pull away. "We'll catch up later, okay, Jay? I'm going for a run, and I have to do some laundry."

"Okay, babe. I'll see you later," Jason says, and then he gives me another kiss good-bye.

Chapter 19

J'm going to a club downtown with Rachel and Laura. I text
Jason as I'm folding my laundry. I figure Laura and Rachel
are due for a night out someplace other than a cop bar. I also text
him the name of the club, as I'm sure that will be his next question
anyway. He asks if I want to meet up at some point tonight, and I
tell him I would like to see him and will let him know once we are
out and settled.

Once at the club, I remember why I rarely go to clubs and
stick mainly to neighborhood pubs and watering holes. Most clubs
in New York City have a dress code, which usually means flashy,
expensive, or barely there. At some clubs, it means all three. Since
I'm not flashy or rich, I decide to go for an outfit that is tastefully
skimpy, if that's possible. I couple a pink top that is barely more
than a bra with white capri pants. I figure showing too much cleavage and stomach is offset by covering my backside and legs. Laura,
on the other hand, decides to barely cover any of her features by
wearing a fashion designer that most cannot afford. Rachel is probably the smartest dressed by showing some leg and keeping the rest
under wraps.

After getting our drinks and surveying the surroundings, I text
Jason to let him know how it is going. I miss him, even though I

really don't want to. I am wondering why I am at this club when I would rather be sitting on a barstool next to him at the local pub. Before I know it, I am texting him to join us if he isn't doing anything else.

"Jason and I hooked up last night," I inform Laura and Rachel as we locate a table to rest our drinks on. I am kind of annoyed that neither one look shocked by the announcement.

"Was it just sex, or are you now coupled?" Laura asks.

"No, it was just sex. Jason doesn't want a relationship. He says he does, but I really doubt it. So we are going to keep it casual," I say carefully because of Rachel's presence. I don't want to reveal too much to her since he is her brother, after all.

"I'm glad it finally happened, Lacey," Rachel says with a smile, and clinks her glass with mine. "Cheers to you and Jason." I don't correct her even though I just stated that we aren't a couple.

It doesn't take long before some guys approach our table and make small talk. I politely excuse myself and head toward the restrooms. I check my phone and see a text from Jason letting me know that the club really isn't his scene and that he is out with Chris. Maybe they would stop in later.

I am disappointed but remind myself that it is my fault. I invited him out as an afterthought; why would he jump at that sort of invitation?

I reapply some lip gloss and start to head back to Rachel and Laura, who are still talking with the group of guys. I decide to veer off and walk toward the bar instead, where I snag an empty barstool.

"Funny running into you here, Lacey," the guy next to me says.

I look over at him and smile when I see who it is. Brady Leary was Ethan Fox's roommate when we were in college. Because Ethan and I dated throughout our college years, Brady and I became friends by default and frequently hung out together.

"Brady, it's nice seeing you. And I never would have guessed this was your type of place either."

"It's not. I'm here with my cousin from Chicago. This is his type of place, so I'm just here to entertain."

"Me too. This is more of my friend's scene, so I'm just suffering through it for her. What have you been up to?"

"I'm working for myself these days. Doing computer-consulting work. After we graduated I got a job working for an engineering firm, and I just couldn't deal with working for someone else. Figured I could make more money on my own and on my own terms."

"Good for you, Brady," I say.

In school, he was always playing with the latest technology gadgets and was somewhat socially awkward. He was a good-looking guy but hid behind glasses, unkempt hairstyles, and drab clothing. Tonight, he is cleaned up with his black hair neatly trimmed and wearing somewhat fashionable glasses with thick, black frames.

"You look good, Brady. I like your new look," I say.

"I like your new look, too, Lacey," Brady says, looking at the cleavage bursting out of my top.

I playfully swat his arm as I see Rachel making her way toward me.

"Lacey, what's going on over here?" Rachel asks.

I make the introductions between Rachel and Brady. Detecting some chemistry between them, I try to steer the conversation around Rachel to keep it focused on her. Brady flags down the bartender and buys us a drink, which I take as a good sign that he isn't looking to escape anytime soon. When I feel as though Rachel and Brady are truly hitting it off and no longer need me to keep the conversation going, I excuse myself to use the restroom.

When I come out of the bathroom, Jason is leaning up against the wall, waiting for me.

"You always hang outside women's bathrooms?" I ask. I am thrilled to see him. "That's kind of creepy, don't you think?"

Without saying anything Jason puts his hand on my neck and pulls me toward him for a kiss.

"What are you wearing? Where's your shirt, Lace?" Jason whispers in my ear as he wraps his arms around me in a bear hug.

"It's not me, is it?" I answer with a giggle.

"No, it isn't. And if there were any stores still open, I would go buy you something to put on."

"Did you see Rachel or Laura?" I ask, nuzzling his neck.

"Yeah, I met Rachel's friend. And Laura pulled Chris onto the dance floor when she saw us."

"Laura isn't shy when it comes to guys, is she?"

"She's no shrinking violet."

"And I went to college with Brady. He's decent," I say, breaking away from Jason and leading him back to the bar, where Rachel and Brady are still talking. Brady is punching Rachel's contact information into his phone.

"Lacey, I'm taking off. It was good seeing you again." Brady leans over and gives me a kiss on the cheek. "Jason, it was nice meeting you. Rachel..." Brady leans into her ear and whispers something that makes her smile.

"He took my phone number and said he would like to go out sometime." Rachel leans forward and whispers to me out of Jason's earshot. Even though Jason doesn't hear what she says, he rolls his eyes.

"Lace, you look amazing, and I'm tired of sharing you with every guy in this club. Let's get out of here," Jason whispers in my ear.

Outside the club Jason flags down a cab for Rachel to take home. Laura and Chris decide to stay longer, as neither one is ready to leave.

"Let's just take the subway," I say as we are walking in the direction of my apartment. It appears as though Rachel has gotten the last available cab in the city.

"Lacey, I love you," Jason says as we are walking. He takes my hand and kisses it.

"I thought we were going to take it slow, Jay. That's not slow."

I want to be annoyed at his persistence at forcing me into a relationship with him. I try to convince myself that I'm annoyed even though I'm somewhat relieved, because I have been falling in love with him for some time now.

"I can't help how I feel about you, sweetie," Jason says, still holding my hand.

"Okay, well thanks for telling me, I guess," I say.

"God, you're a tough nut to crack." Jason laughs as we keep walking.

"Don't take it personal, Jay. But anytime I have loved someone, they have disappeared from my life. And with your track record, I'm not real anxious to hand my heart over."

"Fine. Fight me all you want, but I still love you even if you are in denial about your feelings."

"Whatever," I say, rolling my eyes. "You're a good roll in the hay. That's about it."

"So you're just using me for sex?" Jason turns around so he is walking backward in front of me. He's smiling, clearly enjoying this flirtation. "And what do you mean by good? Don't you mean great?"

"Yes, I am just using you for sex. And I actually meant mind-blowing. But I don't want your ego to get too inflated, you know?"

"That's a relief. If it's only about sex, then I would at least want it to be worth it for you," Jason says. He puts his arms around my waist and gives me a kiss.

"It's so worth it for me," I say, smiling in between kisses.

"Good. Then let's get you home."

Chapter 20

"**L**acey," Jason whispers in my ear.

I think I must be dreaming because I'm sure it's the middle of the night and not sure why he would be waking me. We got home late from the club and, after making love, fell into an exhausted slumber. He's spooning me with one of his legs in between mine and his arms around me. He has his hand lightly covering my mouth as he whispers my name again. He gently shakes me as he starts sliding off the bed, moving me with him.

"There's someone here. Don't say anything," he whispers again as he reaches behind him on the headboard for his gun.

I'm now awake, confused as to why someone would be in my apartment but understanding the need to be quiet. And then I hear it. The soft, subtle creak of one my floorboards as someone is carefully moving through my apartment. Jason pulls us off the side of the bed that is furthest from the door and onto the floor.

"Stay," Jason orders as he makes his way around the bed, closer to the bedroom door.

I'm naked, and my gun is in a drawer in my nightstand on the opposite side of the bed, so I'm not in much of a position to argue. Jason at least has boxer shorts on. I find Jason's undershirt on the floor and slip it on so that I'm not completely exposed. Jason has made his way to the bedroom door and is standing on the side of it, waiting for the intruder to walk through. Since my apartment is tiny, it doesn't take long before the person makes his way into my bedroom.

"Drop it," Jason says as he puts his gun to the back of the person's head.

I can't see the person holding a gun, but Jason must have seen something. That's when I see the person lift his hands. He does have a gun.

"Drop it," Jason says louder, and he nudges the person in the back of the head.

I hear the gun hit the floor. Jason kicks it away from both of them. I crawl over my bed to my nightstand, where my gun and handcuffs are.

Before I can get there, the man turns on Jason and grabs for the gun. The two wrestle for it. I get my gun out of the nightstand, and when the moment comes, I hit the intruder in the back of his head with the heel of my gun. He falls to the floor and writhes in pain. I quickly put handcuffs on him before he regains his wherewithal.

"Who is this fucking guy?" I ask, not fully comprehending what had just happened in my home.

"I don't know, but we're going to find out," Jason says, grabbing the man's arm and dragging him into the kitchen. He pats the man down to see what else he is carrying and finds a small Luger. He pulls out a kitchen chair and pushes the man into it. "Talk."

The man clenches his jaw and looks away from Jason. I pick up my cell phone and call the precinct to report the break-in.

"Who are you, and what are you doing here?" Jason asks.

"I called it in," I report to Jason when I join him in the kitchen.

I'm carrying the intruder's gun and put it on the kitchen table. Jason looks at it, and when he sees the silencer, I know what he's thinking. This isn't a random burglar who is here to steal a few valuables. This man is in my apartment for the sole purpose of killing someone.

"He doesn't have any ID or wallet on him," Jason says, which confirms this isn't a random crime.

"He came here with an intention to murder someone, and if it went wrong, he didn't want to be identified," I say, looking at the stranger in the chair. He has a tattoo on his forearm. I have seen it before but can't remember where.

"What does this tattoo mean, Jay?" I turn the man's forearm toward Jason so he can get a better look. The tattoo is of a rose with a knife with tears falling from the rose petals.

"It's a tattoo common with mobsters. It means death to anyone who talks, and the tears usually represent how many someone has killed. Sal Rizzo has the same tattoo," Jason explains.

When he says Sal's name, it immediately clicks.

"Did Rizzo send you here?" Jason asks, grabbing the man's neck so he is forced to look up at him.

"Uniforms are here, Jason," I say, hearing them in the hallway.

I open my door to let them in. Jason greets them and brings them up to speed on the situation.

"He picked the wrong apartment to rob, huh?" one of the cops says when he sees the man in handcuffs sitting in the kitchen.

"He wasn't here to rob," Jason says, handing over the man's guns. "No ID, and he's not talking. Run his prints, and let me know ASAP when you have a name."

"No forced entry. He come in through a window?" another cop asks.

"The doors weren't locked," I say, somewhat embarrassed.

I try to shrug it off like it is no big deal. Jason gives me a dirty look.

"I was somewhat distracted when I got home last night," I say, returning the dirty look.

The reason I was distracted was because we were practically undressing each other by the time we got in the door, but I am not about to discuss it now.

"Get him out of here," Jason says.

Jason signals to two of the uniforms to remove the man and motions for the other two to stick around. As the intruder is being taken away, Detectives Jimmy Harper and Scott Erikson walk through the door. They are undercover officers Jason and I have worked with in the past.

"Hey, Lacey, you okay?" Harper asks when he sees me.

"Yeah, I'm fine."

"Word on the street is Sal Rizzo has put a million-dollar price tag on your head," Erikson says. "We came over as soon as we heard, but it was obviously too late."

"We let Captain Fuller know, and he is setting up a room in a hotel for you to stay in," Harper adds. Captain Marty Fuller is Jason's and my boss. He's our hard-nosed, no-nonsense, straightforward, but always fair leader.

"Whatever, I'm fine. I'll stay here. Thanks anyway," I say.

"You can't stay here, Lacey. You know who is going to come out of the woodwork for a million dollars? That joker is the first of many who are going to line up to take a shot at you," Harper continues.

I look over at Jason, who is unusually quiet.

"They're right. You can't stay here," Jason adds. "That kind of money is going to attract professionals and amateurs. You'll be dead within twenty-four hours."

"Fine, but I'm not leaving my cat."

"He'll be fine, Lacey," Jason says.

"I'm not leaving him here if there's a chance someone will be breaking in."

"Fine, we'll take the cat to my apartment," Jason offers.

I locate James Bond's carry case and load him into it, along with a few of his toys and food supply. Jason gives the uniformed cops his address and instructs them to take James Bond to his apartment. He feels the need to remind them not to take a direct route and to make sure no one is following them.

Once they are gone, I find a duffel bag for myself and start loading it up with clothes and toiletries, while Jason is discussing my future sleeping arrangements with Erikson and Harper.

"Let's go," I say when I'm done packing.

I'm not thrilled to be leaving and too exhausted to stand around chitchatting. I've pulled a hooded sweatshirt over my head in case anyone is outside watching.

The hotel I'm moved to is very nice. Captain Fuller figured it would be easier to spot those who belong in the criminal world in a more upscale hotel. The room is reserved under a fake name. Erikson checks in, and fifteen minutes after he clears the room, I am allowed to enter. Jason never leaves my side, as I knew he wouldn't. Even though I ask him to go check on James Bond, he calls his neighbor and asks her to check on the cat instead. He also calls his doorman and tells him he will be out of town for the next few days and is expecting no visitors.

"Come to bed, Jay," I say when we are finally alone and I'm ready for sleep.

He sits down on the bed and puts his face in his hands.

"It will be all right," I say, rubbing his back.

"What if I hadn't been with you tonight, Lace? You would have slept right through it. You're such a heavy sleeper."

"You can't do the what-ifs. You were there, and that's all that matters. And I'm only a heavy sleeper when you're with me because I feel safe and can relax. When I'm alone, I wake up when a pin drops."

"That's not exactly true, Lace. I've called and texted you during the night, and it didn't wake you," Jason says, rubbing his forehead. "This is such a nightmare."

"It will be okay, Jay."

"It better be. I don't know what I would do without you. I can't imagine life without you." Jason leans back on the bed and rests his head on my stomach.

"I'm not going anywhere," I say, smoothing back his hair with my hands.

"Like it or not, get used to spending every night with me, sweetheart. We are going to be joined at the hip forever and ever." He turns over and slides on top of me.

"Are you going to protect me and keep me safe?" I ask, trying to keep a straight face. I can't help but smile at his dramatics.

"I'll do my best, but you'll have to do exactly what I say," Jason says, kissing my neck.

"You're in complete control of me," I say, and give my body over to him to show him what I mean.

Chapter 21

When I wake up the next morning, Jason is standing next to the bed, brushing his teeth and watching me sleep. He's already showered and dressed.

"Where are you going?"

"Work, sleeping beauty."

I look at the clock. It's about twenty minutes before our shift starts. "Why didn't you wake me?" I say, getting out of bed.

Jason cuts me off before I get to the bathroom.

"You're staying here, Lace." He puts an arm around me and takes the toothbrush out of his mouth.

"No! Take me with you," I plead with him.

"You're safer here."

"What happened to us being joined at the hip? You're already ditching me?"

"Fine, get in the shower," Jason says, laughing. He gives me a pat on the butt.

He has given in too easily, and that should have tipped me off. When I get out of the shower, there is a note on the bed that reads, "Sorry, Lace. You're staying here."

"Fuck," I say to no one since I'm now alone in the hotel room.

I get ready to head out anyway. If he wanted me to stay put, then he should have handcuffed me to the bed. I open the room door to leave, and I'm greeted by two uniformed cops, Tom Kelly and Paul Morris. I have worked with them before, and Tom frequently drinks with Jason.

"Sorry, Lacey, but you're under house arrest. We have orders not to let you leave," Paul says as he blocks the door.

"You're kidding me, right?" I say, trying to push through him.

"C'mon, Lacey." Tom grabs my elbow and brings me back into the room. "We have orders to restrain you physically if need be. Don't make us go down that road."

I yank my arm out of Tom's grip. "This is bullshit, you know. You can't force me to stay here." I sit on the edge of the bed and put my head in my hands, thinking of what to do next. I am so angry at Jason right now for tricking me and then treating me like a prisoner.

I could try to rush them again to escape, but I don't want this to get ugly. They are, after all, just doing their jobs, taking orders from someone higher up on the food chain. And the order had to come from Jason. Who else would go to this extreme?

"We're here to protect you, Lacey. No one wants to go to your funeral," Tom further explains, obviously feeling bad for treating another cop like criminal.

"Fine," I say, pretending to accept the hand that has been dealt to me. "You want to come in and hang out, or are you going to stand out in the hallway?" I turn on the TV to show them I plan on getting comfortable with the situation.

"We'll hang out in here," Paul says, sitting down in a recliner.

"Want anything? It's on the city," I joke, opening the minibar and taking out water and handing them each a drink.

I make myself comfortable on the bed and flip through the TV channels, settling on a daytime talk show—one of those shows where women sit around a table and discuss current events, interrupting and talking over each other to the point where nothing can really get said. My plan is somehow to escape, even though I don't exactly know how that is going to happen.

"I'm ordering breakfast. Anyone want anything?" I ask, looking over the room service menu.

Paul gives me a distrustful look.

"I *do* have to eat, you know," I snap at him and pick up the phone to put in my order.

Twenty minutes later there is a knock at the door.

"I'll get it," Paul says, holding his hand up, indicating for me not to move.

After verifying it is room service, he opens the door and wheels the cart carrying the food into the room, keeping the hotel employee in the hallway.

"Don't you feel silly, guarding me like a criminal?" I ask no one in particular as I dig into the food. I am really hungry.

"It's not our first choice of things to do today, Lacey," Tom says. "But this is our assignment, and so we are going to do it. And believe it or not, it is for your best interest."

"Right. That's what everyone keeps telling me," I say.

Jason has already texted me, asking how I am doing, and when I don't respond, he sends another text about how it's for my own good. Tom has been avidly texting someone, so I assume he has been sending Jason updates.

Paul gets up and goes into the bathroom. Tom is texting, so I figure this is my chance to get out.

"I'm done with this food. You want any?" I ask Tom.

"No, I'm good," he says, barely looking up from his phone.

"Okay, I'm going to push this cart back into the hallway," I say, opening the door.

I casually push the cart out, let the door close behind me, and run for the staircase. It is way too easy, but I can also see how they would let their guard down. It's not like I am a dangerous convict or something.

I get to the stairway and move down the floors as fast as I can. I'm assuming there are undercovers in the lobby, so I go to the lower level below the lobby. Most hotels have a lower level connected to the parking garage for deliveries, and I'm hoping this one isn't any different. Once I get to the lower level, I put my hood up over my head and casually walk around the hotel employees, who are folding linens and shooting the breeze. I see an exit sign and head that way. Once out into the street, it takes me a minute to figure out what street I'm on. The entrance to the hotel is around the corner from where I just exited, so I make sure to walk in the opposite direction and flag down a cab.

"Rikers Island, please," I say when I get in.

Chapter 22

I show my badge and sign in at the front reception area. Rikers Island is a city unto itself, mainly used as a holding station for anyone who has been arrested and awaiting trial and cannot afford or was not given bail. On any given day, there are approximately thirteen thousand offenders being held at Rikers. Today Sal Rizzo is one of them.

"Warden Lewis," I say to the guard signing me in when asked whom I'm there to see.

The guard nods for me to have a seat while he notifies Warden Lewis that I am here. I check my phone to see the latest text from Jason, asking me where I am. I ignore that one, as I have the other texts that he has sent. I'm so angry at him right now that I'm afraid of what I would say to him.

"Lacey, I'm so glad to see you." Warden Eddie Lewis holds out his hand as he walks toward me.

"I need a favor, Eddie," I say as I give him a quick handshake.

"Follow me." Eddie leads me to his office. "Jason and a few others just left," he says when we get to his office, and he closes the door behind me.

"They accomplish anything?" I ask.

Eddie shrugs. "They pulled Rizzo's phone records and had a nice chat with Rizzo. Not sure if it did any good."

"Then you know why I'm here." I take a seat in one of his office chairs.

"Yeah, I know. And I will do anything you ask. I owe you my life, Lacey. You know that."

"How is Becca doing?" I ask.

Eddie's daughter, Becca, who is about my age, fell on hard times a few years ago. When I was in uniform, I picked her up as she was attempting to sell her body for drug money. Rather than arrest her, I took her to a rehab center and continued to check up on her throughout her time at the center to make sure she stuck with the program. When she checked out a few months later, I let her stay with me while she got back on her feet and even helped her find work as a legal assistant at a law firm, where I knew one of the lawyers. It wasn't until after she got clean that she told me who her father was. She was afraid I knew her father and was embarrassed at her family finding out that she was turning tricks for drugs.

"She's doing great. Been taking evening classes at NYU. The law firm has been paying for it...encouraging her to become a para-legal or maybe even a lawyer."

"That's great. I'll give her a call when things settle down for me," I say, anxious to get to the reason why I'm here.

"I need to see a list of prisoners currently here, Eddie," I say.

"Sure." Eddie takes a seat at his desk and types on his keyboard. Once the information pulls up on his computer screen, he turns the monitor so I can see it better. "It's listed alphabetically by name. Also lists crimes arrested for, arresting officer...and that's our code for how dangerous the person is considered to be," Eddie says, pointing to the last column. "If you need more info on someone, double click on the name, and it will bring you into their personnel database."

"Is there someone in particular you're looking for, Lacey?"

"I'm not sure," I say, scrolling through the list. And then I see the name that may help me: Lee Arcuro. I tell Eddie my plan to see if he's on board.

"Of course I am, Lacey," Eddie says, when I finish telling him what I'm up to. "Like I said, I owe you my life. You saved my daughter, and if anything had happened to her, I would have died with her."

"Thanks, Eddie," I say as we walk toward the prisoner visitation area.

Eddie puts me in a room with a bolted-down table and two chairs.

"I'll be watching through the glass if you need anything," Eddie says as he steps out of the room.

After a few minutes, two guards bring in Sal Rizzo and handcuff him to two rings on top of the table. I notice his black eye and busted lip and can't help but smile at Jason's handiwork.

"What do you want? Your friends were already here, and I have nothing to say," Sal says, looking bored at having to meet with me.

"That's fine. I'll do most of the talking, Sal," I say. "I want to make you a deal."

Sal cocks his head at me, looking a little more interested in what he may get out of this.

"Prisoners die in prison every day, Sal. Some are killed by other inmates, some are found hanging in their cell, and some mysteriously choke to death after taking a bite of their lunch."

"What's your point? I'm not suicidal, and I'm in solitary confinement. No one can touch me," Sal says.

"Right now, no one can touch you. But you see, Sal, the warden and I have been talking and think sticking you in general population might be good for you and might even teach you some social skills."

Sal looks over my shoulder at Eddie, who is standing outside the room, watching us.

"So what?" Sal asks, not looking quite as confident as he was when he first entered the room. "You don't think I can take care of myself in general pop?"

"I think you'll be just fine. As a matter of fact, one of your old friends is also residing here. I'm sure he would watch your back if need be."

I get up and tap on the door that Sal had come through. Four guards escort Lee Arcuro in. Lee is handcuffed and wearing ankle shackles, but when Lee sees Sal, he immediately lunges for him and screams obscenities.

Lee and Sal used to be business partners, working together to get as many illegal drugs out on the street as fast as possible. When Sal was incorrectly informed that Lee was double-crossing him, Sal decided to take revenge by killing Lee's son. Lee was arrested for drugs before he could exact his revenge on Sal. It is just perfect timing they happen to be located in the same prison at the same time.

Sal jumps from his chair and tries to move further from Lee, but the table he is tethered to doesn't move. Lee is an animal, and it takes all four guards to contain him and get him out of the room before his rage takes over and no one can restrain him.

"My deal is a life for a life. My life for your life," I continue, once Sal sits down again. "Call off the hit on me, and Lee Arcuro won't become your cellmate."

Sal leans back in his chair and pretends to mull it over. We both know he has no leverage at this point, and there is only one option for him if he wants to stay alive. I stare at him until he finally speaks.

"Okay, I'll call off the hit for now," Sal says. "But what is going to be your card when I'm sent to a different prison than Arcuro?"

"Who says you'll be sent to a different prison than Arcuro?" I ask. "The warden and I have plenty of pull when it comes to recommending jails that certain prisoners are sent to. Anything happens to me; the warden will make sure Arcuro is your future cellmate. Got it?"

"All right, all right, I'll call it off," Sal concedes. "Arcuro will not have access to me, right?"

"You'll stay out of general population as long as I am alive," I confirm.

"Fine. We have a deal. I'm not sure how long it will take to get the word out, so you may want to lay low for a few days anyway," Sal cautions.

"It's in your best interest to make the word spread as fast as possible, Sal," I say. I get up and walk out of the room.

"I hope it works, Lacey," Eddie says. "The guards are getting him to a phone so he can make the calls. Just out of curiosity, how did you know Lee Arcuro was here?"

"I didn't. I was just looking for someone who Sal has crossed in the past. Fortunately there are many, so if Lee wasn't here, I'm sure another name would have jumped out at me."

Eddie motions for a guard to come over and instructs him to get a car and take me wherever I need to go.

"Take care of yourself, Lacey." Eddie leads me out of the prison. "And it's probably a good idea if you do lay low for a while. Just in case there is someone who doesn't immediately hear about Sal's change of plans."

"Thanks for everything, Eddie," I say, getting into the guard's car. "I'll stay out of sight for a while."

I have the guard drop me off at the precinct so I can try to redeem myself to Captain Fuller for escaping my so-called house arrest.

"Well, look who decided to honor us with her presence," the desk sergeant snaps as I walk through the door.

"Oh, go to hell," I snap back, not feeling the need to explain anything to him.

I head straight for Fuller's office. Fuller is on the phone, but when he sees me, he immediately hangs up.

"What the fuck, Burke?" Fuller yells at me when I enter his office. "You know how many cops are on the street looking for you right now?"

"No one would have to be looking for me if I had been allowed to do my job this morning. Instead I'm held prisoner in a hotel room? That's total bullshit, and you know it!" I scream back at him.

"Sit down," Fuller says, lowering his voice and pointing at a chair in front of his desk. "Jason called from Rikers and told me you just left after meeting with Rizzo. He said Rizzo was calling his cronies to call off the hit. Explain yourself, now."

Jason was a step behind me, as I figured he would be. I told Fuller what happened with me, Eddie, and Rizzo.

"I want you to stay in hiding the next few days until this blows over," Fuller says when I'm done talking.

"Fine, but I'll take care of myself. I don't want anyone standing guard over me, treating me like a criminal."

"It was for your own good, Lacey. No one wanted to go to your funeral."

"No protection," I reiterate.

"Fine," Fuller says, holding up his hands, conceding.

I get up to leave. Before I open the door, I turn back to Fuller and say, "And Captain, I want a new partner."

"Lacey, it's already been done," Fuller says nonchalantly before I can explain my request. "When you return to work in two days, you'll be assigned someone other than Jason. And remember, stay away from your apartment and local hangouts, got it?"

"Got it. Thanks, Captain," I say, feeling as though someone just put a knife through my stomach.

Chapter 23

I debate on what to do. I'm tempted to rent a car and leave the city, maybe take a drive upstate or to Atlantic City. I text Jason to let him know that I am fine and to please take care of my cat. Then I silence the phone so I can't hear back from him. Even though I have requested a new partner, I am somewhat angry and confused as to why he beat me to it and already put in the request. And I am heartbroken. I knew better than to get involved with him and didn't listen to my better judgment.

I decide to slip into a movie theater to get lost in someone else's story so I don't have to think about mine anymore.

After the movie, I head to a bar in lower Manhattan that I used to hang out in when I was in college and has decent bar food. I haven't been there in years, so I figure it won't be a spot anyone would expect to find me.

"Hey, Lacey, nice seeing you here," Ethan Fox says to me as he takes the barstool next to me.

Ethan used to frequent this bar with me when we were dating in college, and I forgot that he mentioned, last time we had lunch together, that he still hangs out there. He said it was because it was close to his apartment.

"I'm glad you're okay," Ethan continues. "I heard about what happened."

"Yeah, I'm technically still in hiding, which is why I came here. Best chicken wings in the city," I say, offering Ethan a wing and ordering another soda from the bartender. I figure it is best not to drink and to keep my wits about me tonight.

"How come you're alone? Where's Jason?"

I shrug. "He put me under house arrest in the hotel room, so I'm not really interested in where he is now."

"Lacey, that wasn't his call. Fuller sent those uniforms over to sit with you. I know because I was supposed to go, but then my captain sent me to an assault over on Wall Street."

"What are you talking about? Tom Kelly was there, and he's one of Jason's friends. The plan had Jason written all over it."

"It was just coincidence. It was Fuller's idea. Trust me, I heard the argument between Jason and Fuller over the radio. Jason didn't want to leave you at the hotel. He knew you would be better off in the field working."

"Regardless, it was a dumb idea. And Jason didn't help it."

"Whatever," Ethan says, shaking his head. "Fuller thought he was making the right decision, and Jason ultimately couldn't go against him. Anyone else would have done the same thing. Including me."

I let out a sigh and look over at Ethan. He's every bit as good-looking as Jason but without the tattoos and facial hair. Ethan is good-looking in a clean-cut sort of way, whereas Jason is more scruffy and unshaven. Ethan is the guy your mother wants you to bring home; Jason is the guy your sister wants to sleep with. Very different men on the outside, but on the inside, they are very similar in that both are testosterone-driven alpha males.

"What are you thinking about, Lace?" Ethan asks when he sees me staring at him.

"I'm thinking I'm glad you were once a big part of my life, and I'm sorry if I ever hurt you," I say, referring to our previous relationship, which feels like a lifetime ago.

Saying no to Ethan's marriage proposal and then ultimately breaking up with him was one of the worst nights of my life. I didn't think he would ever speak to me again, yet somehow we reconnected and are at least on friendly terms these days.

Ethan leans over and kisses me on the cheek. "You did hurt me, but in the long run you were right. We *were* way too young to get married and probably not the best fit for each other, even though I thought so at the time."

"You're a good egg, Ethan. Some woman will be very lucky to land you," I say, squeezing his knee.

"Someday, but I'm in no hurry. You were a tough chick to get over, and right now I'm just enjoying the single life."

"Oh, please. Once word got out we were over, I saw the girls lining up at your doorstep," I tease.

"Ha, right. I have to get going, Lace," Ethan says, finishing his drink and getting off his barstool. "I have to work tomorrow."

"It was nice seeing you, Ethan."

"Where are you staying tonight? You're welcome to stay at my place if you need to," Ethan says before he leaves.

"I'm good. Thanks, Ethan."

"Okay. If you need anything, don't hesitate to call," Ethan says, kissing me good-bye on the forehead.

After Ethan leaves I look at my cell phone. I have two missed calls from Jason and four text messages. One of his text messages says, "Where are you? Just ordered dinner. Please come over and eat. We need to talk."

I agree; we do need to talk. I pay my tab and leave the bar. It is a relief to hear that Jason didn't order the debacle this morning, but I still need to hear his side of the story.

Chapter 24

I knock on Jason's apartment door. I didn't bother to tell him I was coming over. For some reason, I thought it would be best to just show up. I couldn't have been more wrong.

"Lacey, where the fuck have you been?" Jason asks, stepping out of his apartment.

Since he doesn't want me in his apartment, I can only assume it is because he isn't alone. Unfuckingbelievable.

"Move," I say, pushing him aside and opening his apartment door.

And there is Lindsay, the waitress from Shelly's Deli, sitting on his couch, cradling James Bond in her arms.

"Don't mind me, Lindsay. I just came to get my cat," I lie, trying to contain myself. I feel double-crossed by not only Jason but also James Bond, who is now purring in this woman's arms.

"C'mon, James Bond," I say, attempting to get the cat from Lindsay's arms.

James Bond, obviously content in his new home and wanting nothing to do with me anymore, jumps from Lindsay's arms and runs into Jason's bedroom.

"James Bond, please come," I say, following him into Jason's bedroom.

The cat has run under Jason's bed, and I start to crawl under the bed to get him. Jason has followed me into the bedroom and closes the door.

"Lacey, she was just delivering the food. I texted you to come over."

"Fuck off, Jason. And help me get this fucking cat!" I yell at him from underneath his bed. I can't believe this is what my life has come to. I don't know whether to laugh or cry.

Jason crawls under the bed with me.

"Lacey, please. Forget the cat for a minute," he says, trying to crawl up next to me.

James Bond has positioned himself as far away from me as he can so I can't reach him without grabbing a paw or tail, and I'm not willing to do that, out of fear of hurting him.

"Fuck," I mutter to no one, and crawl out from under the bed. "I'll get him some other time. When you're less busy."

"Nice seeing you, Lindsay. Have a good night," I call to her sweetly before I exit the apartment. I figure there's no reason for me to be a bitch to her just because she also fell for Jason.

I hear Jason following me out the door, so I pick up my pace and take the stairs rather than wait for the elevator.

"Please wait, Lacey," Jason calls after me as he chases me down the stairs.

I exit his building and head toward my apartment. I no longer care if there are would-be assassins who haven't heard the latest news that I'm off the hit list. I'm exhausted and just want to go home.

"Goddamn it, Lacey," Jason says, catching up with me and grabbing my arm. "Stop."

"Don't touch me," I say, pulling my arm away. I keep walking. "I hate you so much right now, I can't even look at you."

"We need to talk," Jason says, grabbing my arm again.

I turn with my free arm and punch him square in the eye.

"Fuck," Jason says, bending over and putting his hands up to his face.

"I said don't touch me," I say, surprised at what I have just done. I start running for my apartment.

I figure Jason has given up after my punch because I don't hear him behind me. I check my apartment door to see if anything has been tampered with. I don't notice anything, so I unlock it and cautiously walk in. After doing a walk-through and checking every nook and closet, I determine that no one is there; probably, no one has been there.

After a few minutes, I hear a knock on the door and Jason calling my name.

"Open up, Lace, or I'm coming in anyway. I have a key, remember?"

"God, you're annoying," I say, opening the door.

"And you're the most stubborn, pigheaded broad I've ever met before in my life." Jason is still pressing a hand to his eye, and he walks toward my freezer. He pulls out an ice pack and begins throwing stuff in a plastic bag I had on the counter.

"Get up. You're not staying here," Jason says, standing in front of me as I'm sitting on my couch.

"Go away. I'm exhausted and want nothing to do with you." I lay my head down on one of my couch pillows.

"Don't really care what you want. Get up," Jason says, strongly nudging my leg with his foot. He grabs the throw blanket behind the couch, and before I can ask what he packed in the plastic bag, he grabs my hand and pulls me off the couch.

"You really want an ass kicking tonight, don't you?" I snap, as I'm standing in front of him, trying to twist my wrist out of his grip.

"Bring it, sweetheart. My eye is killing me, and right now I'm in no mood for your bratty tantrums," Jason says as he drags me out the door and toward the stairwell.

We go up toward the roof. When we were still just friends, Jason and I spent many nights on the roof of my apartment building. Usually it was to enjoy a nice summer night, but then we would end up talking the night away. Before we knew it, we would be watching the sun rise. Jason even went to the trouble of buying beach lounge chairs and sticking them on the roof so that we would have something to sit or lie down on and could get comfortable.

The loungers haven't moved since the last time we were up there. Jason lays the blanket over one and tries to push me down on it. I remain standing.

"I'm not staying," I say, folding my arms across my chest.

"Lacey, before we hooked up, you made me promise you that no matter what happened, we would always be friends. Do you remember that?"

"Yeah, so what?" I say, shrugging.

"Well, here I am, doing anything and everything I can at least to salvage our friendship. Do you think you could let down your guard for a minute and work with me for a bit?"

I let out a sigh and sit down on the lounger. I did make him promise that no matter what, our friendship wouldn't suffer.

Jason unpacks what he had stuffed into the plastic bag—ice cream and wine. He scoops out the ice cream into cups and then pours wine into the cups.

"Here," he says, handing me a cup. "I saw it on a food channel or something. It looked pretty good."

I take a sip and get a mouthful of wine and ice cream. It *is* pretty good.

"Who are you madder at? Me or the cat?" Jason asks, apparently trying to lighten the mood.

"That fucking guy. All that I do for him, and he replaces me so fast with another," I say, taking another sip of the wine and ice cream.

"You're talking about the cat, right?" Jason asks, smiling.

"Yes, I was," I say, giggling. "But the similarities are uncanny."

"For the record, I didn't replace you. I ordered dinner, and Lindsay showed up at my door with the food. And then she kind of just invited herself in and got comfortable on the couch. That's when you showed up."

"Then why did you try to keep me out if there was nothing going on?"

"Because I knew you would flip out. And I thought it would just be easier to leave. With you."

I continue sipping my wine. The ice cream has melted some and made it more of a drink. I want to believe him and know I should believe him, but I also don't want to be one of those girls who look like fools because their boyfriends cheat on them left and right.

"I mean really, Lace. Would I tell you to come over if I planned on having someone else there?"

"No, probably not. You're craftier than that."

"Right," Jason says, with an eyeball roll. He finishes his wine, refills my cup, and then lays back on his lounger, placing the ice pack over his eye. "Next issue?"

"I'm angry at you for leaving me in the hotel room."

"I didn't want to do that. No one will protect you like I will protect you, and I thought it was best if you were by my side. Fuller disagreed."

I process what he has said, and it is basically the same story that Ethan told me; I have no reason not to believe him.

"Okay," I say. "It would have been nice if you told me rather than tricking me and then leaving a note."

"Maybe. But I knew you would put up a fight, so the note was easier."

"Fine," I concede.

"What else?"

"That's it, I guess." I lie down on my lounger. Sleep is fast approaching, and I can barely keep my eyes open.

"You're still acting prickly. What is wrong?"

"I was disappointed you asked for a new partner," I say.

Jason laughs. "I think *I* should be mad at *you* for asking for a new partner."

"You were first," I say, closing my eyes.

"Lacey," Jason says, sitting up. "I didn't ask for a new partner. I was promoted to lieutenant. They're taking me off the street."

"Why didn't you tell me?" I say.

"I just found out this afternoon. When was I going to tell you? When you weren't speaking to me this afternoon, or when you were telling me you hated me this evening?"

"Congratulations, Jason. You really deserve it," I say, extending my hand to him.

"Do you still hate me?" Jason asks, taking my hand.

"No, I don't."

"Good, because I still love you," Jason says, lying back down on his lounger.

He keeps holding my hand. I have to smile. We fall asleep like that, lying down on our loungers, side by side, holding hands.

A sudden chill wakes me. It is like an icy wind has blown up and down my body. I sit up on my lounger. Very strange. I look over at Jason, who is still sleeping, undisturbed by anything. I wrap my blanket around me and nudge Jason over to make room for me on his lounger.

"What's wrong?" Jason whispers, barely awake.

"I'm cold," I say, lying down next to him.

He puts his arms around me and snuggles me in to him.

"I love you, Jason," I whisper to him.

"I know. I love you too, Lacey," Jason whispers back, giving me a kiss on my forehead.

Chapter 25

The sun rising over the rooftop of my apartment building wakes us up the next morning. I sit up, stretching. It is such a nice feeling to wake up to the sun warming my bones. Jason puts his arms around my waist and tries to pull me back onto him.

"Get up. Not here," I say, playfully fighting him.

I look at his face and can see better in the daylight the damage I did to his eye. It's badly bruised and slightly swollen.

"I'm sorry about your eye," I say, touching his face. I lower my head, slightly embarrassed.

"I'll live, sweetheart." He sits up and kisses me on the cheek. "And you'll show me later how sorry you are," he adds with a wink.

We head down to my apartment, where Jason hands me one of my duffel bags and says, "Start packing."

"What are you talking about?" I let the duffel bag drop to the floor.

"You're done with this place, Lacey. Pack enough shit so you don't have to come back for a few days. We'll come back at a later time and get the rest."

"I'm fine, Jay. I'm sure the threat has passed by now."

"Not taking any chances." He opens my drawers and puts things in the bag. He holds up a pair of lacy thong panties. "We'll definitely take these."

I sigh loudly and yank the underwear out of his hands. "Do you mind? Stay out of my stuff."

"Then pack, Lace. You're not staying here."

Rather than keep fighting, which I'm so tired of doing with him, I throw some outfits and toiletries into the duffel bag.

"You think Lindsay will still be here?" I joke as we ride Jason's elevator up to his apartment. "Might be awkward."

"God, I hope not. And let's hope the place isn't trashed either," Jason says as he gets off the elevator. "I didn't have her cell number to tell her I wasn't coming back, so Lord only knows what time she left."

He opens the door, and everything appears to be intact. The food Lindsay delivered is still on the counter. I go over and look in the bag. It's two chicken club sandwiches; it's what I always order from Shelly's Deli. I make a silent promise to myself always to give Jason the benefit of the doubt until he gives me a reason not to.

James Bond comes running from somewhere to say hello. I scratch him behind the ears to let him know I've forgiven him, too, even though he has no idea he did anything wrong or that I was ever mad at him.

"Aren't you going to work today, lieutenant?" I give Jason a hug from behind as he's putting my clothes in one of his drawers. "I really am happy for you." I kiss him on the back of his neck.

"I texted Fuller that I wasn't coming in today. Need to punish you properly for how you have behaved the last few days." He turns around and hugs me close to him.

"I don't know what you're talking about. I've been an absolute angel during all this."

Jason laughs. "Angel, my ass. I've arrested gangbangers who were more cooperative and less combative."

He kisses me while he cups my ass with his hands, picks me up, and carries me over to the bed. He lays me down on the bed, moving his hand up my shirt. I move my legs so he's lying in between them and unbuckle his pants. I want him inside me. It feels like forever since we were last together, even though it was just the night before last.

Jason kisses my neck and moves his way down my body.

"Oh, Jay, just take me," I moan.

"No way. I want to kiss every inch of you," he says. He sucks on one of my nipples. His hand caresses my other breast. He kisses my stomach as he goes further down, also working me out of my jeans and underwear. I let out another moan, as I'm already very wet and can't wait to have him inside me. He performs oral sex on me, pushing my legs further open so he can plunge his tongue deeper in. His thumbs part me further open as he flicks his tongue around me and then in me, over and over. He loosely closes his mouth over me and then tightens it around me, sucking lightly and then strongly until I am almost exploding.

"Oh, fuck," I say, as I can't contain myself anymore and feel myself just letting go. I don't usually orgasm during oral sex, instead holding on until intercourse, but this time I cannot help it.

When I'm done, Jason takes a condom from his nightstand and covers himself. He rolls on top of me and inserts his cock into me with one hard thrust. He kisses me on my mouth, and I taste myself on his lips, which turns me on again. I lift my hips to be in rhythm with his movements and feel myself filled by him completely. I wait until he tells me he is ready and then let myself go again. This is the first time I've experienced two orgasms in one sex session. Usually

I'm one and done. By the end I'm totally spent, and I fold, sweaty and trying to catch my breath. Jason collapses on top of me, and I can feel his heart pounding with mine, as though our chests our involved in a game of ping-pong.

Jason kisses me on the cheek before he rolls off me, taking me with him, so I now have my head on his chest with him stroking my hair.

"I love you, Lace."

"I know," I say, kissing him on his chest.

"C'mon. You said it last night. You can say it twice within a twenty-four-hour period," Jason says, nudging me with his arm, which is wrapped around me.

"I was wondering if you remembered. Thought maybe you were sleeping," I say, hiding my face in his side, suddenly bashful.

"How could I forget the most independent woman I've ever known professing her dying love for me?"

"I'm not sure that's how it went down. But I did mean it."

"I just shouldn't expect to ever hear it again?" He flips onto his side so he is facing me.

"Can't you cut me any slack?" I say. I push my forehead into his chest so he can't see my face and the shade of red I have turned. "It was a big deal for me to say it once...baby steps."

"Okay, I'm thrilled you said it once. I won't push my luck." Jason reaches for his phone to check his messages. "We have to go."

Chapter 26

"He didn't tell you anything else?" I ask Jason as we are headed to a precinct uptown.

"No, he just said there was a video we needed to see."

We are holding hands as we walk into the station. I guess because we are no longer partners, Jason feels comfortable letting it be known that we are more than just coworkers. Since I don't know anyone at this police station, I don't care either way. I'm still not about to sing from the rooftops how I'm in a relationship with Jason. That is not the type of person I am anyway. But if he's comfortable advertising it, then I'm comfortable as well.

"We have been doing surveillance on a building over on Eighty-First. There was a woman strangled in her apartment, and we have reason to believe her neighbor did it, but have absolutely no evidence to back up our theory. Anyway, the guy is real quiet, sleeps all night, and is basically boring as hell. We decided to save on manpower during the night and set up a video camera to tape him sleeping," an undercover homicide detective, Ben Kennedy, explains to us.

"Ugh," I say, already knowing where this conversation is headed. My building is on Eighty-First, so this video camera must have picked up something relating to me.

"Exactly," Ben says, putting the memory chip into a computer. "Where the camera is set up catches part of Lacey's roof."

On the computer screen, Jason and I walk onto my roof, sitting on the lounge chairs, eating our wine with ice cream. It's a black-and-white video with no sound, so thankfully, our conversation was not taped.

"Well, at least we weren't getting busy," Jason says with a shrug, trying to lighten the mood.

"Right, but this is where it gets weird," Ben says, fast-forwarding the tape. Jason and I are sleeping on our loungers when a figure appears, standing next to me.

I gasp. I look at the time stamp on the video, and it says 2:05 a.m.

"Who the hell is that?" Jason asks to no one in particular.

The man stands there, staring at me, and then squats down beside me. The video is somewhat grainy, and the man is wearing a hoodie, so his face is partially blocked from view.

I stir in my sleep, and the man stands up and slowly takes a few steps back. Next, the video shows me getting off my lounger and snuggling up with Jason.

"I felt him there. That's why I got chilled and moved over to Jason."

"So that's about it, until he's leaving about five minutes later. For some reason, he turns around and looks directly at the camera," Ben says, as he fast-forwards to the part where the man turns around. He then pauses the video when the man's face comes into view.

"Oh my God," I say, putting my hand over my mouth and taking a step back.

"Freaky, isn't it?" Ben asks.

"Do you know him, Lace?" Jason asks.

"Yes. He's the guy from my nightmares."

"What's his address? We'll go pick him up and find out what he was up to on the roof," Ben offers. "And we'll ask *how* he got on the roof. If you noticed, the rooftop door never opens or closes."

"I don't know his name or where he lives," I say, still dumbfounded over what I just saw. Was that the first time he had been that close to me? I somehow doubt it, which is unsettling.

"Thanks for letting us know, Ben," I say, walking toward the door. I don't know his name or address, but I know where I can find him.

"Don't even think about it, Lacey," Jason says as we exit the precinct.

"Think about what?" I ask. "I'm going to my apartment to make sure no one has been in or out."

"And to get more stuff to bring to my place," Jason says.

"Whatever, Jay. I'm staying with you temporarily. Let's not forget that."

Jason stops me and brings me in for a hug.

"Let's make it permanent. Move in with me?" He kisses me on my cheek.

"No, I need my own place," I say, wiggling out of his hug.

"Why? We already spend all our free time and nights together. It makes no sense to keep two places."

"Please don't push me on this. I've never lived with someone before and don't think I'm ready."

"And what, you think I have a new girl move in every other month? It's a big step for me too, Lacey. But I'm so ready with you."

"I'll think about it, okay?" I say, to placate him.

I can't imagine giving up my home. It would be like handing him too much control over me, and I'm not ready for that yet.

I open the door to my apartment, expecting nothing to be disturbed, and nothing has been disturbed.

"See? All is fine here," I point out.

"You'll never sleep in this place again, Lacey. Even if you tried to, you wouldn't be able to fall asleep. Face it."

I give him a dirty look, tired of his persistence on this subject, even though I know his point is valid. I *would* lie awake all night, eyes wide open, listening to every sound. I grab a suitcase and begin filling it up with more clothes.

"Not moving in with you," I say, more for myself than for Jason. "Just getting more clothes that I forgot to grab earlier."

"Fine. I'm going up to the roof to see if anything looks out of line," Jason says.

I also fill a bag with more of James Bond's food and toys. I do prefer having him at Jason's. It is safer there for him, and I would be devastated if anyone broke into my apartment and messed with him just to get back at me.

A little while later Jason returns to report that nothing looks unusual on the roof. I didn't think he would find anything, but it was worth a look.

"Ready?" Jason asks, grabbing my suitcase.

I have it stuffed it to the max, which I know pleases him. Maybe the more items I move in, the less he'll badger me about living together permanently.

"When do you plan on going to the pool? And don't tell me you aren't planning on it because I know you are," Jason says as we walk through the park to his apartment.

"Tonight," I say, deciding to tell him the truth. "And don't try to talk me out of it because I'm going, like it or not."

"For the record, I think it would be a better idea to send someone else to pick him up. We have a picture of him. Someone will eventually see him."

"He'll come out of hiding when he sees me at the pool tonight. *Alone.*"

"Wrong. You're not going alone."

"You can do whatever you want," I say, shrugging.

Jason puts my suitcase down and then sits down on it, grabbing my hand and pulling me down onto his lap. I laugh at how goofy we must look to the other people walking through the park.

"Why do you always give me such a hard time?" Jason asks, nuzzling my neck.

I try to stand up, not wanting to have this conversation here in the middle of the park, while people are walking around us. He keeps his grip on me so I can't get up.

"Because," I say with a sigh, pretending to be bored with his question.

"Why, Lacey?"

I lower my head, somewhat ashamed of how I had been acting. He's right. I do give him a hard time, and he hasn't done anything to deserve it. I lean into him, resting my head on his shoulder, and begin to tear up.

"Hey, what's wrong? I didn't mean to make you cry," Jason says, pushing my hair out of my face.

"I just feel like once I give myself over to you, you'll cast me aside like all your other girlfriends. Or worse, you won't cast me aside, but you'll just cheat on me. So I fight not to give you all of me," I blabber in between tears.

"Oh, babe. I'm not going anywhere. Hell, I'd marry you today if you would let me. But I can't even get you to move in with me," Jason jokes. He uses his hand to wipe away my tears.

"I know. I have so many issues and problems. I don't understand why you even want to be with me."

"We all have issues and problems, Lace. And I would take over your issues and problems if I could. But I can't, so we'll deal with them together, okay?"

"Okay," I sigh, drying my face with my shirt. What is wrong with me? I feel ridiculous for crying.

When we get back to Jason's, I head for his bedroom and crawl into bed. I think one of the reasons I've been so emotional lately is exhaustion. Jason follows me and puts his arms around me, spooning me. I think this is one of the reasons why I'm hesitant to live with him or anyone else for that matter. There are times when I just want to be alone or at least would like to be left alone on my side of the bed. But when you live with someone, it is difficult to tell someone to leave you alone without the other person copping an attitude or misunderstanding your request. So instead, I adjust to Jason's body holding me close and eventually fall asleep.

Chapter 27

When I awake a few hours later, Jason has his body partially draped over me. His erection is pressed into my thigh. Since I'm feeling amorous myself, I turn toward him so I can take advantage. I kiss his neck and gently push his shoulder so he turns over on his back.

He moans something about being too warm in here, and I agree as I crawl on top on him, straddling him, continuing to kiss his neck. He smirks when he appears to realize what I'm up to, and I feel his hands move down my back and grab my ass. I reach over to the nightstand and grab a condom. After putting the condom on him, I lower myself onto his penis until it slides into me. I take off the T-shirt and bra I'm wearing so Jason has a better view. I know he likes looking at me, and I'm happy to oblige. I move back and forth on him, trying to hit that spot that will be most pleasing for me. He tries pulling me down so he can kiss me, but I remain sitting up, enjoying the position I'm in. Jason and I may fight for control in our relationship, but I can still maintain some control in the bedroom.

He strokes my hips and then moves his hands up to the undersides of my breasts. Anywhere he touches tingles. His hands close over my breasts, and he squeezes and rolls my nipples between his fingers. I let out a moan, and my head falls back, lifting my breasts up and then letting them fall back into his hands. I move up and down on him, feeling him completely inside me and then almost out of me as I rise before moving back down again. Each time I move a little faster. Periodically I tighten around him as I rise but not too often, as I know that drives him crazy and I don't want him to finish before I'm done.

"God, you feel amazing," Jason murmurs, watching me move up and down.

He puts his hands on my hips and tries to control the pace I'm sliding up and down on him. I lift and then drop down on him hard to remind him I'm still in charge. His moan lets me know his approval.

I lean forward and put my hands on his shoulders so I can better manage the tempo, wanting our pleasure to last, but with each slide down his penis, my arousal is becoming almost too much to contain. My breathing is becoming erratic, sometimes stopping completely. I moan as I go up, down, contracting around his almost-ready-to-burst erection.

"I can't last much longer," Jason grunts as he grabs my backside.

"Okay," I pant, "I'm ready."

I lean back, arching my back, and continue to rub myself onto him, trying to take him deeper, not wanting it to end. When my body can't take it anymore, I let out a moan that could probably be heard in New Jersey and then continue to bask in the aftershocks of pleasure as I feel him jerking inside me.

I stretch out on him when I'm done.

"You know Jay, I am on the pill. If you want we could stop using condoms." I feel silly breaking the mood to talk about birth control but figure it's a topic that is long overdue and needs to be addressed. "I'm not carrying any diseases. You said you aren't, and I trust you're telling me the truth about that."

"Up to you, babe. I'm used to condoms, so it's fine with me either way. Whatever makes you comfortable. I've always been very careful and get tested at least once a year to make sure I'm clean."

"I think we could stop using them, then. I'm glad that's settled." I get more comfortable lying across him, stretching out like a cat.

"You're so beautiful, Lacey," Jason says, spreading my hair on his chest.

I give him soft kisses along his jawline as he combs my hair with his fingers. As much as I want to lay here and cuddle, I know I should leave and go deal with my stalker.

He says, "I love you and—"

I kiss him on the lips before he can finish his sentence. "Jason, I should go."

He sighs. "Why, Lacey? We'll go to the pool tomorrow when we're working."

"What happened to you?" I ask, sighing loudly and rolling over onto my back. "A man messes with me last night while I'm sleeping, and you've been acting like it was no big deal. Like you could not care less. But if some guy hits on me in a bar, you break his nose. What's the difference?"

Jason covers his face with his hands and lets out a sigh.

"You're impossible, Lacey. This is different, and you know it. It's not a game. This guy is not right in the head. Someone is going to get hurt if it's not handled correctly."

On some level I guess I know it is a bad idea, but I'm so tired of this man invading my dreams and now also raiding my real life. I just want it to end.

"You promise we'll deal with it tomorrow?" I ask.

"Yes, I promise," Jason says, sliding his arm under me and moving me closer.

"All right, I'll stay put tonight," I say, snuggling into his chest, and I eventually fall asleep.

Chapter 28

The next morning I awake early. When I can't go back to sleep, I decide to go for a run. It's still fairly dark, and because of recent events, I decide to pack my gun into a waist holster that I can keep tucked under my T-shirt.

"Where are you going?" Jason asks, barely awake, when he sees me standing over him getting dressed.

"I'm going for a quick run, and when I get back, I plan on having wild sex with you," I say, leaning over and giving him a kiss on his lips. "Be ready in half an hour or so, got it?"

"Won't be a problem. I just look at you and I'm ready," Jason says, covering his eyes with his forearm.

"All right," I say giggling, realizing that he is still very dopey. I head out the door toward the park.

It's still dark out when I reach the park. I have a flashlight and know the jog routes in the park like the back of my hand, so the dark doesn't bother me. Halfway through my run, it starts to sprinkle. But it's a light, warm sprinkle, so I continue my route. Out of the corner of my eye, I see movement behind a tree, probably someone trying not to get wet. I continue jogging my path. It has now become obvious the person is following me.

"You've got to be kidding," I mumble to myself. When will it end? Only when I end it.

It is still sprinkling. I can sense him in my shadows even though I know there is no way he could be that close. I can almost feel him taunting me. Begging me to catch him. I stop quickly and bend down, pretending to tie my sneaker. He isn't expecting me to stop so suddenly and keeps jogging behind me until he realizes his error and comes to a sudden halt. I slowly raise my head and look over my shoulder, lighting him up with my flashlight. There is nowhere for him to go. He is out in plain sight, exposed. I slowly stand up, not breaking eye contact, and turn to face him. He gives me a small smirk before he turns and runs.

I take off running after him. He tries switching paths, but because I keep him in view, he doesn't lose me. He runs off the path into an overgrown, brushy area, where no one usually walks. I keep him in my sight and still follow. When he realizes he's not going to lose me, he runs out of the park, crosses a street, and then heads down into a subway station. I follow him, determined to end this now. By the time I get to the tracks, he has jumped on a train and the doors have closed. He looks out the window at me and waves good-bye. Doesn't matter. I know where he's going. I wait for the next train to come and hop on.

I pull out my cell phone. There's a text from Jason asking where I am. I've been gone longer than thirty minutes, and he's probably up and waiting after my comment about wild sex. And I did mean it. I was planning to attack him when I returned from my run.

I text him back that I'm on a subway to the Bronx.

As expected my phone rings. Do I answer it?

"Hello?" I say.

"Lacey, what are you doing?"

"He was following me in the park, and I'm so sick of dealing with this shit. I'm going to the Bronx to get answers."

"Lacey, get off at the next stop and wait for me—please. I'm on my way."

I hang up the phone. There's no way I'm getting off at the next stop, Jason and I both know that. I continue, on my way to the pool. By the time I get there, the sprinkle has turned into a light rain. I try the gate. It's open. I walk inside and close the gate, locking it behind me. Daylight is slowly approaching, but it's still not light enough to see without my flashlight. I walk around the pool, which is uncovered. I don't see anyone, but he has to be here. I can feel him watching, just like he did twenty years ago. The lights around the pool come on. It actually makes it harder for me to see because of the rain causing reflections all around me.

"Lacey Burke." He steps out from the shadows. "I have been waiting for you."

"Who are you? Why are you bothering me?" I need answers, and we both know I'm not leaving until I have them.

"You don't remember it at all, huh?" He smiles as though his morning just got better.

"I remember pieces. Who are you?"

"I live across the street." He points to an apartment building that is visible over the white fence.

"So what? You sit in your apartment and stalk the neighborhood?"

He laughs as though it is a funny comment rather than the truth.

"What happened that night? Why were we swimming by ourselves when the pool was closed?" I continue. This man is clearly deranged, but I have to try to get as much information from him as I can.

"Hey, I'm not one to deny little girls' curiosities. You were nosing around the place, so I let you in." He laughs again, even though there is nothing funny about our conversation or this situation.

"Did you push us in?" The thought suddenly occurs to me. Why would two little girls who can't swim jump in a pool?

"You were the ones who said you wanted to go for a swim." He laughs louder but does not really answer the question.

"Did you push us in?" I ask the question again. Tears start to well up in my eyes. I'm surprised by my sudden weakness.

"Really, Lacey? Did you really come all this way to ask such stupid questions?"

"I remember drowning in the pool with Theresa, and then you pulled me out. Why wouldn't you pull her out?" The tears were now falling, as I couldn't fathom how someone could be this cold toward a helpless little girl. "Why? Why wouldn't you pull her out? What did she ever do to you?" I ask more loudly when he ignores my previous questions.

He stands there staring at me, as though he is enjoying being the center of my focus. He shrugs. His back is to the gate, and over his shoulder, I see Jason wiggling the lock, trying to get in.

"Do you have survivor's guilt, Lacey? I've always wondered if you had guilt. I wanted to ask you on the subway that day. A while back. But you looked right through me, as if you had no idea who I was."

"I had blocked everything out. But then seeing you triggered something. Nightmares," I say, putting it together.

"Tell me, Lacey. Do you have survivor's guilt?"

"I don't know. Maybe," I answer. I want to keep the dialogue going so that I can get some answers. I hate that he has total control right now.

"I periodically read about you in the news, you know. Is that why you became a cop, Lacey? So that you could help others because you couldn't help Theresa?" He snickers.

"I was five, and I couldn't swim. How was I supposed to help her? You were the adult. You should have helped her. Why didn't you?" I can feel my anger coming back.

He laughs. "You want to know why?"

"Yes, tell me why now," I say, my voice getting stronger.

He shrugs. "It was the flip of a coin, that's all."

"What? What do you mean?" I ask in disbelief.

"I mean I flipped a coin. You were heads. She was tails. It landed heads, so I saved you."

I gasp at what he is saying.

"That's right, Lacey. The only reason why you are standing before me is because of a coin toss. If it had landed tails, you wouldn't be here." He cackles. "Your whole existence is because of a coin toss."

I close my eyes. I can't believe what I am hearing. I reach behind me, pull out my gun, and cock the trigger.

"How about if we do a coin toss right now on whether you live or die?" I walk toward him, aiming the gun. My tears have turned to anger.

"Lacey, open this door now," Jason yells from the other side of the gate, still trying to get in. "Lacey, let me in, and I will take care of him."

"Go away, Jason," I say.

I keep walking toward this man who has haunted my sleep. He's still laughing, but it's more of a nervous laugh now. He's walking backward away from me.

"You wouldn't kill me. How would that look on your résumé? Cop shoots unarmed man."

"So what? You think I'm afraid of jail time?" I yell at him, still walking toward him as he stumbles backward. "You know how many times I've been to hell and back? You really think jail scares me?"

I am practically standing on top of him now. I can't hear Jason jerking the lock anymore, so I assume he has gotten in even though I can't see him.

"Tell me something, Lacey." He slowly rises to his feet.

"What?" I hiss at him.

"Did you ever learn how to swim?"

"Fuck you," I say as he lunges at me and pushes me into the pool.

I pull the trigger and hear the shot fired, but not before I feel the knife driven into my stomach.

Chapter 29

When I wake up, I'm lying in a hospital bed. I look around the room. Jason is sleeping in a chair beside me. I try to reach over and touch him. A pain pierces through my abdomen, and I let out a moan.

"Lacey." Jason wakes up and grabs for my hand. "Oh, babe, what am I going to do with you?" He kisses my hand.

"How long have I been asleep?" I ask, clutching my gut.

"A few hours. You'll be fine. You were knifed in the stomach."

"My stomach is killing me," I groan.

"I'll get the doctor and let him know you are awake." Jason kisses me on the forehead and leaves the room. A few minutes later, he returns with a doctor in tow.

"Miss Burke, I'm Dr. Shepard, the attending ER doctor tonight." He sits on the side of my bed and takes my hand. "You were stabbed in the stomach right here." He points to the area where I was stabbed. "You're very lucky. The knife missed every major organ, but it did puncture your gallbladder, which we removed. You don't need your gallbladder, so don't worry about that. Some tissue was also cut, but that will heal together with time. You'll have some pain here and there, but it's not life threatening."

"It really hurts. Can I get some painkillers?" I say, wincing.

"I'll have the nurse bring you something more for the pain. We're going to keep you for twenty-four hours to make sure the wound doesn't get infected. You need to rest and not aggravate the tissue that was cut. Okay?" The doctor stands without waiting for an answer. Except for the handholding, he is all business and methodical. I guess when you work in the emergency room, you have little time to linger over patients. "I'll check on you again in a few hours. In the meantime, I'll send in a nurse with stronger meds. Get some rest, Lacey."

"So…how mad are you?" I turn to Jason while we are waiting for the nurse to come back.

"I'm fuming," Jason says, not joking. "But the main thing is you are okay." He takes my hand and sits back in the chair.

"I'm so sorry. I really messed up, huh?"

"Yeah, you really messed up. I messed up, too. I should have taken control of the situation sooner, before it became too late."

"You didn't mess up. I didn't give you a chance to take over. What happened to him anyway?" I close my eyes, knowing the pros and cons of any outcome.

"He died, Lacey. You shot him in the neck."

I keep my eyes closed, not sure how I should feel about that news. The nurse comes in and injects something into one of the tubes hooked into my arm.

"That should help, honey." She pats my arm and leaves.

"Tell me about him," I tell Jason.

"His name was Billy Shanley, fifty-nine years old. He lived in the neighborhood but he kept mainly to himself. None of his neighbors could tell us much about him."

"Go on."

"He was first arrested and sent to a juvenile detention center when he was fourteen for skinning his neighbor's dog. After that he was in and out of prison for various crimes such as rape, assault."

"What's really strange, is all of his victims were foster kids. He dated a woman who worked at Social Services so we think that is how he got his victim's information. She was never tied to any of his crimes and died about ten years ago, so it is not known how involved she was in his criminal activities."

"He was just a bad, unstable dude, Lacey."

"As if foster kids don't have enough to deal with, they had this nut targeting them." I close my eyes when I feel the medication kicking in and fall back asleep.

When I wake up the next morning, Dr. Shepard is standing next to me, writing on my chart.

"How are you feeling?" he asks when he sees that my eyes are open.

"Fine. Where's Jason?" I ask, looking around the room.

"He's outside, talking with your captain." The doctor lifts my shirt to check out the wound. He removes the gauze covering the wound. I wince. "Is the pain any less?"

"Not really," I say.

He pours something on the gauze and covers the wound back up again. "It looks okay. No signs of infection, but we are still keeping you here until tonight. Can I get you anything before I leave?"

"Maybe another dose of pain meds?" I shut my eyes until the doctor leaves, and Jason and Captain Fuller walk in.

"Lacey, how are you doing?" Captain Fuller sits on the side of my bed.

Jason leans against the wall with his arms crossed. He looks annoyed.

"I'll survive," I say.

"Jason filled me in on what happened. I'll just need to get a statement from you when you are feeling better. Maybe in the next day or so? Because it happened when you were off duty, the DA has taken more of an interest in it than other cop shootings."

"Is it really necessary to go over this with her now, Captain?" Jason interjects. "My God, she just woke up."

"Is there anything I should know about what happened, Lacey?" Captain Fuller asks, ignoring Jason.

"No. You can take my statement now if you want," I say, wincing in pain. Where is that nurse?

"No, that's not necessary. Internal Affairs will send someone over in the next day or so when you are home."

"Okay," I say, and I close my eyes.

"The doctor said you should be able to return to work in about four weeks. When you are cleared medically, you'll stay out on routine administrative leave and undergo a psychological examination to determine the effects the incident had on you. Normal procedures anytime a cop is involved in a shooting, Lacey. Usually lasts a few weeks." Captain Fuller's tone is soothing, even though I am not upset. I know the drill. "So, if all goes well, you'll be back to work in about six weeks, okay?"

"Fine," I say, looking over at Jason. "Can you get the nurse, please?" My insides are on fire.

Jason returns, followed by a nurse. "Can you please give me something more for the pain?" I say, holding my breath. If I stop breathing, perhaps the pain will go away.

"Sure, honey." The nurse indicates for Captain Fuller to get off the bed and injects something into my tube. She then lifts my shirt so she can feel my wound. "You're a little warm." She sticks a thermometer into my mouth and feels my forehead. "I'll be back with the doctor. You're starting to run a temperature."

Jason and Captain Fuller discuss something in hushed voices. I close my eyes, hoping sleep will come.

The doctor comes in. "Miss Burke, what's going on? You were just fine when I left you a little while ago."

"My stomach feels like it's on fire," I say to him, writhing on the bed.

"You're running a fever. It's an indication of infection. We're going to start you on antibiotics. You'll definitely be here another night."

"No, I don't want to stay here any longer. Just shoot me up with something and let me go. *Please*," I say, pleading with the doctor. "I just want to go home." Jason sits on the bed and takes my hand.

"I'm sorry, Lacey. I can't discharge you yet," the doctor says. "We need to stop this infection before it does any serious damage. I'll increase the pain meds, so you should go back to sleep."

"Okay." This placates me some. I shut my eyes and go back to sleep.

Chapter 30

When I wake up, Jason is sitting in the chair next to me, playing with my phone.

"Hey." He puts down the phone when he sees I'm awake. "How are you feeling?"

"Better. I'm really hungry. What time is it?"

"It's about eight. You've been sleeping. They have been pumping you full of meds all day."

"You don't have to stay here, you know. You must be bored to tears."

"I'm fine. I went home and showered. There's been people stopping to see you all day long, so I had plenty of company."

"Mmm. Did you move my stuff back to my apartment? I figure after this, you'll be kicking me out," I say, closing my eyes.

"Yeah, I did move your shit back. But I'm keeping the cat. He's growing on me. We've bonded over nutty women."

I smile and push the nurse button on the table.

"Lacey, how are you doing?" the nurse asks as she walks into the room. "You look much better." She takes my temperature and lifts my shirt to look at my bandage. She unhooks some of my tubes. "You shouldn't need these anymore."

"I'm starving. Do you think it would be okay if I ate something?" I ask her.

"I think that's a good idea. We stopped serving dinner two hours ago, but the cafeteria is still open."

"There's a burger joint around the corner. I'll run out and get you something." Jason kisses me on the forehead and leaves.

"You are one lucky girl," the nurse says, watching Jason leave. "I would never get out of bed if I had him next to me. Mmm."

I laugh. "He is cute, isn't he?"

"That he is, my dear. The doctor will be in a little later," she calls back to me as she leaves.

I close my eyes and wait for Jason to return with my food. My stomach still hurts, but it's a different kind of pain. No longer an on-fire kind of pain.

The only reason you are standing here is because of a coin toss.

That statement keeps flashing into my brain, torturing me. What if?

The smell of greasy food fills my room. Jason moves the food tray in front of me and unpacks the bags he's carrying. He lays out cheeseburgers, hamburgers, curly fries, a Diet Pepsi, and a chocolate milkshake.

"Oh, Jay, you certainly know how to please me," I say, digging in.

"I'm so relieved you're feeling better, Lace," Jason says, while also digging into a hamburger. "And there is no way I was going to let you eat that cafeteria food. I ate breakfast there. It was disgusting."

"Thanks," I say, looking at him and smiling.

The doctor returns, interrupting our food party.

"Miss Burke, glad to see you are feeling better. Don't stop because I'm here. I'm just going to give you a final check before I finish my shift tonight. If the night goes all right, the nurses have instructions to discharge you tomorrow morning," the doctor informs me.

"I feel well enough to go home tonight, you know."

"Well, that's not going to happen," he says, lifting my shirt and redoing my bandages. "Everything looks okay. Stitches will need to come out next Tuesday. The nurse will set up an appointment time for you to come back. I'm also going to give you a prescription for painkillers for one week. The pain shouldn't last any longer than that. And here's my cell phone number. Call me if you need anything." The doctor writes his phone number on a piece of paper, which Jason takes out of my hand and puts in his pocket.

"I'll call you if anything comes up," Jason says, glaring at the doctor.

"Anyway, Miss Burke," the doctor continues, ignoring Jason, "take care of yourself. The nurse will go over the medications and a list of things you can and cannot do over the next few weeks. I'll see you next week."

"Relax, Jason. He was just being helpful," I say when the doctor leaves my room.

"I've been to the hospital many times, and the doctor never gave me his cell phone number to call if I need anything."

"Yes, but how many nurses have given you their cell phone numbers?" I say, smiling at him.

Jason stares at me without answering, seeming to know it's in his best interest to keep his mouth shut. Instead he leans back in the chair and starts texting.

"Wait, what are you doing?" I ask when I see it's my phone he has open and is texting with.

"I'm responding to the text messages you've been getting. Keeping everyone updated on what's going on."

"That's very sweet of you. Now can I have my phone please?" I lay back on the pillow and stretch my hand out to get the phone.

"Did you realize you have twenty-two unread texts from Tyler?" Jason asks while still scrolling through what's on my phone.

I let out a loud sigh when I realize I'm not getting the phone back. "I don't care. Delete them. I'm not going to read them anyway. He'll give up eventually."

I see him punching away on the keys. "Now what are you doing?"

"I'm going back and forth with Laura. I let her know you are leaving here tomorrow. She and Rob are getting along splendidly, just so you know. And I also let someone named Nicole know what was going on. Who is Nicole? How come I've never met her?" Jason is clearly enjoying his latest game.

"Jason, will you please give me my phone? I'm awake and can respond to my own messages, thank you." I outstretch my hand again in the hopes that he'll give me the phone.

"Hmm. A text just came in from Kellan Walker. He wishes you well and would love to take you out to dinner sometime and make you feel better."

"Jason, give me the damn phone. I'll take care of Kellan."

"No, *I'll* take care of Kellan." Jason types a reply message.

"You're impossible," I say, closing my eyes and giving up. The morning cannot come soon enough.

When I wake up during the night, Jason is sound asleep in the chair. He's going to have neck and back issues after these last two nights. I reach over and tap his knee. When he wakes up, I move over on the bed to make room for him. He takes the hint and climbs in next to me, kissing me on my forehead before putting his head down and falling asleep.

"Okay, you two. Wake up," the nurse says when she walks in the door the following morning.

"This isn't a hotel, you know," she says, shooing Jason off the bed. "Lacey, how are doing today?"

"I feel well enough to go home," I say.

"Well, as long as everything looks good, you'll be on your way." The nurse starts running tests and taking notes. She double-checks my wound and redoes the bandage. "Okay, honey. You are good to go. Here are your painkillers and written instructions on how to care for the wound. Here's a list of what you can do and when. Here's your appointment card for next Tuesday, when you need to come back and have the stitches removed. Any questions?"

"No. I'll be fine."

"Good." She hands the paperwork and pills to Jason, who puts everything in his pocket. "Get dressed, and I'll be back with a wheelchair."

I sit up, and the pain pierces my stomach.

"Careful. Are you sure you're good?" Jason says, helping me up.

"Positive. Where are my clothes?"

"Here."

Jason helps me change into the sweatpants and a sweatshirt that he brought back when he went home to shower. I lay back down while he puts on my socks and sneakers.

"Are you sure you're all right to leave?"

"Jason, I can't stay here another minute. I will feel 100 percent better when I get out of here."

"Okay." Jason looks at me skeptically.

The nurse bounds through the door, pushing a wheelchair.

"Oh, please. I can walk," I say, standing up.

"Sorry, honey, hospital policy. You get wheeled out." The nurse helps me into the chair.

"Okay, but it really isn't necessary."

"Duly noted. You can walk but will still get pushed." The nurse rolls her eyes as though she has this conversation multiple times a day.

"Couch or bed?" Jason asks when we walk into his apartment. He has his arm wrapped around under my armpit, holding me up and steadying me as I walk.

"How about couch? That way I can at least watch TV."

He leads me over and gently eases me into the seat. He pulls out the footrest and tips the seat back so I'm practically lying down. "You want a pillow, blanket?" he asks, looking at me. "You don't look comfortable."

"I'm fine, really." I smile up at him. The nurse was right: I am so lucky.

James Bond jumps up on the cushion next to me and butts his head into my thigh—his way of saying he's happy to see me.

Jason places a bottle of water next to me.

"Jay, please sit. You don't have to wait on me. I can get anything I need. Thank you."

"You can barely walk, Lacey. Just relax. I don't have anything else to do today but take care of you." He sits down next to me and turns on the TV. "You want to watch a movie?"

"Yeah, that's a good idea." I reach over and hold his hand.

Jason scrolls through the list of movies available for download. We settle on the latest action movie and call it a day. Halfway through the movie I fall asleep. When I wake up, I'm in Jason's bed. It's about seven o'clock, but it's very dark in the room because Jason has the all the shades down. I can hear the TV and assume Jason is still in the living room. My wound is killing me. I pop a painkiller, take a sip of water, and fall back asleep until the next morning.

Chapter 31

J feel Jason kissing me on the forehead, and I open my eyes.

"Hey, I didn't mean to wake you."

"Where are you going?" I ask when I see he is fully dressed. "What time is it?"

"You've been asleep forever. I'm going to work. How are you feeling?"

"Better. Those painkillers really kicked my ass, huh?"

"Go back to sleep, babe. I'll stop back during the day and check on you." Jason kisses me again before he leaves.

I feel as though I've been asleep for a week. My wound is feeling better. I get out of bed and walk to the kitchen. I'm starving. How long ago has it been since I've last eaten? Jason's kitchen is stocked with food. When did he go grocery shopping? I have a bowl of cereal with a glass of orange juice. James Bond jumps up on a kitchen chair next to me, looking for his breakfast. I place a small plate with moist cat food in front of him on the table so that he can eat with me. When I'm done eating, I decide to try to take a shower. I feel disgusting and smell like a hospital.

Around lunchtime I'm sitting at the kitchen table, reading a magazine, when Jason comes home.

"Wow, you look much better," he says when he sees I've cleaned up.

"I feel better. Oh, Jay, what am I going to do for six weeks? I'm already bored out of my mind." I get up and give him a hug.

"You're going to rest and take it slow, Lacey. Just because you're feeling better doesn't mean you're back to 100 percent."

"I know. I'm still sore. But I am so bored." I push my face into his chest. "Are you home for the day?"

"No. I just stopped in to see how you're doing."

"Someone from Internal Affairs is going to be here in about an hour," I say, looking at my watch. "Fuller called me earlier to give me the heads-up. He made it clear that I should be alone, and no one else should be here."

"I know. He told me the same thing this morning. Just tell the truth, Lacey. You didn't do anything wrong. He stabbed you, and you shot him. End of story."

"Okay," I whisper and push my face back into his chest.

"Don't worry about it. You'll be fine."

He tilts my head back and kisses me on the mouth. Oh, it feels like an eternity since we've had sex. He cups my neck and kisses me harder.

"I want you so bad," he whispers in my ear.

"Then take me, *please*."

"We can't. It's on your list of things you can't do until stitches come out." Jason pulls away, trying to restrain himself.

"Really? Since when did you ever follow instructions?" I kiss him again.

"Lacey, please. I would be devastated if I caused you to be reinjured." He backs away again.

"Fine." I pout and sit back down in the kitchen chair. "What do you want for dinner tonight? Maybe I'll cook something."

"Lacey, I really don't want you overdoing it. I'll pick something up from Tino's on my way home."

I shrug. "It's really not a lot of work."

"Not tonight. Maybe tomorrow, okay?"

"Okay."

"I'm going to get going. Call me as soon as you're done giving your statement. Everything will be fine, I promise."

Jason gets up, and I walk him to the door. He puts his hand on my neck, gently pulls my hair, and pulls me in for another kiss on the mouth.

"You're going to be in such trouble on Tuesday," he whispers in my ear.

"Can't wait. I'll call you later," I say, smiling.

Shortly after Jason leaves, there is a knock on the door. I open it to find an attractive man in his late thirties, wearing a crisp black suit and carrying a computer case. He's about six feet tall with a medium build and dark-brown hair, combed neatly to the side. His eyes are a very light blue.

"Miss Lacey Burke," he states as though he wouldn't expect anyone but me to answer the door. He stands there, staring at me.

"Yes, and you are?"

I can guess who he is but also know its procedure for a cop to identify himself, and I certainly am not going to let him in without knowing exactly who he is. Strange. If he doesn't find his tongue, it won't be much of an interview.

"Um, I'm Louis Harvey with IAB." He awkwardly sticks out his hand that I shake and then invite him in.

"Have a seat, Mr. Harvey." I lead him into the kitchen and pull out a chair for him. "Can I get you something? Coffee? Tea? Water?"

"Water would be great, thank you. Call me Lou, please." Lou takes a seat at the kitchen table and sets up his computer. "This is just a formality, Lacey. I'm just here to gather information so everyone has all their bases covered and no surprises come out with the DA."

"Okay." I take the seat opposite Lou. He continues to stare at me with his piercing blue eyes while his computer warms up.

"Oh, you wanted a water, didn't you?" I say, standing up and getting him a bottle of water.

Lou starts with the basic questions. My name, DOB, and so forth. He then wants me to explain how the morning in question started. I tell him I was jogging through the park when I noticed a man following me. I walk him through to the last part I remembered, which was a knife going in my stomach and pulling the trigger. The whole process takes maybe thirty minutes. Lou doesn't ask a lot of questions. There are times when I feel as though he isn't really listening to me and instead just gazes at me. What is this guy's problem?

"Well, Lacey, I think we are done for now. You told me what happened. I don't see how anyone could question your actions that morning. I have to write a formal report that I will need you to sign when it is done and then send it to the DA. He'll then decide whether further review is needed and if additional information should be gathered."

I get up and walk Lou to the door. "Lacey, it was a pleasure." He shakes my hand and holds on to it for far too long. "I'll be in touch with you in the next day or so." He finally releases my hand.

"Thank you for taking the time to meet with me," I say, trying to remain professionally courteous, and close the door behind him.

What was that all about? I pick up the phone and call Jason.

He answers on the first ring. "Hey babe, how'd it go?"

"Fine. It went fine."

"What's wrong?"

"Nothing's wrong. It's just he wasn't here very long. Maybe half an hour. And he didn't really ask any questions. It was kind of weird."

"Did he question your actions and why you did it?"

"No. That's just it. He really didn't ask any questions and just said everything should be fine."

"Okay, well, I'm sure everything will be fine then. I'll see you in a little while, okay?"

"Okay."

When Jason comes home, I'm resting on the couch. He has dinner from Tino's, as promised. He sets up the food around the table. I walk over to him and give him a hug from behind as he's pouring our drinks. He brings my hands up to his mouth and gives each one a kiss. He then pulls out a seat for me to sit down.

"Sit, Lacey. I want to hear more about what happened today."

I sit down and shrug. "I don't know what else to say. It was fast. Not very detailed because as I said, he didn't ask any questions. That was that."

"Then why are you acting so weirded out?"

"I don't know. It was just weird. He kind of creeped me out. His name was Lou. Harvey," I say, looking at the business card he gave me because I couldn't remember his last name.

"Oh, I've met Lou. I don't know much about him. What do you mean, he creeped you out?"

"I can't explain it, Jay. You know how you get a feeling about someone that he's a creep? That's the feeling I had while he was sitting in front of me. It's probably just me. I'm so full of meds that my head is fuzzier than normal." I start eating the pasta Jason has put in front of me.

"Did he do something, Lacey?" He is staring at me, as though trying to read more into what I'm saying.

"No, he didn't. I think it was just me. Forget I said anything. He said he'll call me in the next day or so. I'll find out more then."

Jason is still staring at me, looking as if he is trying to get me to keep rambling and tell him more. I shove a forkful of ravioli in my mouth to stop myself from talking. I imagined the awkwardness and handshake, right? Telling Jason would only make him fly off the handle, and then the situation would be made worse.

"Okay then. We'll wait and see." He finally relents and eats his food.

Chapter 32

*E*ach day I'm feeling better and stronger. I begin taking short walks in the park, resting on park benches here and there so as not to exert myself. I also am getting more comfortable at Jason's apartment. He has cleared half of his closet and drawers to make room for me and clothes that I had previously brought over. He's trying to make it official, even though it has not officially happened or been confirmed. There's plenty of room for my stuff. I have never been a clotheshorse, so it's not like I have a lot to hang up anyway. I left the nicer dresses that Tyler bought me at my place. Not sure if I should keep them or donate them.

The longer I stay at Jason's, the more I like his apartment better. It's much more spacious than mine. I can't imagine what the rent is here. I know Jason is many pay grades above me since he made detective six years before I did and is now a lieutenant, but I'm not sure how much more he makes. I never cared, so I never asked.

Detective Lou Harvey calls me a few days after we initially met to tell me that his report is done. He lets me know he is working down by Wall Street that morning, and asks if it would be okay if we meet somewhere in the middle to review it and sign. He sounds normal on the phone, so I agree to meet him at a restaurant located in midtown.

I let Jason know what the plan is. He isn't thrilled with the meeting, but at least it's a public place. That pacifies him somewhat. Fortunately, Jason is tied up with an arrest, or I think he would probably show up. I promise to call him afterward.

I show up at the restaurant on time. Lou is already sitting at the bar, drinking a soda.

"Lacey, it's nice to see you again." He gives me another long handshake. Maybe that's just how he shakes hands?

"Lou, it's a pleasure. You have the report?" I ask, cutting to the chase.

"Yes. It contains everything we discussed." He pulls it out of a briefcase. "Please read it over. Can I get you a drink?"

"I'll just have a Diet Pepsi, thank you." I read the report. It is verbatim what we discussed the other day. I read it over again. "Lou, I think this is fine."

"You just need to sign here then." Lou points to the last page.

I sign on the dotted line that the statement is true to the best of my knowledge.

"And here is a copy for you to have." He hands me a copy of the report. "That should be it, Lacey. Like I said before, it's pretty clear-cut. Not sure why anyone would give you a hard time over it."

I soften up. "Thanks, Lou. I just want to move on and go back to work."

We sit for a few more minutes, finishing our sodas and making small talk and then saying our good-byes. It must have been my fuzzy head from the meds. He's almost a different person.

Chapter 33

*T*uesday is finally here. Jason takes me to the hospital to see Dr. Shepard and have my stitches removed. The doctor has me lift my shirt so he can examine the wound.

"You have healed very nicely. There is no infection, and the wound has completely closed." He begins cutting the stitches off. Once they are removed, he wipes the area clean and puts a bandage over the raised scar. "I'm just putting the bandage on for additional protection. Keep it on for twenty-four hours, and then you can take it off. Nothing strenuous for a few more weeks, and you should be back to full recovery."

"What do you mean by nothing strenuous? Can I have sex? Can I go running?" I bluntly ask, regarding my two favorite pastimes.

"Yes, you can have sex, and maybe work up to the running. Start with a slow jog, and see how that goes. Since you were stabbed in the stomach, you should avoid any activities that are particularly hard on your abs. Like sit-ups, twisting, Pilates. Stuff like that. And if you are doing something and feel any pain, you should stop immediately."

"Okay, sounds good."

"Take care, and I'll see you in a few weeks when you need to be cleared for work," the doctor says as he leaves the room.

"Oh, I'm so relieved to have these stitches gone. What a pain in the ass they were. Let's get out of here," I say to Jason, pulling my shirt back down.

We are the only ones on the elevator going up to Jason's apartment, so I begin my attack to cut down on foreplay time. Before I can get very far, Jason pulls away from me.

"Lacey, I have to go back to work."

"No," I whine. "Stay home this afternoon."

"I can't. I have to wrap some stuff up today." He's holding my arms back so that I can't touch him.

"What stuff?" I huff.

"*Stuff.* Crime didn't stop because you're on disability," he teases me.

"Fine." I move to the other side of the elevator and cross my arms to show him I'm not happy.

"Rest, okay?" he says, opening the door to his apartment.

"Fine," I say again, and kiss him good-bye on the cheek.

I change into sweatpants and a tank top, put on my headphones, and take a walk down to the park. I walk around at a leisurely pace for a few hours, stopping at various benches to enjoy the day and people watch. I don't feel as though I'm ready to get back into running yet and don't want to push it. When I get home, I lie down on the couch and take a nap.

I'm woken up by Jason carrying me into the bedroom.

"Hey, what are you doing?"

"I'm going to finish what you started," he says, kissing me as he puts me down on the bed and lying down on top of me.

"Finally," I say as I pull off my sweatpants and help him get out of his jeans.

"Oh, babe, I have missed you," Jason says as he kisses me and strokes me to see if I'm ready. I was ready a week ago. He inserts himself inside me.

"Oh, Jason," I cry out as he slowly grinds himself into me. A week's worth of unmet sexual need is building up inside me, ready to explode.

I lift my hips up and into him to try to get him to move faster.

"Oh, please don't tease me anymore," I groan.

"You promise you'll tell me if I hurt you?" Jason whispers in my ear.

Is he kidding me? "Yes, I swear to God, it feels *so* good."

"Okay, then."

He moves faster and harder until I just can't take it anymore, and a rush surges through my body.

"Oh, that was heaven," I say, as we are lying next to each other, catching our breath.

"Are you sure you're okay? I didn't hurt you?"

"Positive. It was exactly what I needed." I climb on top of him and softly kiss him on the lips. "You're so perfect in every way, you know that?" I lay back on my side so that I can stare at his beautiful face. I *am* in love with this guy.

Jason brushes a piece of hair off my face and lies on his side so that he is facing me. "You know, Lacey, we really need to talk about that night."

Mood killer.

"What's there to talk about?" I shrug the shoulder that I'm not lying on.

"Well, for starters, why wouldn't you wait for me? Listen to me?"

"Because I didn't want to get you in trouble. I knew you would try to take over, and if anything happened, I didn't want you involved."

"Well, I am involved. I couldn't be more involved. And maybe if I did take over, then maybe you wouldn't have been stabbed."

I close my eyes. "Please don't lecture me. I know I screwed up. I don't need you reminding me."

"I'm sorry. But I can't help thinking if the knife went in two inches to the left or three inches higher...it drives me crazy to think you might not be here."

"If the coin toss had been tails, then I wouldn't be."

"Babe, I'm sorry." He slides his arms around me and pulls me closer to him. "Please don't believe that."

"I keep thinking about what he said to me. The only reason I'm alive is because of a coin toss. I so easily could have been the one he didn't save. And maybe I shouldn't have been the one to survive."

Jason grabs the blanket that had been kicked to the floor and wraps it around me. He pulls me closer to him. I push my face into his chest.

"You've given him too much power, Lacey." Jason kisses my forehead. "Who's to say you wouldn't have survived without his help?"

"How could I have?"

"You're the toughest girl I have ever met. You don't think you could have eventually pulled yourself out of the pool? I mean, look at all the rough situations you've been in. And you survived them."

"I never thought about it that way before. Maybe you're right. I just keep thinking maybe Theresa would have served more purpose on this earth. Maybe it should have been her who should have lived."

"Oh, Lace. I think you would have lived either way." Jason hugs me tighter. "He tried to kill you last week, and you lived, right? What makes you think you wouldn't have survived twenty years ago without his help?"

"You're right. I need to change my thinking. I would have saved myself with or without him."

"I have no doubt you would have saved yourself." Jason kisses me on the mouth. "Now back to us. Promise me you will never pull that shit ever again."

"I promise," I whisper.

"Good." Jason keeps kissing me. "I have a surprise for you. I was going to tell you tomorrow, but maybe it will make you feel better."

"Mmm. You've already done enough to make me feel better," I say, pulling the blanket tighter around me and snuggling into his chest.

"I took next week off from work so we could spend more time together."

I reach up and give him a kiss. "I'm so happy. I've missed being with you during the day."

"And I think it would do you good to get out of town, so I've booked a trip to help you recuperate."

"Where?" I eye him suspiciously. "I don't need to go anywhere. I'm happy right here."

"I know, but I thought if we escaped to the Cayman Islands, it would help you feel better. We can relax on the beach and drink cocktails all day in the sun."

"Oh, Jay, you're too good to me." I kiss him on the mouth, letting him know I am ready for our next lovemaking session.

Chapter 34

"This place is amazing," I say as we walk to a pair of loungers on the beach. The sun is beginning to set. We flew into Grand Cayman earlier in the day and just had dinner at a beachside grill. I am wearing one of the sundresses that I purchased in New York yesterday. Jason is wearing khaki shorts and a white short-sleeved shirt. He is carrying a bottle of wine with two glasses that he snagged from the grill's bar.

"How can this place be on the same planet as New York?" I say, looking at the clear blue water. "It's a far cry from the East River, huh?"

"Here," Jason pulls the two loungers closer together and indicates for me to sit on one.

I get comfortable on the lounger and take the glass of wine Jason has handed me. I close my eyes and listen to the soft waves the ocean is pushing along the shoreline. Jason sits down on the lounger next to me and takes my hand to hold.

"It doesn't get any more relaxing than this, does it?" I say, looking over at Jason. "What's wrong? You've been very quiet."

"Nothing's wrong. I'm enjoying the view," Jason says, smiling at me and taking a sip of his wine. He continues, "Lacey, I absolutely love and adore you. I want to spend the rest of my life with you."

"I know. And I love you, too," I say, getting off my lounger and climbing on top of him. I kiss him on the lips.

Jason kisses me back and then pulls away, shifting himself underneath me so I am not lying directly on top of him. He reaches into his pocket and pulls out a ring box. It suddenly occurs to me what is about to happen. And surprisingly, I am okay with it. My fear of being controlled, losing my independence, and depending on another human being is replaced with an excitement of what my future could be like with this man.

"Lacey, will you marry me?"

"Yes, I absolutely will," I answer, smiling from ear to ear.

Inside the ring box is the ring that I had told Laura was my favorite when we were at her jewelers. Jason puts it on my finger.

"There. Now it's official," he says, kissing my hand.

I am stunned. "How did you know?" I ask, looking at the emerald-cut diamond ring I had previously admired on my shopping day with Laura.

"I called Laura to get advice on diamonds. I figured if anyone knew diamonds, it would be her. She knew exactly where to take me."

"Wow," I gasp still looking at the ring. "It's absolutely stunning."

"No, *you're* stunning." Jason kisses me on the cheek.

"You know, you really shouldn't have. This is all too much. I would have been happy with a ring from a gumball machine," I say, suddenly feeling guilty at how much this vacation and ring must have set him back.

"You deserve something beautiful." Jason refills our wineglasses.

"I'm just saying."

"Lacey, please," Jason says, cutting me off. "Don't worry about it."

"Okay." I put my head back on his chest and close my eyes. Before long, I feel Jason's breathing become more labored. My poor baby. He's exhausted.

I feel sand being poured on my leg and think I must be dreaming. I slowly open my eyes and see the culprit. He stands about three feet tall and I'm guessing is around four years old. He's staring at me as he dumps sand from his bucket onto my backside. I look around. We are surrounded. I nudge Jason and quietly whisper to him to wake up.

"Wake up," I whisper again.

He opens his eyes.

"We fell asleep out here," I inform him.

Jason looks around at the people who are now lying around us and frolicking in the ocean. "What time is it?"

I look at my watch. "It's a little after eight," I say, brushing the sand from my face and getting off him. Jason gets up and finds his shoes buried in the sand.

"Cute kid," he says, looking at the mother of the four-year-old as he dumps the sand out of shoes. Jason gathers up the empty wine bottle and glasses, then grabs my hand and leads me into the hotel.

"What a little asshole," he says in the elevator as he wipes more sand off himself.

"I can't believe we slept out there all night." I'm starting to laugh at the situation. "Did you see those people looking at us like we just crawled out of a sewer or something?"

"Mmm-hmm." Jason doesn't seem to see the humor as I do, but he at least cracks a smile.

When we finally get inside the hotel room, Jason grabs me and kisses me. He turns me around and kisses my neck while his hand makes its way down my front and into my underwear. I've learned that whenever Jason goes from behind, it usually means he just wants a quickie. I don't mind since he is normally such an unselfish lover. I step out of my underwear and let my dress fall off my shoulders and onto the ground. Jason continues kissing my neck and rubbing my nether region.

"Lacey, you are so beautiful."

Jason moves me toward and onto the bed as he removes his shorts. He inserts his finger into me to see if I'm ready. I was ready in the elevator. I cry out when he finally penetrates me. He feels so good. He continues to rub my clitoris as he thrusts into me from behind. His other hand is massaging my breasts. It's amazing how fast he can bring me to my knees—*literally.*

"Oh, God, you are amazing," I say, moaning and crying out.

He keeps pushing himself farther and deeper into me. When he wraps his arms around my waist to pull me back into him, I can't hold back anymore. I explode around him. He lets himself go when he sees I'm finishing. I collapse on the bed when we are done. Jason lays next to me, gasping for air.

Chapter 35

"I'm hideous," I yell to no one as I'm looking in the mirror while wearing my new red bikini. The four-inch scar to the right of my belly button stands out like a disco ball in a dark room. "I think it's getting bigger," I say, walking over to Jason, who is sitting on the bed, laughing at me.

"You're perfect." Jason places his hands on my waist. "And besides, with a rack like this, no one is going notice a scar on your stomach," Jason says, while kissing the tops of my breasts.

"You really know how to sweet-talk me," I say, slightly annoyed.

Jason continues kissing my breasts and then says, "If you want to see the beach anytime soon, then we need to get out of here."

We settle on two lounge chairs located under an umbrella that are not close to the youngster who tried to bury us alive earlier this morning. I settle back with my book and periodically glance at Jason lying next to me. His lean, muscular body is glistening as the heat stirs up his sweat glands. I love studying his body and have always been fascinated by his tattoos.

I'm looking at the Gaelic sun on his forearm when I inform him, "I'm going to get a tattoo."

"No, you're not," Jason says, not even humoring me.

"Why not? I think I should get one over this scar so that it blends in."

"Unless it says, 'Property of Jason' across your ass, it's not going to happen," Jason says as he reaches over and grabs my behind.

"Whatever. Why is it okay for you but not for me?"

Jason sighs. "First of all, your scar will fade. So that's a stupid reason to get one. Second, I got mine many years ago when I was a teenager and going through a phase. I'm not getting any more."

"Well, we'll see. I may get one."

"Not going to happen," Jason says, clearly insisting on having the last word. "Let's go for a swim." He grabs my hand and pulls me up off my lounger and toward the water.

The water is like bathwater. It is so nice and calm, hardly a wave. Jason dives into the water in front of me while I slowly immerse myself. When he sees me hesitating, he swims back to me.

"I'm sorry, Lacey," he says, taking my hand.

"I can swim now, silly," I say, pulling away from him. "I'm just taking my time."

"Are you sure?"

"Yes, I'm sure. I can tread water, and I can do a mean dog paddle."

As if to show him I'm okay, I jump into the water and start dog-paddling. He watches me for a minute and then starts swimming after me. I stay where I can touch bottom, whereas Jason swims way out, over his head. When he sees I'm not following him, he swims back.

"I'm not going where I can't touch," I explain before he asks.

"Here, get on my back," Jason says, turning around and moving closer to me.

"No, I'm all right," I say, swimming away.

"I promise I won't go out far," he says, following.

"You'll stay where you can touch?"

Jason rolls his eyes. "Yes."

"Okay, then," I say, getting on his back and wrapping my arms around his neck. He swims out farther. "This is far enough."

"Lacey, I can still touch here." He stands up to show me.

"Okay, but not much farther."

Jason moves out a little bit farther and then stops. He stands up, and the water is just below his shoulders. "See, I can still touch here." He takes my arm, moves me around to the front of him, and kisses me.

"I should have known you had an ulterior motive to get me in over my head. Now I'm trapped." I wrap my legs around him and run my hands through his hair, kissing him back.

He slides his hands into my bikini bottom and grabs my butt so that he can pull me closer to him.

"This is such a bad idea, you know that, right?" I ask.

"I think it's a great idea," Jason says in between kisses.

"Jason, we are on a public beach, and I'm not exactly quiet."

"There's no one around us, and you'll have to be quiet." Jason moves his hand past my butt and reaches in between my legs.

"You're evil, you know that?" I say, tensing up as he strokes me.

"Just relax. No one is looking."

I let my body go limp so that it is easier for him to maneuver. I keep kissing him on the lips to quiet any sounds escaping my mouth. He moves my bikini bottom over to one side and inserts himself into me. I push my face and mouth into the side of his neck to muffle the sounds I'm aching to make.

"Shh, you have to be quiet," he tells me.

Jason pushes himself further into me. He's trying to make small moves in order not to disrupt the water around us too much. Because we are so still, I can feel every pulsating move his body makes. I press my mouth harder into his neck when I really just want to scream out.

Jason puts his hands on my hips to hold me still while he moves in and out of me, still trying not to disturb the water around us. I keep my arms wrapped him and my face buried in his neck. Then he wraps his arms around me and pushes into me. We stay like this for what seems like an eternity. I hear people moving around us, but I don't dare look. *Crap.* Because we are so still, I can feel him throbbing inside me.

"I can't stay like this much longer," I whisper to him.

"I know." He walks backward into deeper water to get farther away from the people around us.

I take deep breaths, hoping that will slow down what's coming. Jason goes back to moving around inside me.

"Really, not much longer," I whisper to him again in case he has forgotten what I said a moment ago.

"Okay, there's no one around us now, and a boat is going by. We'll get some waves in two seconds."

If I weren't so horny for him, I would have laughed at his methodical planning. Instead I wait for the waves. Jason grinds harder, taking advantage of the disruption in the sea that the boat has caused. I keep my face and mouth pressed into his neck, trying to keep my train of thought as he blows my mind. It is one of the most intense orgasms I have ever experienced, and long after the waves calm down, I am still shaking from pure bliss. When I'm done I peel my face off his neck and my nails out of his back. Jason laughs.

"I am so mad at you right now. Just take me back to shallow water, please," I say, trying to keep from laughing. I straighten out my bikini bottom and pull myself around so that I'm on his back. "Everyone is looking. I'm mortified."

"No one is looking, Lace," Jason says, still laughing but not moving.

"Back," I say, pointing to the beach.

"You know I was thinking we should work on your self-control more often."

"Fuck you," I say, laughing. "Now take me back to where my toes can touch, please."

When we get back into shallow water, I hop off his back, make sure my swimsuit is in the right place, and then walk back to our loungers. Jason hangs out in the water a little while longer, no doubt shifting things around. I, along with the other female beachgoers, watch him walk back to me when he decides he has had enough of the water. He bends down and kisses me on the lips before settling into his lounge chair.

"Still mad?"

"No, I'm not mad. Just embarrassed," I say, looking around.

"No one knew what was going on. Last thing I would do is put you on display out here."

"True," I agree.

Now that that's settled, I go back to reading my book. Jason falls asleep.

I put my book down and look at my watch. I'm starving. I can smell hamburgers cooking on a grill somewhere. It's been about an hour and a half since our sex romp in the ocean. Jason is still sleeping. I should really wake him, or he's going to have way too much energy tonight, but he looks so peaceful. I get up and find the beachside grill, from where the delicious aroma is coming, and put in my order. I can see Jason from the grill and keep an eye on him in case he wakes up. I get my food and carry it back to our chairs. I decide Jason has slept long enough and straddle him to wake him up. He opens his eyes and looks at the food I have laid out on his chest.

"How lucky am I?" Jason asks shielding his eyes from the sun. "I wake up to a beautiful girl sitting on me in a bikini eating a hamburger. Life doesn't get any better."

"I couldn't wait any longer. I needed food," I say, dipping a french fry into ketchup and putting it in his mouth.

"What time is it?"

"About four. Too early for dinner," I say, taking a bite of my hamburger and then offering it to Jason so he can take a bite.

"What do you want to do tonight?" Jason asks. He raises his knees so that I can lean back and get more comfortable. "And before you get any ideas, I promised Rachel that we would not get married down here. So don't plan on getting me drunk and dragging me into some chapel."

"She and your mother would be heartbroken if we did that." I give him another bite from my burger and finish up the fries. I close my eyes while leaning back further on his bent knees. "Let's not leave here. We can buy a shack and be beach bums."

"Sounds good, but what would do for money?"

"I could periodically pimp you out to bored housewives who are here on vacation," I say, nodding in the direction of a forty-something-year-old woman who has been watching Jason behind her sunglasses all day. "And I could comb the beach each day with a metal detector. I can't imagine the stuff people drop and leave behind. I would think that would be enough to cover any shack-living expenses."

"That sounds like a plan, but I'm not real crazy about being pimped out," Jason says, sounding somewhat amused.

"Well, I'm not crazy about it either, but you would have to make some sacrifices until we found another way to make money. I'm just dreading going back home. I'm nervous about this whole shooting investigation getting wrapped up."

"The shooting is out of your hands, so there is no point in worrying about it."

"You're right. How about if we go for a swim and then have a nice dinner somewhere later tonight?"

"Hmm, another swim, huh?" Jason says, tugging at the side of my bikini.

"No more water sports for you. I am staying in the shallow end," I say, finishing up my burger and fries.

Chapter 36

Returning to New York is dreadful after spending a week in the Caribbean. Jason has to go back to work the day after we return, and I am back to puttering around the apartment. I still have about ten days left of disability and then the mandatory administrative leave whenever there is a cop shooting. Rachel and Jason's mom have been calling me, wanting to meet up so that we can plan the wedding. I've been putting them off. Of course I want to marry Jason. I just don't want the ceremony that it involves. I have no family to invite and no one to walk me down the aisle. It depresses me whenever I think about it.

My phone is ringing, and I look at the caller ID. Lou Harvey.

"Hi, Lou," I say cheerfully, hoping he has good news.

"Lacey, we need to talk. The DA has some questions, and he asked me to get more information from you."

"No problem. Why don't you give me his number? I'll set up a time to meet with him. It will be a lot quicker that way, don't you think?" I just want this over with.

"Sure, it would be quicker, but that's not how our procedures work. I have to cross my t's as well, you know?" Lou says, getting a little huffy.

"Fine. Can we do this over the phone, or do you want to meet somewhere and discuss?"

"Can you meet me at the same restaurant in midtown? The one we met at last time? In about thirty minutes?"

"Sure, I'll see you there." I hang up, slightly annoyed but a little happy that I now have a reason to get out of the apartment. I text Jason to let him know, and he doesn't respond. Must be busy. I fix myself up and head out the door.

Lou is sitting in the same chair at the bar. I hop on the seat next to him and order a Diet Pepsi.

"Lacey, I'm sorry to bother you again. Thanks for meeting me here," Lou says, without the huffiness he previously displayed.

"No problem. I'm anxious to clear anything up and get this over with."

"Well, you see, the DA really has a problem with why you were there that morning." Lou turns his body so that he is facing me. His knees are touching my chair. I take a sip of my drink, and he sees my ring.

"Congratulations. You think you've tamed Reed, huh?" Lou says, smirking.

"I already told you why I was there," I say, ignoring Lou's last comment. "The guy was stalking me, and I wanted to find out who he was and why. I wanted to know why he was following me."

"Right. I believe you, Lacey. It's just the DA finds it difficult to believe you went there by yourself with no intent of hurting anyone. Now if there is more information you could provide, that would certainly help," Lou says, still smirking at me. "If you give me the right answers, I can make this go away for you."

"What do you mean, right answers? All I can tell you is the truth. I'm not a monster. I went there to talk to him. He stabbed me. I shot him. It was either he dies, or I die. I didn't go there with any intention of shooting anyone." I take another sip of my Diet Pepsi. This is not going well.

"I'm just saying I could really help you out of this jam if you let me spin it how I want to." Lou puts his hand on my forearm and rubs my arm with his thumb. "I've worked with this DA many times before, and he listens to what I have to say. He trusts my judgment."

I sit there, stunned.

"And there is even talk about looking at Jason's actions that morning and maybe he should have done more to stop you." Lou continues to rub my arm with his thumb.

"What do you mean? He couldn't have done anything."

"He could have done a lot more, Lacey, and you know it. The DA mentioned charging him with conspiracy or aiding and abetting. Something along those lines. And if the DA doesn't charge him with something, then I will at a *minimum* suggest he be reprimanded. I can make it all go away for you if you let me."

"What do you want from me?" I say very quietly, even though I already knew the answer.

"I just want to get to know you better, that's all. I want to know what makes you tick. Why should Reed have all the fun?"

My cell phone starts buzzing. It's a text from Jason. I look at my watch. "I have to go, Lou. I'm already late for a lunch date," I lie. As I climb off the barstool, I grab his hand. "You promise me you'll make this go away if I agree to what you want? I don't even care about myself, but you have to fix this for Jason. He did nothing wrong."

"I'll see what I can do, Lacey. But I'm not going to stick my neck out and get nothing in return. Got it?" His eyes turn ice blue.

"Yeah, I got it," I say, moving my hand to his thigh and giving it a squeeze. I lean in and breathlessly whisper in his ear, "You know, I felt something for you when we first met. I'm glad it wasn't just my imagination."

"Lacey," he says, putting his hand over mine, "I can make you very happy if you let me."

"Can we discuss this later? Maybe in a more intimate setting?" I say, cocking my head at him and giving him a sly smile. This guy makes the hair on the back of my neck stand up, but I've gone undercover enough times to know how to play dirty.

"I look forward to it, baby. Oh, and Lacey, don't tell anyone about this conversation, or I will for sure have Jason's badge," Lou says, smiling at me, and then he gives me a wink. "I'll be in touch, honey."

I calmly walk out of the restaurant when what I really want to do is run as fast as I can home. What am I going to do? I can't sleep with this guy, but I also cannot let Jason face charges for something he didn't do.

I continue walking for a few blocks and then duck into a pub when I'm sure Lou is not following me. I order a drink at the bar and then find the ladies' room, where I throw up anything and everything that was in my stomach. My insides are in knots over my conversation with Lou. I wipe my face clean and then go back to the bar. I sit down and sip the beer that I ordered. I look at the text from Jason. He wants to know why I'm meeting Lou Harvey again and asks me to put it off so that he can go with me. Too late.

A few minutes later, my phone rings. No doubt it's Jason, wanting to know what's going on since I didn't respond to his text.

"Hi," I say into the phone, trying to sound cheerful.

"Hey, babe, what's going on?"

"Nothing. Everything's fine." I'm so sorry I got him into this mess.

"Where are you?"

"I'm in a bar near midtown," I say, not wanting to lie.

"Why?"

"I was hungry, so I thought I would stop in here."

"What's wrong, Lacey?"

I'll never be able to fool him.

"Nothing's wrong. I'm fine. The meeting was fine. He asked a few more questions, that's all."

"You sound funny. What bar are you at?"

"I don't know. I just popped in. I'm fine."

"Lacey, what bar are you at?"

"Excuse me, sir." I flag down the bartender, knowing Jason won't let up until I tell him where I'm at. "What is the name of this bar?"

"O'Grady's on Forty-Sixth," the bartender says, while he continues to wipe down some glasses. He's an elderly man, probably in his seventies. Not a care in the world, just happy to be alive and still be working.

I repeat the name back to Jason. "I'm fine. And I'm not going to be here much longer, so don't bother showing up."

"I'm on Thirty-Ninth. I'll be there in two minutes. Stay put."

I need to get my act together before he gets here.

"Honey, are you okay?" the bartender asks me as he puts another beer in front of me. "You don't look so good."

"I'm fine. Thanks for asking," I say, putting a smile on my face.

I can't even fool a bartender I don't know. I go back to the bathroom to try to freshen up somewhat. When I return to the bar, Jason is sitting in the seat that was next to mine talking to the bartender. I have to smile; just seeing him makes me feel better.

"Hey," I say, kissing him on the cheek and sitting back down on my barstool.

Jason stares at me for a few moments and then asks, "What's wrong? You look green."

"My stomach hurts," I say, grabbing my wound. "I tried to go running this morning and think maybe I overdid it. This pain shoots through me every once in a while."

"So you thought it would help to stop in here and drink?" Jason asks, seeming to look right through me.

"Yeah, I thought it would help with the pain. And besides, what's the rush to get home? It's not like I have a lot to do today anyway." I laugh nervously.

"Lacey, what did Lou want? And don't lie."

"He wanted to discuss why I went to the pool again. He said he needed more detail. I told him the truth. I think I'm just really nervous about the whole situation." It's not a total lie.

"It will be all right, I promise you. Please don't worry about it," Jason says.

"I know. I'm just a little uptight right now." The bartender replaces my empty with another beer.

"Are you going to sit here all afternoon and get drunk?" Jason asks, looking annoyed.

"Don't you have to go back to work or something?" I ask, getting equally annoyed.

"Finish your drink, and then we are leaving."

"Please quit bossing me around," I say, firmly.

Maybe if I piss him off enough, he'll dump me, and then it won't be cheating if I sleep with Lou. Worst plan ever, but right now, it is all I have.

Jason waves the bartender over and asks him what the bill is for my drinks. Jason then gives the bartender money to settle up.

"Lacey," Jason says, turning toward me and trying to keep his voice calm, "I have to go back to work, and I'm not leaving you sitting here in this bar. Get your shit together, and let's go."

"Okay, I'm ready," I say very sweetly, and I slip my hand into his. What am I accomplishing sitting in a bar anyway?

Out on the street, Jason gives me a kiss good-bye. "We are going to talk later, right?"

"Yes," I say, smiling at him.

"And you are going home now?" Jason asks.

"Of course. I'll see you later," I say. I have no intention of going home.

I turn and walk toward the subway station that would take me home. Not absolutely trusting Jason not to follow me into the station, I actually hop on the train that would take me home.

On the train, I take a seat and dial Captain Fuller's cell phone number.

"Hi, Lacey."

"Hi, Captain. Listen, I need to speak with you about something."

"Sure, what's up?"

"I can't do it over the phone. Are you going to be at the station for a little while?"

"Yeah, I'll be here until seven tonight."

"Are you expecting Jason to come back to the station anytime soon?" I ask.

"No, Lacey. He's busy down around Thirty-Ninth with a suspected terrorist bust. Is everything all right?"

"I'll be there in ten minutes," I say, and hang up the phone.

I don't know what else to do. There's a chance Fuller will tell me to get out of his office and that he has no interest in taking on Internal Affairs. If he does, then so be it. I'll have to figure something else out.

When I get to the station, I'm relieved to see there is hardly anyone there.

Captain Fuller stands up when I walk into his office. He motions me to have a seat and then closes his office door.

"Lacey, what is going on?"

"I met with Lou Harvey again today. He said the DA had more questions about my shooting and wanted to meet and discuss what happened again. So I—"

"Wait a minute, Lacey," Fuller interrupts me and holds up his hand. "I thought this issue was settled. Who has more questions?"

"He said the DA did."

Fuller picks up his phone and punches in some number. "Alicia, this is Marty Fuller. Can you put DA Fitzpatrick on the phone, please?"

After a few minutes, the DA gets on the other line. "Steve, this is Marty. What the fuck is going on over there? You tell me the Lacey Burke case is closed, and now I hear it isn't. Is it, or isn't it?" Fuller pauses for a minute. "Yeah. Uh-huh. That's what I thought. Then you don't have any more questions for her? All right, fine. Thanks for letting me know. Later." Fuller hangs up the phone. "Case is closed, Lacey. Fitzpatrick doesn't have any concerns over what you did and has closed it. What is the problem?"

"The problem is Lou Harvey. He said I needed to sleep with him to make this go away. And he said IAB was also looking into Jason's actions that night and he would take Jason's badge if I didn't sleep with him."

Fuller stares at me as though he is not sure how to process the information I just told him. "That's pretty serious, Lacey. You know I'm not a fan of poking lions with a stick. And that's exactly what I would be doing by questioning Internal Affairs. But I'm also not a fan of losing my best cop because a prick like Harvey wants to sleep with his girlfriend."

"Just tell me what to do, and I'll do it," I say. "If you think the only option is to sleep with him, then I'll do it. I won't be responsible for Jason losing his job."

"I don't want you to do that. Let's come up with a better plan, okay? Did you tell Jason?"

I shake my head no.

"Good. Or I think we would be pulling a gutted Harvey out of the East River tomorrow," Fuller says sardonically.

I smile somewhat, knowing it is more of a truth than a joke.

"When are you supposed to meet Harvey again?" Fuller asks.

"I don't know. He said he would contact me."

"Okay. We'll treat this as though we would any other scumbag on the street. When he wants to meet, we'll put a wire on you and get him to convict himself. That's all we can do, Lacey. Otherwise it's your word against his, and nothing will get accomplished." Fuller looks as if this is the last thing he wants to do but has no choice.

"Thanks, Captain. I'm sorry to involve you, but I didn't know who else to tell."

"Lacey, that's what I'm here for. Don't ever hesitate to talk with me. By the way, congratulations. When is the wedding?"

"Thanks. We haven't set a date yet," I say, getting up to leave. My cell phone buzzes with a text message.

"It's Harvey. He wants to meet tomorrow at the Empire Hotel in midtown. One o'clock," I say, reading the text back to Fuller.

"All right, tell him you'll see him there. Come here first around noon, and we'll fix you up with a wire. I'm going to set up surveillance while you're meeting him in case anything goes wrong and so we can pick him up as soon as he admits it. Don't worry, Lacey. You've been wired up a thousand times before. You know exactly what to do."

"I know. It's just different when it's personal. You're not going to have Jason do the surveillance, are you?"

"No. That wouldn't end well." Fuller laughs as if reading my mind. "He'll be busy somewhere else. Don't worry about it."

"Okay, sounds good. I'll see you tomorrow at noon."

I feel much better leaving the station and having a plan to deal with Harvey. My only concern is tonight and how I will avoid Jason's cross-examination of me. He definitely knows something is up and isn't the type to back down until he gets answers. And I hate lying to him.

When I get on the subway to go home, I text Harvey that tomorrow works for me and I look forward to seeing him again. I add a flirty wink at the end of my text so he thinks I'm game for what he has in store. Then I text Laura to see if she would like to meet for dinner tonight and do some catching up. The less time I have to spend with Jason, the easier it will be. Laura texts back that dinner would be great and recommends a French restaurant on the upper East Side. After we firm up the time and place, I close my eyes and sit the rest of the ride home in silence.

Before Jason is due home, I text him to let him know that I'm going to dinner with Laura and will see him later tonight. I know that will royally piss him off, but at this point I just can't bear to face him. As expected as soon as I send the text, Jason is calling me.

"Hi," I say, picking up the call. If I let it go to voice mail, that would have pissed him off even more.

"Lacey, I was hoping we could spend this evening together. I had a shit day at work and really need to be with you tonight. And I was hoping we could talk about what happened today."

I feel so guilty.

"I can't," I say quietly into the phone. "I'll see you after dinner. I promise it won't be a late night. We can talk when I get home."

"Fine," Jason sighs. "Promise you won't be out late?"

"I promise."

I fix myself up for dinner and then head out the door. I'm very early but don't want to be home when Jason gets there. If anything, I'll hang out at the bar in the restaurant until Laura arrives.

"Lacey!" Laura gives me a hug when she sees me sitting at the bar. I've been there at least an hour alternating between alcoholic and nonalcoholic drinks to keep my sobriety in check.

"Laura, it's great to see you."

"Look at you. All tanned up and everything. You look stunning. I want to hear all about the wedding plans."

"Thanks for helping Jason with the ring, Laura. I'm amazed at how beautiful it is."

Laura grabs my left hand and looks at the ring again. "I *so* love this ring, Lacey. I was happy to help him when he called me. He was so cute in the jewelry store. He must have asked a thousand times if I was positive that this was the ring that you liked. He was so worried about making sure he got the one that would make you happy." Laura sighs as she gazes at the ring. "You're so lucky to have him."

"Things okay with Rob?" I ask her.

"Sure, it's going okay. He just doesn't make my stomach do backflips, you know? He's a very safe boyfriend."

"What does that mean?"

"We act like an old married couple already. All he wants to do is relax at home and then top off the evening with the usual missionary sex."

I laugh at Laura's frankness.

"Tell me about the wedding plans," Laura broaches the subject again.

"We haven't planned anything yet, Laura." I say, picking at my food.

I'm surprisingly not hungry. I haven't eaten anything all day and even threw up anything that was previously in my stomach.

"Really? How come?" Laura gives me a raised-eyebrow shocked look.

I shrug. "I don't know. Just have been busy."

"You're not working right now, Lacey. If you don't have time now, then when will you?"

"It'll get done, Laura. I just don't know what type of wedding I want. We can't plan anything until that is determined."

"Hmm. I've always known since I was a little girl what type of wedding I wanted."

Well, I had other things to worry about growing up. Like when was I going to eat next.

Laura continues going on about what her fairy-tale wedding would be like. When she's done she asks, "Promise me you'll take me dress shopping with you?"

"Absolutely, Laura. I wouldn't dream of going without you," I say, smiling, somewhat relieved that I will at least have someone to go with and give me an opinion.

My phone buzzes. No doubt a text message from Jason. An appetizer, salad, dinner, dessert, and two bottles of wine later, I am definitely past being "out late."

"Lacey, let's go out this weekend. I'm getting itchy watching movies with Rob and need a fun night out. What do you say?"

"It's a plan," I say, giving her a hug good-bye.

My walk home is a slow one. My stomach is in knots at having to look at Jason and know the mess we're in, which I have caused. And what's even more difficult is that I can't even tell him the mess we are in.

I walk in the door, and Jason is in the kitchen, pouring himself a glass of water.

"Hi," I try to say, somewhat cheerily, as though it is just another ordinary night.

"There you are," Jason says, greeting me with a kiss and giving me a hug. "I have missed you."

"Bad day at work? I'm sorry I didn't come home earlier, but you know how Laura loves to talk. It was tough to pull away."

"That's all right." Jason is still hugging me and kissing my neck. "I'm just glad you're finally home. I've been worried about you. How's your stomach?"

"What? My stomach is fine. Why?" I pull away and set my purse and phone on the kitchen table.

"You said earlier your stab wound was hurting today, remember?"

"It's fine, Jason," I say, remembering my lie from earlier and giving him a look that lets him know I'm not playing this game tonight. We know each other too well. "I'm tired. Going to bed."

I walk into the bedroom, and that's when I hear my cell phone buzzing on the kitchen table with a text message notification. Who would be texting me this late? My heart drops, and I quickly walk back toward the kitchen to get my phone. Too late. Jason is standing in the kitchen holding my cell phone with a look in his eyes that makes me wish God would strike me down with immediate death.

"Lacey," he says, trying control his voice. "Why are you getting a text message from Lou Harvey that says, 'Can't wait for tomorrow, baby'?"

Jason looks at my phone again and scrolls through the rest of my text messages with Lou. "And why did you write you would look forward to meeting him at a hotel, wink?"

"Give me my phone please, Jason. It's not what you think. And how *dare* you go through my text messages." Maybe it's the booze, but I'm suddenly very angry at his lack of respect for my privacy.

"Tell me about it then. If it's not what I think."

I stand there, unable to speak. I have never seen him this angry. And I've seen him awfully angry. Like when the drug addict took a swing at him and dislocated his jaw. He was pretty angry then. Or when the drunk pissed on his leg. He was pretty angry then, too. But I have never seen him as angry as he is right now.

"I'm waiting for an answer." He clenches his jaw shut and tries to control his breathing.

"Yeah, and I'm waiting for an answer as to why you think you can check my text messages," I counter, trying to take the heat off me.

"Because you've been acting funny all day," Jason says.

"Whatever. I have never cheated on you, and I never will. And the fact you don't trust me and think you can just go through my phone is total bullshit," I snap at him.

"Why would I believe anything you have to say right now? You've been lying to me *all day*, Lacey. I can't deal with you if I can't trust you."

"I have never cheated on you. But you obviously don't trust me, or you wouldn't feel the need to snoop and interrogate me. Believe it or not, I'm not cheating on you," I reiterate.

"Then tell me what this shit is about."

I don't say anything. I don't know what to say at this point. On one hand, I'm angry as hell at him for reading my text message; on the other hand, I feel like crying because of this situation that I can't fully explain to him. I sit down on a kitchen chair, put my face in my hands, and cry.

"It's not what you think," I whisper through my hands that I still have covering my face.

"Then what is it?" Jason yells at me, which makes me cry harder.

I don't say anything. I want to tell him what is going on, but I am not sure if that would make the situation worse.

"I'm done. I don't even want to look at you right now, let alone deal with you." Jason grabs my purse and cell phone, opens the door, and throws everything into the hallway. "Get out," he says, while holding the door open.

I stare at him in disbelief. My anger has returned, as I can't believe he would put me out on the street. I guess I don't move fast enough because the next thing I know, he grabs my elbow, drags me toward the door, pushes me out into the hallway, and then slams his apartment door shut. I'm standing in the hallway, not believing what has just happened. I gather up my purse and cell phone and brush everything off. I'm not sure what to do at this point. Do I try to go back in and at least get James Bond and some of my other stuff or come back after he has cooled off?

I knock on the door, wondering if he will even answer. I hear the doorknob turning, and my heart races, hoping that maybe he will see how wrong it is for him to kick me out and at least let me back in for the night.

"What?" Jason says with a sigh, only partially opening the door.

I pull off my engagement ring and throw it at him. It hits him squarely in the face, and then I hear it land somewhere on the floor behind him. I turn and walk away.

Chapter 37

The next morning doesn't come fast enough. I'm in my apartment, lying on my bed, which has no sheets or pillows. Doesn't matter. I cried most of the night, falling asleep for a brief time here and there. Comfort wouldn't have made the night any better or go by any faster. I look at the clock. It's about six. I'm tempted to go get James Bond, but I know Jason hasn't left for work yet, and I'm terrified of running into him. I look around at what I have left at my apartment.

I see a pair of old sneakers and decide to go for a walk/run. I'm still not able to run as I did before the knifing, but I do what I can to keep progressing and getting stronger. My headphones are at Jason's, so I have to forgo running with music. It will force me to clear my head without any distractions. The park is already bustling with activity. It's another beautiful day in New York City. My emotions overcome me at certain times, and I find myself pushing too hard. I have to stop and find a bench to rest on. My side is splitting, as if I just ripped something open. Wonderful; this is all I need to deal with today. I pull up my shirt and look at my scar. No blood. I get up and walk home.

I lie down on the couch and put an ice pack over my face to lessen the swelling around my eyes. My cheeks feel as though they are burning from all the tears, so the ice pack feels very soothing. I fall back asleep.

When I wake up, I get ready for my meeting with Lou Harvey. I have enough old toiletries to take a decent shower and clean myself up for the meeting. And falling asleep with an ice pack on my face did wonders for the puffiness around my eyes. I throw on a pair of jeans that I had left behind, as well as a pink tank top. The outfit is sexy enough to show off my body but not so revealing that I could be mistaken for a hooker sitting in a hotel bar. I style my hair and throw on some makeup with some old beauty products that I hadn't bothered to move or throw out yet. Overall, I think I do a pretty good job throwing myself together, considering the night I had. I grab my purse and cell phone and head to the station.

I'm relieved once again to find the station somewhat empty and Captain Fuller sitting in his office.

"Lacey, how are you?" he asks when he sees me. "Jason told me what happened last night. I had all I could do not to shake the shit out of him."

"I'm fine, Captain," I say, lifting my chin up. "Show must go on, right?"

"Right. Let's go." I follow Fuller down to the surveillance van parked in the street.

"You're going with us, Captain?" I ask.

He usually sits in his office and doesn't go out on the street.

"I'm going on this one because it involves another cop. I want to make sure it is done correctly and nothing can be disputed."

He slides open the van door for me and indicates for me to get in. I climb inside, and there are two other detectives, Wilson and

Peters, sitting inside playing with the surveillance equipment. I've worked with these guys before, so I'm feeling more comfortable that everything will go smoothly. Detective Wilson is a very good friend of Jason's, and he and I have spent many hours sitting in a bar, talking while Jason worked on some random skirt. How much does he know? Wilson gives me a wink as I take seat, as if he can read my mind.

"You know how this gig goes, Lacey," Wilson says as he hooks me up with my earpiece. "I'm putting the microphone in your purse. It's supersensitive, so it will pick up anything, even though it's inside your purse. Harvey is too smart. I don't want anything visible that would give you away. Just put your purse on the bar or hang it over the back of your chair so we can get clear audio."

Peter's tests my earpiece.

"I can hear you," I let him know.

"All right, Lacey, we're almost there. We're going to park about three blocks away. We'll move closer once we know Harvey is inside," Captain Fuller informs me as we arrive at our destination. "When you get to the lobby, ask someone where the bar is. That will be our test if we can hear you. Peters will then repeat back what you said to let you know the audio is working. If you don't hear Peters, then return to the van so we can fix it."

"This isn't my first time, Captain," I say to Fuller.

"Right. Off you go then," Fuller says, opening the door for me.

As I'm getting out of the van, Wilson grabs my arm and whispers to me, "Nail his balls to the wall."

"I plan to," I say with a small smile.

When I walk into the lobby, I find some random hotel employee and ask where the bar is.

"It's over there to the right, miss." The hotel employee points me in the direction of the bar.

"Thank you," I say. As I walk toward the bar, I hear Peters repeat back our conversation.

Lou Harvey is already sitting at the bar, sipping what looks like scotch.

"Hi, Lou," I say as I hop onto the empty seat next to him. I hang my purse over the back of my chair.

"Hey, Lacey, can I get you a drink?"

"An Absolut with a twist of lime," I tell the bartender.

"Where's your ring?" Lou asks, staring at my bare hand.

"I gave it back to Jason. Wasn't working out," I say, shrugging my shoulders and taking a sip of my drink.

"Well, that was fast. I can't say I'm sorry. He didn't deserve you. Especially since he was still banging that union rep behind your back."

Ouch.

"Well, it's a moot point now, isn't it?" I say, recovering from another dagger that has just been driven into my heart. I clink his glass with mine. "Cheers."

"Does this mean you don't care if I fuck with him or not?" Lou asks, looking kind of disappointed.

"Who?" I say, pretending to be distracted by a piece of fuzz on my tank top.

"Jason. Do you care if I still fuck with him?"

"Why would you still bother?" I say, as if this conversation is boring me. "He and I are over."

"Sometimes it's just fun to fuck with people and their careers."

"Wow, the kind of power you have is incredibly sexy, you know?" I whisper to him as I lean forward and place my hand on his thigh.

"It's very good to be me. All you have to do is name someone, and I can make their life a living hell."

"Oh, get out of here," I say, swatting his knee playfully. "You're just putting me on, aren't you?"

"No, I'm not. Name someone who you can't stand, and I'll get rid of him or demote him. That is, if you play your cards right," he says, taking a sip of his drink. "Go ahead; name someone. I'll prove it to you."

"What do you mean, you'll prove it to me? What will you do?" I ask. I cannot believe how eager he is to talk.

"I'll make up shit and put it in his file. Name someone."

I pretend to think about it. "Well, like Captain Fuller drives me up a fucking wall some days. What would you do to him?"

"Depends on how bad you want the reprimand to be."

"Well, what if I just wanted him off my back? Like he's so anal about paperwork. The other day he chewed me a new one because I stapled something instead of using a paper clip. I mean, give me a break already," I say, rolling my eyes.

That ought to give them something to chuckle about in the van. Captain Fuller is notoriously anal about paperwork, but the paper clip is something of an exaggeration to get my point across.

"Well, that's pretty minor. But for something like that, I would make up a complaint filed by a private citizen, put it in his folder, and then meet with him to discuss it. During the meeting, I would mention how favorably you talk about him and maybe he should treat you better. He'd get the point."

"Hmm, so what if I wanted something more severe to happen? Like a demotion or firing?"

"That usually requires an accusation of discrimination, harassment, or illegal act."

"I don't understand. Who do you get to make the accusation?" I ask, pretending to be totally confused. He must think I'm real naïve, so I play it up to get him to talk more.

"Oh, honey, it is so easy to find someone. Take you. I can't stand Jason Reed. If I heard you two just broke up, I would contact you to make sure you didn't feel pressured into the relationship, or maybe he treated you differently while working because you're female, or maybe you overheard him make a racist comment, or perhaps you saw him do a wrongdoing sometime. It's very easy to capitalize on human relationships gone awry and get someone to say what you want them to say."

"And what if I wasn't willing to say anything bad? Then what would you do?" I ask. I do not believe how stupid this man is for talking so much.

"I would find something to hold against you until you said what I wanted. If that still doesn't work, then I would make shit up. Fabricate something from a private citizen. Produce skeletons to put in people's closets."

"Now you're really putting me on, aren't you? I mean, who have you done this to before?"

"Lots of cops."

He names off his previous victims. One of the names I recognize: Pete Cooke. Pete was fired when a sexual harassment suit was filed against him. Everyone knew he didn't do anything wrong, but he was terminated anyway.

I gasp and hiss at him, "Pete was a good cop. And he had a wife and five kids. That accusation not only destroyed his career but his family as well."

Lou looks at me and for the first time realizes that maybe he has said too much. Shit. Get a grip on your emotions.

"But I guess you had your reasons for doing what you did." I switch gears and purr again. I take my hand and move it further up his leg to let him know I'm still playing his game.

"Finish your drink, and let's go upstairs. I already have a room," Lou says, still sounding slightly annoyed at my outburst.

"Now, Mr. Harvey, what is your rush? I have *all* afternoon. Hell, for that matter, I have *all* weekend," I say, leaning further into him so that my breasts are practically falling out of my tank top. "I mean, you could handcuff me to the bed and do whatever you want to me for two days straight, and no one would miss me until Monday. What's your rush, sweetie?" I ask as I move my hand further up his leg and lightly brush his groin area.

"Well—" Lou fidgets in his seat and takes a gulp of his drink. "I guess when you put it like that, there is no hurry, huh?"

"No hurry. Now let me enjoy a cocktail or two and relax. You're very intimidating, you know? I need a little liquid help before I take you on." I take a sip of my drink and give him a wink. "And you need to tell me, Lou," I continue, "exactly how do you plan on getting me out of this jam that I'm in?"

"Oh, that's easy. I'll meet with the DA and convince him you didn't really go there to kill someone. Like I told you before, the DA and I have a pretty good relationship. He trusts what I have to say." Lou takes another sip of his drink. "That is, of course, if you give me something in return."

"And what if I don't give you what you want?"

"Then I'll take a different approach with the DA. I'll let him know I'll get him more information to corroborate any charges he wanted to file against you and Reed."

"And that information will probably be framed, huh?" I ask, already knowing the answer but needing him to say it out loud.

"You got it, honey," Lou confirms.

"Hmm. So I basically get fucked either way," I say, chewing on an ice cube from my drink.

"Yep," Lou says. "You might as well pick the fucking you'll enjoy. Now excuse me for a minute while I find the bathroom."

When I see him leave the bar area, I whisper toward my purse, "Why the fuck aren't you moving?" They have more than enough to nail him.

"Oh, I'm sorry, miss. What else can I get you?" the bartender asks, mistakenly thinking I am talking to him.

"Top me off," I snap at him, and slide my drink in his direction so that he doesn't get suspicious.

"This is good shit, Lacey. Keep him talking," Peters says in my ear.

"Yeah, well I'm ready to vomit all over this bar," I hiss back.

"Can I get you a bucket and some crackers, miss, for your upset stomach?" the bartender asks. Damn, he has good ears.

"*What?* No. No bucket, but some crackers would be great. And keep my drink topped off," I bark back to him.

The bartender returns with some saltine crackers.

"I'm sorry, miss. These were all I could find for you."

"Thank you," I say, smiling sweetly at the poor kid. I'm actually starving and nibble on one.

"What's this?" Lou asks when he returns and sees that I'm eating. "Now you've ordered a meal?" he huffs.

"No, just a little snack. I have a feeling I'll be exerting a lot of energy later and should fuel up." I take a cracker and offer to put it in his mouth. He reluctantly takes it and chews. He'll wish it was poison when he finds out what's in store for him.

"So, Lou," I continue, "are you the only one who operates this way in IAB, or are there others like you?"

Lou shrugs. "I don't know. It's not really something we sit around and discuss."

"Yeah, but you must have some idea if anyone else is as crafty as you. A smooth operator like yourself?" I place my hand on his forearm and stroke it with my thumb.

"Well, maybe Testoni plays games with people. Other than that, I really don't know. Like I said, it's not something that's openly discussed." He's watching my thumb rub against his arm.

"And what about the DA? Is he aware of what you do?"

"Oh, hell no. He thinks I legitimately get him what he wants. What, do you think I'm stupid?"

Yes.

I take a sip of my drink and eat a cracker. I'm officially bored with this man.

"So why did you and Jason break up?"

"Oh, you know how those work hookups are. All hype and no substance. Why do you dislike him so much?"

"Do you remember when you and I first met?"

"Yeah, after the shooting you came to take my statement."

"No, Lacey. You and I met two years ago at a Christmas party near the financial district. I forgot who was throwing it. Doesn't matter." Lou sits there staring at me, waiting for me to remember.

"I remember that party," I say slowly. "It was down by the Seaport."

"But you don't remember me," Lou says, reading my mind and getting pissed. "Well, *I* remember *you*. I can even tell you what you were wearing that night and how many beers you had to drink. And I have followed your career ever since. I know you better than you know yourself, and I have waited for this moment for *two years*."

I sit, looking at him in total disbelief.

"So when this moment finally comes, and I see you are involved with Jason, it pisses me off. Why the fuck should he get to have all the fun?" He grabs my arm, clearly angry at this point. "Now here is what is going to happen. I'm tired of talking. We're going to go upstairs, and you're going to do whatever I want, or your whole career as a cop is over. Got it?"

"You're done, Lacey. Get out," Peters says in my ear.

"Sure, I got it. Excuse me for a moment while I freshen up in the ladies' room. I'll be right back." I walk out of the bar and head toward an exit near the back of the hotel lobby. I run into Captain Fuller walking in as I'm leaving.

"Lacey, you did great. We got more than enough out of him. Listen, honey, Jason is in the van." Fuller puts his hand on my shoulder as he's talking to me.

"What? I thought——" I look at Fuller as though he had just stabbed me in the back.

"I know. But he saw your texts last night, remember? He knew the time and place and was going to show up here anyway. I had to tell him what was going on to keep him out of the hotel."

"Okay, I'm done here, right, Captain?" I say, handing him my earpiece and mic.

"Yes, you're done."

"Good. Then if you don't mind, I'm going to disappear for the rest of the day. I need to relax and clear my head. I'll come in tomorrow and do the paperwork." I start to head out the door.

"Go relax. You were great today. Oh, and Lacey——" Fuller stops me from leaving. "I'll take care of any paperwork. I know where the paper clips go."

"Thanks, Captain," I say, giving him a big smile. I head out into the street.

Chapter 38

I get off the subway and inhale the salty air from the Atlantic Ocean. Coney Island. It's one of my favorite places in Brooklyn to visit, and I'm positive no one will look for me here. I turned off my phone on the subway after receiving a text from Jason. I didn't read it and just wanted to be left alone for a while.

I make my way toward the boardwalk and buy a salty pretzel and a Diet Pepsi. I walk the boardwalk and find a bench to sit on and people watch. I find the waves from the ocean to be very relaxing and peaceful. The Caribbean, it is not, but it is peaceful nonetheless.

An elderly man with a cane sits down next to me on the bench. I nod at him.

"Hello, missy," he says. "You're not from around here."

It's not a question but more like an observation to no one in particular.

"No. I live in Manhattan. Thought I would spend some time here today."

"Who or what are you running from?" the old man says, looking at me.

"You're quite perceptive, sir," I say, laughing. "What gave it away?"

"Pretty girls from Manhattan don't hang out alone in Coney Island unless they are trying to hide."

"I actually spent some time growing up in Sea Gate," I say, referring to a Coney Island neighborhood where I lived for a few months when I was fourteen.

"Oh, so you're back to reminisce *and* hide?"

"Something like that," I say, smiling at the old man.

"It's changed over the years, hasn't it?" he says, waving around at his surroundings.

"Yes, it has. More commercialized. But it still is one of my favorite places to visit."

"I have lived here my whole life. Grew up here. Raised a family here. My wife of sixty-seven years died last November," the old man informs me.

"Oh, I'm so sorry," I say, reaching over and touching his arm.

He waves me off. "It was a good sixty-seven years. I was blessed to have her in my life. Every morning we would take a walk down the boardwalk and then sit on this bench and people watch. Some days it was for half an hour, some days it was for hours. Just depended on how we felt, weather, blah, blah."

"What was the key to staying married to someone for sixty-seven years?" I ask.

He thinks about it some and then says, "Communication. We always spoke freely to each other and told each other exactly what we thought. There was no dishonesty. But speaking freely to someone will also lead to fights," he says, winking at me. "And you should fight fair," he continues. "We fought. But it was always a fair fight. The fight was about the issue. Not attacking each other personally. I never said anything to her that I regretted. Never. I think that is important."

I nod in agreement. I wonder if turning off my cell phone on Jason constitutes good communication.

We sit in silence for a few minutes while I think about Jason. The old man looks as though he's remembering his wife.

"Does the pain ever go away?" I ask him.

"Sure. We had a great life together. I'm ninety-two years old, so I'm thankful for every day I wake up. I know when my time expires, I'll meet up with her again. But right now, I'm grateful for each additional minute I have in this world."

"That's beautiful," I say, looking out into the ocean. "We should all be so lucky."

"A pretty girl like you must have them lined up around the block."

I shrug. "Can I buy you a hot dog? I'm starving and have been looking forward to a Nathan's hot dog all day. What do you say?"

I return with the hot dogs and drinks for me and the old man. We sit and eat on the bench. He continues with stories about the old days and complains about his two sons who don't come around as often as he would like.

I tell him stories about growing up in foster care and how I would kill to have a living parent. He shrugs and says, "You don't appreciate what you have until it's gone."

Daylight starts to turn to dusk. I can't believe how late is has gotten and how long we have been sitting on this bench talking.

"Well, missy, it's been a pleasure speaking with you, but we are fast approaching my bedtime."

"Yes, I should be heading back. Can I walk you home?" I stand up with him, and he slips his arm through mine.

He's so frail. It takes us about thirty minutes to walk to his apartment, a walk that would have taken me about five minutes if I had been alone.

At his door, he gives me a small bow and says, "Thank you for spending the day with me."

"It was my pleasure. Have a good night, mister," I say, and walk away.

Maybe I'll come back in a few days and look for him on the bench. Probably not, but it makes me feel better to think I may see him again.

By the time I get home, it is dark. I can't believe how great my day ended, considering how bad it started. I turn on my cell, which notifies me I have unread text messages and a voice mail from Jason. There's also a text message from Rachel, asking if we can hang out tonight. I'm sure Jason put her up to it in hopes that he could find out where I was. There's also a text from Laura, asking if I want to go out tomorrow night. I ignore everyone, wrap myself up in a blanket, and get comfortable on my recliner. I had previously canceled my cable and Internet service, so my entertainment for the night is the few local television channels that I can tap into for free. But it doesn't matter what my entertainment is for the night, as I'm exhausted and can feel sleep approaching fast. I'm surfing my thirteen free television channels when I hear a knock at the door. I ignore it since I know who it is.

"Lacey, I know you're in there. I can hear the TV. Please let me in," Jason says, and he knocks on the door. He waits a minute and then says, "I have a key, remember? I'm coming in either way. We need to talk."

I get off the recliner and open the door. When I see him standing there, I remember how he physically removed me from his apartment, and I decide I really don't have anything to say to him. I thought I had left my anger on Coney Island, but I feel my annoyance coming back again. I try to slam the door shut, but Jason sticks his foot in the door to stop it from closing.

"Whatever," I say, throwing my hands in the air and walking back into the living room.

"Lacey." He grabs my arm and tries to turn me around to face him.

"Don't fucking touch me," I snap at him and yank my arm away. "Talk if you want to talk, but don't fucking touch me."

I sit in my recliner and point for him to sit on the couch. I know as soon as he starts touching me that I will melt in his arms, and I don't want that right now—not after how he behaved.

Jason looks pained and almost shocked that I won't allow him to touch me, but he takes a seat on the couch, facing me, while I sit back in my recliner.

"Lacey, please. I am *so* sorry. I couldn't have been more wrong," Jason says. "Please forgive me. I can't be without you."

"Whatever, Jay. You had no problem putting me out on the street last night. And you survived the night just fine without me. So, *yes*, you can be without me," I growl at him.

"It was a miserable night for me, Lacey. I had all I could do not to pay Harvey a visit."

He tries to reach for my hand. I move it so it is out of his reach.

"Don't care about your anger issues," I say, leaning my head back on the recliner and closing my eyes. I am past exhausted.

"I know it's my issue," Jason says. "I really screwed up. I'm sorry for how I treated you."

"I am exhausted and don't feel talking anymore. Please leave me alone." I wrap my blanket tighter around me and try to get more comfortable.

"I am begging you to forgive me. Please. I made a huge mistake. I will do whatever you want to make it up to you," he says, getting off the couch and kneeling in front of me. He takes my hand and holds it up to his face, kissing it. "Please. I don't want to live without you."

"I am just so incredibly disappointed with how you acted. Knowing my past and how I've bounced from home to home—and then for you to kick me out of yours. It was one of the worst things you could have done to me." I pull my hand away and stand up. "I don't want to do this right now. I need time alone." I walk over to the door and open it for him. "Please leave."

"I'm so sorry. I will do anything you want to make it up to you. *Anything.*" He stands up and walks toward the door.

"Just go," I say, looking at the floor.

I can't look at him without crumbling and giving in. Not that crumbling would be a bad thing, but I need time to think this relationship over. I need time to think about whether I can be with someone who takes so much control away from me. I gently close the door behind him.

The next day, when I'm sure Jason has already left for work, I go to his apartment and move James Bond and my stuff back to my apartment.

Chapter 39

*I*t's been seven days since I've seen Jason. He has texted and called, asking when he can see me again. I have responded to his texts with vague answers, basically telling him I need more time alone. I miss him terribly and am miserable without him but still haven't decided if our relationship is best for me. Basically, I am once again terrified of losing my independent self and becoming dependent upon him, or anyone else for that matter. Growing up, anyone I had ever depended upon disappointed me by having me removed from his or her home and sent back to foster care. Jason has proven to be no exception.

Today I am browsing in a department store in lower Manhattan, not really shopping for anything, just trying to stay busy until I am cleared to return to work. My phone buzzes, indicating that I have a text message. It's from Captain Fuller, asking where I am. I tell him the name of the store and where it's at. Fuller tells me to go outside and wait for him. It's an unusual request, but because he's still my boss, I do as he says.

I'm standing outside the store when an unmarked police car with tinted windows pulls up to the curb. The front passenger window rolls down. Fuller is sitting in the front seat.

"Lacey, get in," he barks and thrusts his thumb toward the back.

I walk toward the car and bend down so I can see who is driving.

"What's going on?" I ask when I see it's Chris driving. Chris works in Brooklyn and doesn't work for Fuller, so I'm immediately cautious as to what is going on.

"Get in," Fuller barks again.

I slowly open the back door.

Jason is sitting in the back seat.

"Oh, fuck this," I say. I slam the door shut and start walking away from the car.

"Burke, get in this car, *now*!" Fuller yells at me again.

He pounds his fist on the side of the car. Something or someone had pissed him off long before he showed up at my feet. Since Jason is riding in the back seat, I'm assuming he had something to do with Fuller's foul mood.

"Not going with you, Captain," I say, walking.

Chris slowly drives alongside of me so that Fuller can keep yelling at me.

"Burke, you are still under my command. And I am ordering you to get in this car, *now*," Fuller barks at me again.

I stop walking, take a deep breath, and get in the back seat of the car. Chris pulls away from the curb and merges into traffic.

"What do you want from me?" I ask, crossing my arms and looking out the window. I refuse to look at anyone else in the car.

Fuller turns around from the front seat and wags his finger at me and Jason. "I want whatever is going on here to be fixed. That's what I want from both of you."

"Kidnapping me won't fix anything," I bark back at him.

"Want to bet, missy?" Fuller looks at me, daring me to talk back to him again. "I'm sick of his miserableness at work," Fuller continues, pointing his finger Jason.

"Not my problem," I sass again. I'm really annoyed and angry at being forced into the back of a cop car like some criminal.

"I'm making it your problem. You two are not leaving this car until whatever is going on gets resolved. Got it?" Fuller asks while Chris hits the lock button, locking Jason and I in the back seat.

I lift my leg and kick the back of Fuller's seat, making him jerk forward. Chris and Jason stifle laughs, as it's something we have all experienced from some jerk who was just arrested and fuming in the back seat of a cop car. Fuller doesn't think it is funny and turns around to glare at me. I glare back at him and am thankful for the mesh partition separating the back seat from the front.

"Did you put them up to this?" I ask, now directing my anger at Jason.

"No, I was tricked into this. And I don't need to go around kidnapping women, Lacey," Jason says, equally miffed.

"Oh, that's right. You just text, and they come running," I snap.

"Get your head out of your ass, Lacey, and cut the shit. If need be, we will ride around in this car all night. Got it?" Fuller says, turning around and facing the front.

After about thirty minutes of driving around in complete silence, Chris pulls off to the side of the street and parks the car.

"Hey, Captain, you getting hungry? There's a restaurant here I've been meaning to try," Chris says as he turns off the ignition and points to the restaurant that he parked in front of.

Fuller looks at his watch. "Well, it's too late for lunch and a little early for dinner, but why not?"

"You think we should leave the car running or crack the windows? I wouldn't want them to die from heat exhaustion," Chris says before he gets out of the car.

"You can't leave us back here," I say, shaking the screen in front of me.

"Crack the windows," Fuller says, ignoring me. "I also don't want them to be too comfortable."

Fuller and Chris get out of the car and walk into the restaurant. I sit back in my seat, trying to figure my next move. I know it would be fruitless to try to break out of the cop car; the back seats are designed for the specific purpose of confining people. But I can't help but wonder about a way out.

"Why have you been so quiet?" I ask Jason. "Aren't you pissed?"

I really look at him for the first time. He looks awful. His facial hair is no longer just scruffy but is now a full-blown beard. And he looks very tired.

"Of course I'm pissed, but it's not going to get us anywhere to piss off Fuller even more."

"This is bullshit. Whose idea was this?" I ask.

"Probably Chris's idea, with plenty of input from Fuller. I went out drinking with him last night and was an asshole the whole time. Today Fuller tells me I have to help Chris with an arrest in midtown, and next thing I know, I'm trapped in the back of a cop car."

"At least they are creative. So how do we get out of this?" I ask.

Jason holds up his phone. "Smile. I'll send Chris a pic of you smiling and tell him everything is good."

I give Jason my toothiest smile, and he takes the picture and forwards it to Chris.

Within seconds Jason reads me Chris's text saying, "Nice try."

I smile. It wasn't a horrible idea but obviously not good enough.

"Lacey, I really am sorry about everything that happened between us."

"I know you are. You aren't totally to blame. I'm sorry for the way I acted too," I say. "Sometimes I think I have too much baggage to be in a healthy relationship."

"We all have baggage. But, yes, because of your childhood, your baggage is definitely heavier than most," Jason says, taking my hand and holding it in his lap.

It feels nice to touch him, so I don't pull it away.

"All I know," Jason continues, "is that I love you more than anything else in this world. And I totally adore you and your baggage. And my life royally sucks without you in it."

I cave and move closer to him. "I love you too. And these last few days without you have been absolutely miserable for me."

I put my hand on his face and lean over so I can lay a kiss on his lips. He puts his arm around me. I snuggle up to him and lay my head on his shoulder.

"You know, Lacey, when we were just friends, we would talk for hours on end…about anything and everything that was happening in our lives. Then it was like sex replaced the talking."

"What are you saying, Jay? You don't want to have sex with me?" I look at him in disbelief.

"That's not what I'm saying at all," Jason says, laughing. "But I think we do need to work on communication. If you had felt comfortable enough to talk to me about Harvey, then none of this would have happened, and we wouldn't be locked in the back of a cop car. If we were just friends, you wouldn't have had a problem telling me. What changed?"

"Our relationship changed," I say, giving him the short answer. "I would have expected you to handle it more rationally as just a friend."

"I guess that makes sense. But let's make a promise that we will tell each other everything from now on. Even if we think the other person will react in a way that we may not like."

"You're right. We do need to tell each other everything, regardless of the outcome," I say, remembering the old man in Coney Island telling me how he stayed married for sixty-seven years.

"Good." He kisses the top of my head. "And I wish I had handled myself differently that night. I'll never forgive myself for throwing you out and how I treated you."

"As you were dragging me out of your apartment, I was thinking how bad it would look to show up to my meeting with Harvey covered in bruises, which is why I didn't put up a fight. Bet let's be clear, Jay, if you ever try to remove me forcibly from a room again, I *will* kick your ass," I say, poking him in the ribs.

"I was somewhat surprised you didn't fight, but then I chalked it up to you feeling guilty. And if I ever act that way again, then I deserve an ass kicking."

"You think maybe we should slow down a little bit? Everything has been moving so fast." I run my hand along his stomach. "Maybe it was too soon to live together."

"No, Lacey," he says, squeezing his arm around me tighter. "It wasn't too soon. But we will move only as fast as you are comfortable moving."

"It just scares me how much control I have given you. To get comfortable somewhere and then have the rug yanked from under me is a road I've been down too many times. And I can't ever go down that road again."

"Whatever you want me to do, babe, I'll do it. You want me to change the name on my lease to your name, you want me to move into your apartment, you want to find another apartment so it will be new to both of us? Whatever, I'll do it. Just don't make me live without you." He hugs me tighter.

"I'm not sure what I want to do. Let's think about it." I wiggle around somewhat so that he loosens his grip.

"So how was Harvey after I left?" I ask, realizing I never heard how his arrest went.

"Oh, he was interesting." Jason continues. "He put up a real fight."

"Really? I thought he would have walked out of there with his tail between his legs."

"No, he went out swinging. Peters got his clock cleaned and had to go to the hospital. If Wilson hadn't gotten Harvey's gun away from him, I think we would have had a shootout."

"I'm surprised to hear that. He came across as more bark than bite. Peters will be okay?"

"He'll be fine. He just got punched a few times. You were great, by the way." Jason gives me another hug and kisses my head again.

I shrug as though it was just another day at work.

"Did you go to that Christmas party two years ago that Harvey mentioned?" I didn't know Jason two years ago, and I'm pretty sure he wasn't at the party. I would not have forgotten meeting Jason.

"No, I wasn't there. You know, he really had a thing for you, Lacey," Jason says, leaning back so he can see my face. He runs the back of his hand down my jawline and then twirls a piece of my hair around his fingers. "We found some stuff at his apartment."

"Hmm. That's nice," I say, not really interested.

"No, I mean we found some stuff having to do with *you* at his apartment. It was kind of like a shrine or something."

I shrug. "So what? I'm surprised you don't have a shrine of me at *your* apartment," I say, trying to lighten the mood.

"I'm serious, Lacey. He's a twisted individual."

"Okay, so he had a shrine. What do you want me to do? Nothing. There's nothing I can do about it, so I'm not going to worry about it," I say.

"My point is he isn't going away forever. He'll be charged with fraud, resisting arrest, assault, and maybe a few other things. But none of it will result in a life sentence. Maybe five years at most. And in the meantime, he'll make bail and will be out on the street in a few days." Jason is still twisting my hair and looking intently at me.

"I'll keep my eyes open and will watch my back," I say. I am not really worried about it.

"Please be extra careful when you're out and about by yourself. And I know you don't like to wear your gun when you're not working, but maybe it's a good idea if you start to," Jason says. I can tell he is trying not to be preachy, when preaching to me is exactly what he wants to do.

I nod my head as though I'm really considering what he's saying, which I am—just not as sincerely as he would like.

"I'll be more careful of my surroundings," I promise. I pause for a few seconds while remembering something Harvey had said to me. "Harvey mentioned something about you and a union rep. What is that about?"

"I don't even know any female union reps, Lacey. I have no idea what he was talking about," Jason says, looking me in the eye and brushing a piece of hair off my face.

I keep staring at him, looking for a sign on his face that lets me know if he is telling the truth or not. I don't think he has ever lied to me before so I really have no reason not to believe him now.

"Lacey, since we have hooked up, I have been with no one else," Jason continues. "*No one.* You are the only one."

"Okay," I say, feeling better. "I believe you. Because I have zero tolerance for cheating too. Don't ever expect me to put up with it either."

"You're the only one I want." Jason kisses me on the forehead. He picks up his phone and reads a text message. "Chris wants to know if we have made any progress."

"Tell him to stay in there and get dessert. I'm enjoying this time with you," I say, reaching up and pulling Jason toward me for a kiss.

After a while a knock on the window interrupts our kissing and talking. Then both front doors open, and Chris and Fuller hop in the car. They are discussing the meal they just had, so Jason and I resume our private conversations, not really interested in how their hamburgers were cooked.

"Okay, Lacey, you're free to go," Fuller announces when Chris pulls the car to the curb in front of my apartment building.

"Well, thanks for the ride, I guess," I say, when I hear Chris unlock my door for me.

"Hey," Jason says, pulling me back to him and whispering in my ear. "I'll see you later, okay?"

"Yes, I'll be at your apartment when you get off work," I whisper back to him, and I give him a kiss good-bye.

With that I go upstairs and spend the rest of the afternoon moving James Bond and some of my belongings back to Jason's apartment.

Chapter 40

When I wake up the next morning, Jason is sleeping next to me, lying on his side as he was when I fell asleep. He's facing me and has his arm draped over my stomach. I don't want to move his arm and wake him, so I lie there, studying his beautiful (yet still hairy) face.

"You know, it's tough to sleep when you're staring at me," he says, with his eyes still closed, totally busting me.

I burst out laughing, and he tickles me to keep the laughter going.

"I didn't want to wake you," I say, in between giggles, and I try unsuccessfully to get out of bed. He keeps his arm draped over my stomach, making it tough for me to get up.

"What do you want to do today?" Jason asks, not moving his arm.

"I don't know. Maybe go for a walk. Maybe shave your beard. How about you?"

"I was thinking we could go to the Yankees game. They have a doubleheader. First game is at one. What do you say?"

I don't say anything and instead roll my eyes. I forgot what a die-hard fan he is. It's not that I don't like going, but it isn't something I want to do on a weekly basis either.

"You go," I say, patting his arm. "You'll have more fun without me."

"No, I want you to go. I want to spend the day with you. It's supposed to be a beautiful, sunny day. Perfect baseball weather." He is moving his arm back and forth across my stomach, as though slowly rocking me will change my mind.

"All right, I'll go," I say, after thinking about it for a few minutes. "But I don't want to stay for the second game. You can stay if you want, but I'm leaving after the first one."

"Good. We'll just stay for the first one then," Jason says, smiling at me.

"Sounds good," I say, smiling back. I look at my watch. "I can't believe how late we slept. You know, it's almost nine. We should get going."

"We have plenty of time," Jason says, kissing my neck and moving his hand down the front of my underwear. "Plenty of time for me to kiss every inch of you." He moves his mouth down my neck. "You are so beautiful, Lacey. I could just stare at you all day,"

Jason kisses my neck again. He moves his mouth along my neck and kisses my collarbone. He slides his tongue from my collarbone down in between my breasts and then moves over to my left nipple. He places the nipple in his mouth and gently pulls on it with his lips.

"You drive me crazy," I moan.

He continues sucking on one nipple and caresses the other one with his hand. Then he moves his hand down my body and caresses me. He pushes my legs open wider and slides further down my body. He stops to kiss my belly button and scar. The buildup is making my whole-body ache. He moves further down, and his tongue caresses me.

I gasp as a wave of heat surges through me. Jason continues to maneuver his tongue in and around me. He then pulls back and lightly brushes his tongue over me. Barely touching me and teasing me, he makes me beg for more. I cry out in sheer joy and let myself go all around him.

When I'm done, Jason turns me over so I'm lying on my stomach and then pulls me up until I'm on my hands and knees. He thrusts his penis into me and grinds in and out. I'm still hot from his tongue and feel myself climaxing again. I wait until he is ready, and then I orgasm again.

"You are *so* skilled," I gasp as we lay next to each other on the bed, recovering.

"All right, beautiful," Jason says, getting up and pulling me off the bed. He puts his arms around me and kisses me on the mouth. He breaks away and says, "We do need to get going."

"I know," I say, kissing him back and then make my way toward the shower.

When I get out I throw on a pair of capri jeans with a blue Yankees T-shirt and pull my hair into a side braid. I put on one of Jason's Yankees baseball hats.

"You look incredibly cute, but you are missing something," Jason says, getting dressed.

"I'm not missing your facial hair," I tease as I run my hand down his shaven cheek. He has left his trademark stubble, which is fine with me.

Jason reaches into his jeans pocket and pulls out my engagement ring.

"What about it?" I say, shrugging and not taking it.

"Here. Put it on," Jason says, still holding it out for me.

"Hey, you threw me out. You want me to wear it, you'll have to ask again," I say, trying to give an attitude and biting my cheek to keep from smiling. "Ready?" I say, walking toward the door.

"You're impossible," Jason says, walking toward me and dropping to his knees. "Lacey Burke, will you please marry me already?"

"Yes, Jay, I will marry you one of these days."

I give him my left hand so he can put the ring on it. Then I lean down and give him a kiss.

"You're not going to embarrass me if we run into Ethan, right?" I ask as we are walking toward Yankee Stadium.

"Would I ever embarrass you, Laces?" Jason says, with a glint in his eye.

"Yes, you do it all the time. You get off on it or something. Please, *please* don't," I plead with him.

"I won't."

"Promise?"

"I promise," he says, and kisses me on the cheek.

"Okay, good," I say, not totally believing him.

Jason spots a uniformed officer he knows working near the gate, and the officer leads us past the ticket line and into the stadium. One of Jason's friends who works on Wall Street purchases a suite every season and has made it known that police officers are welcome to watch the games from there. Sometimes it can be very crowded, but today, there are only a handful of people in the suite. I don't see Ethan, but I do spot Chris, talking with a few other guys who don't look familiar to me.

"What's the deal with him and Marie?" I whisper to Jason before he sees us.

"I don't know. I haven't asked," Jason says. "You've provided me with enough drama lately. Why would I want to listen to his drama?"

"True," I say, slightly embarrassed at all the craziness I have created these last few weeks.

We walk over to the refrigerator in the suite, and Jason pulls out a beer for each of us.

"Hey, glad to see the ring is back on," Chris says, giving me a wink. He lifts up my hand and looks at my engagement ring. He kisses me on the cheek and congratulates us.

"Thanks, Chris. How is Marie doing?" I ask him.

"She's here. Around here somewhere," Chris says. He looks around the suite and then points to Marie, sitting alone in the exterior seats overlooking the ball field.

"I want to go say hi. Excuse me for a moment," I say, stepping away and leaving Jason and Chris alone to talk.

"Hey, Marie," I say, walking up behind her and sitting down in a seat next to her.

There is no one around, and we are sitting in the stadium seats overlooking the first base line. The players are on the field warming up.

"Hi, Lacey," Marie says, turning toward me and giving me a smile.

I'm immediately taken aback by how awful she looks. She must have lost twenty pounds since Atlantic City. Her face has a grayish tone, and her eyes are sunken in. I feel as though I just sat down next to a corpse. Her eyes have a glassy look, and I presume she is high or medicated. Or both.

"Marie, how are you?" I ask, touching her arm.

"Good. I'm good, Lacey," she says, giving me an insincere smile.

"You've lost weight since I last saw you," I state the obvious.

"A few pounds," she says, shrugging. "Congratulations on your engagement, Lacey. I told you he was in love with you."

"Yeah, you were right, Marie," I say, nodding.

"Can I give you some advice, Lacey?"

"Sure," I say, not really wanting any.

"Have a long engagement. Enjoy each other without being married. Cause once the vows are said, everything changes. He's got you, and he knows you will never leave." Marie looks blank as she is speaking.

"Oh, Marie." I put my arm around her. "I'm sorry you are so unhappy."

"No, I'm not unhappy, Lacey," Marie says, suddenly changing her tune and trying to be upbeat. "I'm sure you heard about Chris and his love child. I was devastated when he told me. But, you know, we have started to go to couples counseling, and I think we are going to get through it."

"Good. I'm glad you are talking to someone about it," I say, grabbing her hand and giving it a squeeze.

"We'll be okay, Lacey," Marie says—trying to convince me or herself, I wasn't sure. "It will just be weird when the baby is born and then trying to fit him or her in with our kids. But that is what the counselor is helping us with."

"Well, if you ever need help or someone to talk to, I'm here for you, okay?" I say, truly feeling bad for her situation.

"Thanks, Lacey. And remember what I said. Have a long engagement, and enjoy each other."

The game is starting, and I turn around to see what Jason is doing. He's talking with Chris and a few other guys I don't know. Marie has gone back to staring blankly at the field. I watch the game and sip my beer.

"Hey, Marie, how's it going?" Jason asks, taking the seat next to me. He leans over and kisses me on the cheek.

"I'm fine, Jason. Thanks for asking." Marie goes back to staring at the game.

Jason puts his hand on my knee and asks me if I want to go to the lower level and watch the game.

I shrug. "It's up to you. I don't care."

"All right, let's go walk around." Jason grabs my hand.

"Marie, can I get you something?" I say, getting up. "A water or soda?" I'm hesitant to offer her any alcohol, considering the state she is already in.

"No thanks, Lacey. I'm good."

"We'll see you in a bit, Marie." Jason leads me out of the suite and down the stairs to the seating on the lower level.

Jason finds an usher he knows and asks him what seats are available. The usher leads us to two empty seats along the first base line.

"Do you know everyone here?" I ask, always amazed at how many people Jason knows.

"Lacey, I have been coming to Yankee Stadium since I was a little kid. Along the way I have met a few people." Jason waits for me to get settled in my seat before he sits down. "These seats are better, don't you think? I didn't want you to sit next to Marie all game."

I shrug. "She was messed up, don't you think?"

"Chris said her doctor prescribed her a heavy dose of antidepressants. And some other stuff."

"Well, that's too bad. Why doesn't she just leave him already? She's setting a horrible example for her kids by staying with him," I say, slightly annoyed.

Jason shrugs. "Don't know, Lacey. And it's really none of our business." Jason buys a bag of peanuts from a vendor walking along the aisle.

"Baseball, beer, and peanuts. It doesn't get any better than that, does it?" I say, smiling.

"No, it doesn't," Jason says, smiling at me. "I am so in love with you, you do know that, right?"

"I have some idea," I say, resting my head on his shoulder.

Since I'm having such a good time, I let him know we can stay for the second game of the doubleheader if he wants to.

"No, we'll leave after the first. Maybe we'll stop at McGinty's for happy hour on the way home?" Jason asks, referring to one of the bars near the stadium.

"Whatever you want to do," I say, patting his knee.

I text Laura to let her know where we'll be for happy hour in case she is interested. She is, of course, interested.

Chapter 41

After the game, we walk out of the stadium and head over to McGinty's. It's a nothing-fancy drinking bar where Yankees fans usually gather before and after games. Some of the guys who were in the suite and who also decided not to stay for the second game are already there. Not too long after we arrive, Laura shows up, and one of Jason's friends immediately hits on her.

"I love hanging out with you, Lacey. You are always surrounded by men," Laura whispers to me.

I look around the bar and notice for the first time that she is right. The bar is made up of mostly men, with a handful of women.

"Just be careful. This isn't my usual crowd, and I don't know much about these guys," I warn her.

I look at Jason, who is talking with a couple of guys I have never seen before. He glances at me periodically, probably to make sure I'm okay.

"I'm a big girl, Lacey," Laura jokes.

"Right. How is Rob anyway?"

"He's okay. We had a talk last night that we still want to hang out but we are free to date other people."

"Oh, Laura, I'm sorry."

"It was my call, Lacey. I really like him but pretty sure he's not the one. I want to keep my options open."

I smile at her, relieved at what a contrast she is from Marie. As we are talking, a guy leans up against the bar and ask us if he can buy us drinks.

I politely decline, and when I see Laura take an interest in him, I quietly slip away and walk over to Jason, who is now sitting on a barstool. He immediately pulls me in between his legs and wraps his arms around me. I stand like this for a minute and then slowly try to untangle myself from his grip. He makes no attempt to release me, and so our game of disentangling begins. My alpha male.

"You know I'm not a big fan of you pawing me in public," I say, giving up for a minute and leaning back into him. "And it's too hot in here to be this close."

I start to wiggle away again. Jason tightens his grip.

"Quit wiggling, or I'll take you out back and bend you over a dumpster," Jason whispers into my ear.

Oh my. I feel a tingle go through my body and go limp in his arms. "I love it when you threaten me with a good time," I whisper back.

"You drive me insane."

He kisses me on the cheek and releases me from his grip. I keep my hand on his knee but slowly move away from him and lean up against the bar.

"Who here is datable?" I ask, looking around the bar.

"Excuse me?" Jason says, pulling me back to him.

"For Laura," I sigh, and unravel myself again.

Jason looks around the bar. "No one."

"Really? There are no nice guys in this bar?"

Jason rolls his eyes. "She's no saintly virgin, you know. I get the feeling she doesn't want a nice guy. She threw Rob back to the wolves, didn't she?"

"He told you that?"

"Yeah, more or less. Don't worry about her. She can take care of herself. And she keeps herself busy with Chris anyway," Jason says, looking over at Laura, who is still talking with the guy who offered to buy us drinks.

"Chris? What are you talking about?"

Jason cocks his head looking at me. "She didn't tell you?"

"Tell me what, Jay?"

"She and Chris have been hooking up."

"What? When did this start happening?" I ask, not fully comprehending what I'm hearing.

"Lace, I thought you knew. She and Chris hooked up that night they met at the club. They've been periodically meeting up here and there to fool around."

"I didn't know," I say, fully disgusted. I turn to face Jason and let my forehead rest on his chest.

"I thought she told you, babe. Sorry," Jason says, stroking my hair.

"No, she didn't share. Probably too embarrassed, as she should be."

"Well, maybe Ethan can teach her a thing or two," Jason says, smirking at me.

"Whatever," I say rolling my eyes. "Don't start."

Wait. Why did Jason just bring him up?

I turn toward the door and see that Ethan and two other guys have walked into the bar a moment ago. I turn back to Jason, who is still smirking at me.

"You promised, remember?" I say, almost pleading with Jason, who is staring at me, clearly loving how uncomfortable he can make me feel.

"Hey, Lacey." Ethan comes up behind me and plants a kiss on my cheek. "It's nice to see you. I hear congratulations are in order." Ethan extends his hand to Jason. "Jason, congratulations, man."

"Thanks, Ethan," Jason says, shaking his hand. "What are you drinking?" Jason flags over the bartender and orders Ethan a drink.

"So how are you feeling? How's the stab wound?" Ethan asks me.

"I'm fine, thanks. I lost my gallbladder. No big deal," I say, waving him off.

Out of the corner of my eye, I see Laura straining to see who I am chatting with. She decides Ethan is a better option than the man she is currently talking with and comes over for introductions. Jason sits on his barstool smiling, obviously pleased with how everything is turning out for me.

"Ethan works down by Wall Street," I inform Laura after introductions are made.

"What's new?" I ask Ethan.

He gives me updates about so-and-so, with whom we went to college. Laura is hanging onto his every word, as though he is the most interesting man alive. While he is talking, I also take notice at how good he looks. His brown hair has lightened a bit from the spring sunshine, and he looks as though he has been working out more. He always had a great body, but it looks slightly more defined and chiseled. When he smiles he has a dimple in his right cheek. I glance at Jason, who is watching me watch Ethan. Great.

"Lacey, I have to go to the bathroom. Come with me," Laura says, grabbing my hand.

I reluctantly get dragged away, not wanting to leave Jason and Ethan alone and still disgusted with Laura at this point.

"He is beautiful," Laura says, reapplying her lipstick once we get into the ladies' room. "You think I have a chance with him?"

"I don't know, Laura. I don't know if he has a girlfriend or is seeing anyone."

"You two go way back, huh?" Laura says.

"Yeah, we went to college together." I then add, "But I wouldn't have a problem if you hooked up with him. It feels like I was with him in another lifetime."

"Really?" Laura asks.

"No, I wouldn't have a problem with it," I say, not lying. "But I do have a problem with you screwing Chris. He's a married loser, and you should be ashamed of yourself."

Laura lowers her head, staring at the floor. "I know. I'm not proud of it. He's been like a drug that I can't kick."

"I've said all I have to say on the matter. I'm not going to lecture you on it. You're an adult," I say. I walk out of the bathroom.

When we walk back to the bar, Jason and Ethan are laughing at something like old high school chums. Hmmm.

"What's so funny?" I ask, walking up to them.

"Nothing," Jason says unconvincingly. "Anyone ready for another?" Jason waves to the bartender.

"I got this round, Jason," Ethan says, handing money to the bartender when he places our beers in front of us.

"Thanks." I move closer to Jason, still curious about what transpired when we were in the bathroom.

Laura turns to Ethan, and they begin a private conversation.

"What were you talking about?" I whisper to Jason.

"Don't worry about it," Jason says, smiling at me.

"Rude," I say, pretending to be mad.

It's hard to be mad at him when he's smiling at me.

"When do you want to get out of here?" Jason asks, finding a piece of my hair that has come loose from my braid and twisting it around his fingers.

I shrug. "Doesn't matter to me, but I'm not comfortable leaving Laura alone in this bar."

Jason nods. "We'll put her in a cab when we decide to go."

I look over at Ethan and Laura, who are laughing about something. I have to smile. They could make a cute couple if she kicks her Chris habit.

"You know, if they couple up, you'll have to hang out with him more," I say to Jason.

Jason rolls his eyes. "It's asking a lot of me to hang out with the guy who stole your innocence, you know that, right?"

"Oh, Jay, don't be so dramatic. I never should have told you that," I say.

"I've hung out with him before, so I guess it would be all right," Jason says reluctantly. "And I do actually like the guy. I wish I didn't, but he is a decent guy. The question is, how would you feel about it?"

"I would only care if Laura continues to screw Chris. Ethan is too nice of a guy to deal with that." I take a sip of my beer.

"True. And I will require full disclosure of whatever happened between you two besides the deflowering incident. I don't want to be hanging out with him and be hit with any surprises," Jason says, putting his arm around me and drawing me nearer to him.

"What are you talking about?" I ask, innocently.

"Oh, I don't know, like you were actually married and then had it annulled. Or there is a love child floating around somewhere."

"You're insane," I say, smiling. "But if it makes you feel better, we'll talk about it later, okay?"

"Okay," Jason says, kissing me on my forehead.

"You know I have to meet with the department psychologist in a few days," I say, changing the subject.

"I know. I think you should pretend you're struggling with what happened and push to stay out on disability."

"I can't do that," I say.

"Why not? Then you'll have more time to focus on me and my needs." Jason puts his arm around my waist and pulls me closer.

"Are you feeling neglected? Deprived? Not satisfied?" I ask in disbelief.

"None of the above. But I wouldn't fight you if you pressed for more."

"Well, I'll keep that in mind. But I'm still not going to fake a mental illness." I look over at Ethan and Laura, who are still talking.

After a few more rounds, I let Jason know that I want to go home. I interrupt Ethan and Laura and tell them we are leaving. Then I pull Laura aside and tell her Jason is getting her a cab.

"I'll be fine, Lacey," Laura says, waving me off.

"No, you are not hanging out in this bar alone," I whisper to her looking around. "Say good-bye to Ethan."

"Okay," Laura says, agreeing that it would be a bad idea to stay here alone.

She says good-bye to Ethan, who saves her phone number in his contact list. This makes it much easier for her to leave.

"Lacey, it was great seeing you." Ethan kisses me on the cheek again. "I really am happy for you."

"I know. It was great seeing you too. Take care, Ethan."

Chapter 42

"Maybe we should turn the air on?" I ask when we get home. For some reason, it is incredibly warm in Jason's apartment. I open a few windows and strip down to my bra and panties.

"Are you feeling okay?" Jason asks, looking amused. "Not that I'm complaining about the view, but it is comfortable in here."

"I'm all right. Maybe it's just from sitting outside in the sun all day," I say as I open the refrigerator and let the cool air linger over me while I get a bottle of water. I walk into the living room, turn on the television, and plop down on the couch.

Jason follows me but doesn't sit down. "What are you doing?" he asks, standing there and looking at me.

"I'm going to watch some TV before bed," I say, trying to look around him to view the screen. I pull my hair tie out and undo the side braid my hair was in. I know I'm teasing him, which is part of my plan.

"Let's go to bed," Jason says, still standing, and offers me his hand.

"No, I'm not ready. I want to watch some TV," I say, flipping through the channels.

"Really?" Jason keeps staring at me while he sits down on the couch next to me. He tugs at my panties like a little kid waiting to get permission to open his Christmas present.

"Not now," I say, removing his hand. "Later, okay?"

He sighs and leans back on the couch to get more comfortable. I move to get more relaxed and in the process let my underwear slide over, exposing some of my ass.

"Are you kidding me?" Jason asks.

"What?" I pretend I don't know what his problem is.

We sit in silence for a few more minutes.

"Fuck this," Jason says, standing up and lifting me off the couch.

"Jason, put me down now," I hiss as he carries me into the bedroom and lays me onto the bed.

He kisses me on the mouth, teasing me with his tongue until I just want him inside me. But I hold off and cross my legs at my ankles.

"What is your problem?" Jason asks laughing when he realizes access has been denied.

"Nothing," I say, smirking.

"Then open up," Jason says, kissing me again and trying to pry my legs open.

I hold them closed. "Try to make me," I whisper in his ear.

Jason stops what he is doing and looks at me to make sure he heard me right.

"Oh, Lacey, you really do entertain me."

Jason kisses me again, and before I know it, he is holding my hands above my head. He then puts my wrists together and holds them with one of his hands, freeing up his other hand. I put up a mild struggle to keep the game going. I don't want this to get too violent.

"Now do you want to give up?" Jason asks as he moves his hand down to pry my legs open. I keep them closed and try to get my hands free. "Because you know all I have to do is flip you over and you're done."

"You always promise me such good times," I say, laughing and still struggling against his grip.

"All right, that's it. I've had enough of your shit," Jason says, while turning me over on my stomach with his free hand.

He keeps a hold of my wrists with his other hand. Before I know it, he is laying on my back and in between my legs. He pushes himself inside of me and reaches around to my front, where he strokes my clitoris with his free hand. Neither one of us lasts long as the buildup is too intense. Game over.

"So Miss Lacey wants to do some role-playing, huh?" Jason asks as I rest my head on his chest and he puts his arm around me.

I shrug, not really knowing what to say.

"Well, what was all that about then?"

"I thought we could mix it up sometimes," I say, almost embarrassed. "I don't want you to get bored with me." There, I said it.

Jason laughs. "No more talking to Marie, okay?"

He can read me like a book.

"She said we should have a long engagement because marriage changes everything."

"I'm not taking relationship advice from Marie." Jason sighs and pauses for a moment. "You know Chris cheated on her before they were married. And she still married him. He cheated on her right after they got married, and she stayed with him. He cheated on her after the first kid, after the second kid, after the third kid, and after the fourth kid. And she still kept pumping out kids, thinking another one would change him. So, yes, Chris is a cad. But Marie also needs to take responsibility for allowing herself to be unhappy in a shitty marriage."

"I think she just discovered his cheating," I say, still trying to stick up for her.

"No, Lacey. She has known the *entire* relationship. Chris hasn't changed one bit since the day he met her. She knew exactly who he was but chose to think she could change him."

"Okay, I didn't know that."

"And guess what? I'm not him, so stop comparing me to him," Jason says, kissing me on the forehead.

"I know you're not." And then I add, "But I still don't want you to get bored. So if there is anything you want to try, let me know. I'm open to it."

"Okay," Jason says, looking amused.

I have a feeling he has already had his fantasies satisfied, but I'm not going to ask. I don't want to know.

As if reading my mind, Jason rolls onto me and kisses me again.

"You know what my fantasy is, Lacey? To stay inside of you forever because you feel so amazing," he says as he kisses my neck and inserts himself into me again.

Chapter 43

*J*ason has insisted on coming to the psychiatrist's appointment with me.

"I can do this myself, you know," I say. I let the receptionist know that I am here.

"I know you can. But I want to be here with you," Jason says, rubbing my hand as we take a seat in the waiting area.

"This isn't a big deal. I know it's tough to believe, but I *am* mentally sane. It's not like it's going to be a difficult judgment call for him and you need to be here to help him decide."

"That's not why I'm here, Lacey. After the whole debacle with Harvey, I'm not letting you meet with any man by yourself."

I laugh. "So for the rest of my life, I'm not allowed to be alone with any other man but you?"

"Basically, yes," Jason says, smiling.

"Do you know how silly you sound?"

"Lacey, Dr. Greene will see you now," the receptionist informs me as she gets up and opens the door to Dr. Greene's office.

Dr. Greene stands from behind his desk, and introductions are made. He is a thin, frail-looking man in his mid-fifties. His gray hair is parted on the side and swept over.

"Dr. Greene, if you don't mind, I would like Jason to sit here with us," I say, needing to explain why Jason was entering the office with me.

"That's fine for this appointment, but at some point before you go back to work, I will need to speak with you alone," Dr. Greene says, indicating for us to sit down in a pair of leather chairs facing the one in which he sits down.

The appointment runs along smoothly. Dr. Greene is very warm and easy to speak with. His questions are straightforward; there is no hidden agenda or any attempt to twist my thinking process. The only time I feel uncomfortable is when he brings up my parents.

"Lacey, let's discuss your mom and dad," Dr. Greene requests while writing something on his notepad. He's been taking notes all meeting.

"Let's not," I say curtly.

Dr. Greene stops his writing and looks up from his notepad.

"My parents had nothing to do with this shooting," I say.

"You're right," Dr. Greene says, smiling. "I only bring it up in case it is something you would like to talk about."

"No, I'm fine, Dr. Greene," I say, smiling back.

After talking for a bit more, the appointment winds down. Dr. Greene informs me I'll need to meet with him three more times over the next two weeks—preferably *alone*. We set up a date and time for the next appointment with his receptionist, and then we leave.

"That wasn't too bad," I say to Jason as we get into the elevator.

"No, it wasn't bad at all. I liked him more than I thought I would," Jason says, taking my hand. "Come. I'll buy you lunch before I go back to work."

We decide to eat at a semi-casual Italian restaurant for lunch. After ordering half the menu because I'm famished, I check my cell phone and see I have missed a text from Rachel. I haven't spoken to Rachel in what feels like a very long time, mostly because I know she wants to get together and plan the wedding.

"Your sister wants to hang out sometime soon," I say, letting Jason know what the text is about.

"So why are you avoiding her?" Jason bites into a mozzarella cheese stick.

Damn, he's perceptive.

"I don't know what you mean," I say, pretending to be busy buttering a piece of bread.

"Shall I put in a request to Dr. Greene to discuss wedding phobias with you?" Jason leans back in his seat and stares at me.

"No. There's no phobia," I say, not willing to admit my issue.

"Spill it, Lacey. What's your problem?"

I take a deep breath. "We decided to take it slower, remember?"

"There is no reason to take it slower. You are the one I'm spending the rest of my life with. Whether we go slow or not, the outcome will be the same. So why wait?"

"Fine. And your mother and Rachel want a big ceremony, and I will have no family there. It's depressing for me."

"So then tell them what you want."

"I want something very small and simple."

"Then why don't we just go to Vegas like I wanted?"

I shrug. "Maybe we should."

"You should at least pick a date already," Jason says.

"Why is this all about me? Why don't you pick a date?" I ask, getting annoyed at the pressure.

"Because I would have picked two years ago," he says, staring at me as if trying to read my facial expression.

I roll my eyes. "You were in lust two years ago."

"I was in lust for the first hour after I met you, and then I fell in love," Jason says, twirling a piece of my hair around his fingers. "Tomorrow then."

"We're not getting married tomorrow."

"All right, Lacey. Just pick a date then."

"Right. I'll see if Rachel can do lunch sometime this week or next." I pick up my phone and text Rachel back that I want to meet her for lunch.

Jason smiles, and I immediately feel guilty for how difficult I can be. He is right about the outcome being the same, so there really is no point in taking it slow. I run my hand along his stubbly jawline.

"You know how sexy you are?" I ask, rubbing his chin.

He just smiles again and gives me that look that makes me blush. I squirm in my seat, trying to pretend I don't notice how uncomfortable I've become, which amuses him even more.

"Stop it," I say, buttering another piece of bread.

"Stop what, Lace?" Jason says.

"Stop staring at me that way," I whisper.

"I have no idea what you are talking about, but okay, I'll stop staring," Jason says, smiling.

After lunch Jason heads back to work, and I stroll back to my old apartment. I've decided it's time to give it up so that I can save some money. Jason changed the name on his apartment lease to my name after the Lou Harvey debacle. The super looked at Jason as if he had two heads when Jason explained what he wanted to do, but because he has been a good tenant, the super didn't have a problem doing it. If the rent is paid, the super really doesn't care who is renting the place. I know the name change is only a symbolic gesture, but it does make me feel better.

My plan is to surprise Jason with a trip to Vegas, and a couple of months without paying for rent would come in handy. I'll just have to run the idea by Rachel and Jason's mom and hopefully get their blessing.

When I find the super to my apartment building, I let him know this will be my last month here. He's okay with me breaking my lease, as I knew he would be. The building is full, and we both know he can charge a new tenant more. I always suspected he gave me somewhat of a break on the rent because of what I did for a living and because I never caused any problems. It's an amicable break. Before leaving I take a mental note of what still needs to be moved and wonder what I should do with it all. Storage would be a waste since none of my furniture is particularly special or worth anything. And Jason's apartment is fully furnished, so there is very little I would bother keeping. I text Laura to see if she knows the best way to sell or donate household items. She seems to be an expert when it comes to retail, and I also want an excuse to talk with her and find out what is happening with Chris and Ethan.

She texts back, wanting to know where I'm at. I let her know I'm walking through Central Park. She asks if I want to meet her at Lotus. I agree to meet her there.

Lotus is a lounge bar located off the west end of Central Park. It's not far from Jason's apartment. There is an outdoor patio, which is why I agree to meet her there. It's a beautiful day, and the last thing I want to do is sit inside somewhere.

I get there before Laura and snag an outdoor table overlooking the park. The bar is somewhat crowded. It's mostly filled with women who have decided to take a break from shopping and have a cocktail. There are a few men in suits who look as though they are conducting some sort of business over drinks. I order a peach sangria and wait for Laura to arrive. As I sit at my table people watching, I see Kellan Walker talking with someone in the park. Shit. I try to duck down in my seat in the hopes he won't see me. No such luck. Kellan finishes up his conversation and strolls over to me.

"Lacey Burke," he says as he takes a seat at my table. "Tell me the rumors aren't true. For my heart's sake, please tell me you aren't marrying Reed."

"It's true, Kellan. I'm officially off the market." I smile at his dramatics.

He takes my hand, looks at my engagement ring, and whistles.

"Wow. I didn't know cops made that much. Sure he's not bought?" Kellan says, joking.

"Positive. Last person who would take bribes is Jason."

"Yeah, I have to agree with you there," Kellan says. "You know, Lacey, you and I have had our differences. And Lord knows Jason and I have had our differences. But when it's all said and done, I just want you to be happy."

"Thanks, Kellan."

After a few minutes, Kellan continues. "I am kind of surprised Jason is getting married, though. No offense, but he's not the monogamous type. Just make sure you know what you're getting into, okay?"

"I know what I'm getting into, Kellan." I take a sip of my sangria.

We again sit in silence for a moment. Where is Laura?

"So how come you and Jason don't get along?" I start making small talk.

"My cousin Deanna is on his booty call list. Poor girl. Jason texts, and she goes running. Doesn't matter when or where, she's always willing. She's got it bad for him, and he takes advantage."

"Well, it takes two to tango," I say, feeling a pang of jealousy. Why have I never met this Deanna? "Why didn't you talk some sense into her?"

"I've tried. Just like I've tried with you." Kellan smirks.

"I'll be okay, Kellan. Thanks for your concern," I say slightly sarcastically.

Laura finally arrives and takes a seat at our table. I make the introductions before Kellan gets up to leave.

"A dog doesn't forget his tricks, Lacey," Kellan whispers in my ear before he leaves.

"Isn't that the guy who was pawing you in the bar, and Jason took him outside?" Laura asks when Kellan is gone.

"Yeah, that's him. Don't ever date him, Laura," I say, in case she gets any ideas.

"I'm in love with Ethan, Lacey."

I have to laugh. "That was fast. What happened?"

"Oh, nothing happened. I just can't stop thinking about him. Tell me more about him. Why did you break up?" Laura orders a peach sangria from the waiter when he stops over.

I shrug. "He's a nice guy. We dated in college. Relationship wasn't going to the next level, so why stay with someone? It was time to move on."

"He told me he proposed," Laura says, calling my bluff.

"He did. I haven't told Jason about the proposal yet. I didn't want to marry Ethan, so once I declined, the only thing left to do was break up."

"Why didn't you want to marry him?"

"Honestly, Laura, I never thought I would get married. I didn't exactly have a happy family life growing up. I just figured marriage wasn't in my plan. Jason changed that."

"So, there's like nothing drastically wrong with Ethan?"

"No! I told you, he's a real sweetheart. And dreamy to look at," I say, smiling at Laura.

"He is beautiful, isn't he?" Laura has a faraway look in her eyes.

"And what about Chris?" I ask when I realize she's not going to bring him up.

"I told him not to contact me anymore," Laura says, looking away at me. "I am embarrassed at my behavior."

"We all make mistakes," I say, and then change the subject, not wanting to harp on her bad decision. "I have an apartment full of crap that I need to unload. Short of hauling it to a dump, what else can I do with it? The furniture is gently used—nothing expensive but not trashy either."

"Donate it. I volunteer at a woman's shelter in the Bronx. They are always looking for furniture to furnish the rooms with. They'll send over a moving truck and move everything into it. You won't have to lift a finger."

"That's a great idea. I told my super I'll be out by the end of the month. You think they could take everything away next week?"

"I'll double-check, but I don't know why not. You're finally giving up your apartment? Now how about setting a wedding date?" Laura asks.

I explain to her my concerns about the wedding and my idea for surprising Jason with a trip to Vegas.

"What do you think?" I ask her when I'm done talking.

She shrugs. "You have to do what you want to do. It's your wedding. Me? I've always wanted an over-the-top wedding with horses, carriages, flamethrowers. You name it, I want it at my wedding. But that's me. I also have always had a huge family to support whatever I want. I can't imagine growing up like you did."

I nod, thinking about what she just said. "Yeah, the big wedding thing just isn't my cup of tea."

"Can I still take you dress shopping? Even though it will be in Vegas, you'll still have to wear a white wedding dress," Laura says.

"Absolutely. We'll still go dress shopping."

"And then from Vegas, you should fly to Mexico for your honeymoon. Like Cabo or somewhere nice like that. That would be cool," Laura says.

"Yeah, we'll see. That is a good idea."

We talk and have a couple more cocktails. I look at my watch. I want to be home when Jason gets there. I text him and let him know where I'm at and ask what he wants for dinner. He says he doesn't care what's for dinner. Easy enough. I stop on the way home and pick up sandwiches. I decide not to confront him about Deanna tonight.

Chapter 44

Friday night comes, and we are off to Manny's Bar. Laura has a date with Ethan and said they might stop in later. Jason is wearing jeans and a white short-sleeved shirt. I look at him and wonder what he is doing with me. He could have any girl in this city—why me? He stops suddenly on the sidewalk and pulls me in for a long kiss on the lips.

"You always know when I need a kiss, don't you?" I say, grinning at him.

He takes my hand, and we continue walking to the bar.

"Let's not stay long, okay?" Jason asks as we walk in the door.

"Fine with me," I agree. We only agreed to go out and get some air tonight after a marathon lovemaking session.

We make the rounds once we get in the bar. Jason, of course, knows almost everyone here. My social butterfly. We eventually make our way to two open barstools and have a seat.

"Laura let me know earlier that her charity can take my furniture next week. Is there anything you think we should keep?" I say.

"I have everything we need. It's up to you if you want to keep anything. We can always make room," Jason says, rubbing my knee. "We'll make a trip over there this weekend and pack up miscellaneous items and whatever else you decide to keep, okay?"

"Sounds good. Once I'm out though, you're pretty much stuck with me," I say, smiling at him.

Jason laughs. "You make it sound as though you've been sprinting to the finish line. More like I've been dragging and pulling you over the line."

"Whatever. I haven't been that bad," I say, rolling my eyes.

"Yeah, you kind of have been that bad. And you also never gave me the full scoop on Ethan. Don't think I haven't forgotten about that, even though I'm expected to hang out with him tonight," Jason says, playing with a piece of my hair.

"Really, Jay? It's no big deal," I say, somewhat annoyed.

"Then let's hear it."

I sigh. "He proposed. I said no. That is basically why the relationship ended. I told him I didn't ever want to marry him, so there was no reason to continue the relationship."

"Ouch," Jason says, somewhat surprised.

"No, it wasn't an ouch ending," I say, shaking my head. "Ethan was a great boyfriend. He didn't do anything wrong. I just didn't want to be married. *Ever.* Until, of course, you came along." I lean over and gently kiss him on the lips.

"Good answer," Jason says, kissing me back.

I lean back against the bar and try to remember anything else that Jason should know about regarding my relationship with Ethan. "That's really it, Jay. It was a typical college romance. Nothing earth-shattering. Happy?"

"Yes, I'm happy. Thanks for sharing," Jason says, smiling.

"You think you will be okay hanging out with him?"

"Yes, I'll be okay. We aren't going to become best friends, Lacey," Jason says. "But I will be able to hang out with him here and there without breaking his neck."

I sigh and roll my eyes.

Our talk about Ethan comes to end as he and Laura arrive at the bar. As the night progresses, mutual friends of Ethan and Jason also show up so they are not stuck with only hanging out with each other all night. The group of guys has moved toward the back of the bar, while Laura and I sit at the bar and talk. She cannot stop telling me how wonderful Ethan is.

"I know. He is a great guy," I agree for the tenth time.

I *am* truly happy for her and hope their relationship lasts for the long haul.

I break away for a bathroom break, and as I am walking out of the bathroom, I run into Kellan. Ugh.

"Hi, Kellan," I say, and try to keep walking.

All I need is for Jason to see us talking. I look over to where Jason was previously standing to see if he has noticed, but I no longer see him standing there.

"What's the rush, Lacey? You know, I really enjoyed talking to you the other day," Kellan says, taking my hand.

I immediately remove it from his grip and start walking back toward Laura.

That's when I notice Jason. He has moved to the back corner of the bar and is leaning up against the wall with his back to me. He's talking with a very attractive brunette.

Kellan cuts me off and forces me to stop in my tracks. "Jason's not holding his breath waiting for you, so can't we just talk a little bit more?"

"Sure, Kellan, what's up?" I am trying to act as if I don't care who Jason is speaking with. I look over Kellan's shoulder and can see Jason laughing at something the brunette just said.

"Who is that anyway?" I ask Kellan nonchalantly.

"Oh, that's my cousin Deanna," Kellan says coolly. "Why don't you give them a minute? I'm sure he's telling her all about you."

I look at Jason and Deanna, who are giggling like high school kids. She's got her hand on his arm, and it looks like the last thing they are discussing is me. I could kick myself for not asking Jason about her before tonight.

Kellan, all of sudden, looks sorry for me. "I'm sorry, Lacey. I tried to warn you."

"Please don't," I say, holding up my hand, irritated that he would pity me. "I'm fine. I'll just go over and introduce myself."

"If you think that will make a difference, Lacey."

"Well, we will see, Kellan," I say, remembering the talk Jason and I had about better communication.

I walk over to Jason and Deanna to see for myself what the situation is.

"Lacey," Jason says, pulling me closer to him and putting his arm around me. "This is Deanna. Deanna, this is my fiancée, Lacey."

"Hi, Deanna," I say, shaking her hand and so relieved at my decision not to listen to Kellan.

"Lacey, it's nice to meet you," Deanna says.

"Deanna was just informing me what Kellan was up to tonight," Jason says.

"My asshole cousin asked me to come here tonight and hit on Jason when you weren't looking. But I couldn't go through with it and was just telling Jason his plan to start a fight between you two," Deanna explains, looking somewhat embarrassed.

"Thanks for letting us know, Deanna. I really appreciate it," I say sincerely.

I look up at Jason, who is looking around the bar, no doubt for Kellan, who has now vanished. My alpha male.

"Excuse me for a minute," Jason says to us, and he walks away. I still don't see Kellan, but something seems to have caught Jason's eye.

"My cousin always had a thing for you," Deanna continues, trying to explain his behavior. "He always thought if you two hooked up, it would be the ultimate revenge against Jason."

"Yeah, I kind of guessed that. Kellan is an interesting character. Just not my type, you know?"

I don't want to tell her what I really think of Kellan since she is still his blood relative, and I want to keep things kosher between us. She has, after all, taken the high road tonight when she easily could have started a fight between Jason and me.

"It was nice meeting you, Lacey, but I'm going to mosey out of here," Deanna says. "I have to work early tomorrow morning."

"Thanks again, Deanna," I say, and make my way back to Laura, who is still seated at the bar.

"Everything okay?" Laura asks when I take the seat next to her.

"Perfect," I say, finishing my beer.

Chapter 45

"Tell me about Deanna," I say to Jason when we finally get home.

"It was a total setup, babe," Jason says, taking a seat at the kitchen table.

"Right. I got that. But I want to know about your relationship with her. It's embarrassing for me to walk out of the bathroom and see you talking with a girl you used to hook up with. You know how that makes me look to the rest of the bar? Like I'm out of sight for a minute, so you immediately start talking to someone else."

I'm not mad at him because I know what happened tonight wasn't his fault. But I want to let him know that I am not happy with the situation either.

"No one in that bar even knows who she is. I've never been out in public with her. It was a purely sexual relationship, nothing more." Jason grabs my hand and tries to pull me onto his lap.

I resist and stay standing. "Is that supposed to make me feel better?" I ask.

"Yeah, it should. She doesn't mean anything to me. Just someone I used to call when I was bored."

"Kellan said she has a thing for you."

"Who cares? I was always clear with her about what I wanted."

I hear Jason's phone buzzing in his pocket, and I hold out my hand for him to give it to me.

"Fine," he says, pulling his phone out and giving it to me. He sighs loudly.

"It's a text message from Deanna," I inform him.

"Whatever. Read it," he says, surely already knowing I plan to.

"It says, 'Lacey seems very nice. I wish you a wonderful life. Take care.'"

"Are you happy now?" Jason smirks.

"Almost."

I delete all his text messages and then go into his contact list and hit "delete all." It takes a few minutes for his hundreds of contacts to fly into the little trash can picture.

"Please tell me you didn't just delete all my contacts," Jason says as I hand his phone back to him. He looks down at the phone and tries to maintain his cool.

"Done," I say, smirking and daring him to explode.

"Lacey. Those weren't all ex-girlfriends, you know. Most were family, coworkers, old friends. People I have no way of getting in touch with now."

I shrug nonchalantly. "Anyone who should be in your life will find a way to get a hold of you. You needed a fresh start."

"I don't know anyone's number, not even yours. That phone was my memory," Jason says, taking a deep breath and closing his eyes. I can tell he is trying to keep his composure.

Maybe I went too far, but it's done now and can't be reversed.

I stand there staring at him when I notice the cut above his eye.

"What happened to your eye?" I ask, getting a couple of ice cubes from the freezer.

"Nothing," Jason says.

I wrap the ice in a paper towel and apply it to his cut.

"I'm fine, Lacey. Fuming. Pissed. But my eye is fine."

I keep the ice on his cut and straddle his lap. "Don't be mad. It made me feel better to do it."

I take his phone back and type in my contact information and hand it back to him. "There, now you at least have my number."

He laughs when he sees I have saved my name as Lacey Reed.

"You are forgiven, babe," he says, giving me a quick kiss on the mouth.

"So how did you get this cut?" I ask again.

"You know I wasn't going to let Kellan get away with what he did. He managed to get in a good punch. That's all."

"Does it hurt?"

"No. I wouldn't have known it was there if you didn't ask about it." He closes his eyes and sighs again. "You're good at fixing me up, you know that?"

Since we started working together, there have been numerous times when I have fixed cuts and bruises Jason had suffered from one rumble or another. Some were work related; some were not.

"When I was about ten years old I was living with this couple in Staten Island. Every Friday after work, the husband would get drunk and come home and beat the shit out of the wife. I would stay in my room until it was over, and when I heard him leave, I would come out and help her clean herself up. He used to do some serious damage to her. I would beg her to go to the hospital or call the cops. And all she would say to me was 'You fix me up so good, Lacey. Why do I need to go to a hospital?'"

"That's awful that you had to go through that," Jason says, opening his eyes and staring at me.

"One time he came home and hit her so hard, her cheek opened completely up. I told her I couldn't fix this one and begged her to go to the hospital. She told me to get a needle and thread and do the best that I could."

"Then what happened?" Jason asks.

"I threaded a needle and began stitching her cheek together. She was so pretty too. I felt horrible—like it was my fault she had this gigantic cut on her face. I kept pleading with her to go the hospital so a doctor could do it right and maybe minimize the scarring. But she didn't care. She kept telling me not to worry about it and do the best I could. The whole time I kept thinking I was destroying this woman's face even, though it wasn't me who hit her."

"I'm sorry you had to go through that," Jason says, rubbing my back. "No ten-year-old should be put in that position. What happened to her?"

"I came home from school one day, and the house was on fire. The husband had come home from work for lunch, and she clubbed him over the head and then torched the house. He died. She walked." I shrug.

"She never went to jail?"

"No. I was her best witness. I realized that was the only reason she wanted me there, so someone else could verify how he beat her. Once she got off, I never saw her again. I always wondered if I saw her on the street, would I recognize her because of the scar on her face? Or did the scar eventually fade?"

"Oh, Lacey," Jason says, pulling me close to him and hugging me tight. "I am so sorry you had the childhood you had. I would fix it all for you if I could."

I laugh. "Don't feel bad for me. I survived. A lot of kids out there have it much worse than I ever did."

I stand up and dump what's left of the ice in the sink. When I come back I sit in his lap and bury my face in his neck.

"Are we good?" Jason asks, stroking my hair again.

"Yeah, we're good," I say, closing my eyes.

"Good. I think we have a whole new set of issues for you talk about with Dr. Greene next week," Jason says, smiling. "I'm going to start a list for you to take."

"Get the fuck out of here," I say, laughing.

"First on the list will be the potty mouth you have recently acquired. So right now, we have potty mouth and wedding phobias. I'll also add trust issues."

"Fine. I think we both have major trust issues, so put it on your list too," I say, nuzzling his neck.

"Not true. I trust you. I just don't trust any man around you," Jason says, hugging me tighter.

"I'll also be adding control issues to your list," I say.

"Okay. I'll give you that one," Jason agrees.

"And bossiness," I say, continuing our banter.

"I think that falls under control issues. So you are up to three, and I have one."

"You have two. Trust and control. You still don't trust me to handle the men you don't trust," I say, correcting him.

"I don't think that's a trust issue for me. More like a bad judgment issue for you. So now you have four, and I have one."

"That's not fair. Then I don't trust your willpower to say no to other women," I say.

"That's still *your* trust issue, Lacey. And I also want to add communication issues to your list," Jason says, pushing my hair off my face.

"Hey, tonight was a huge step for me. When I came out of the bathroom, I was very close to leaving the bar. But I sucked it up and went over to you to hear what you had to say."

"It *was* a big step for you," Jason says, amused. "And look how much better things turn out when you communicate with me."

"Much better," I say, kissing his neck.

"But I'm still going to add it to your list since it's still a work-in-progress issue. So now you have five issues to work on, and I have one."

"You never would have looked at my phone if you trusted me with Harvey. You have two," I counter.

"Fine. I have two," Jason concedes, picking me up and carrying me into the bedroom.

Chapter 46

The rest of my time off from work flies by. Dr. Greene clears me mentally to go back to work, and Dr. Shepard from the hospital clears me physically.

Jason and I clean out my apartment. Laura's charity takes most of my items. The stuff I decide to keep we pack up and make room for in Jason's apartment. He is thrilled when it is all done. I am somewhat saddened. I have been on my own for so long, it's the end of a very long chapter—the end of my singular lifestyle.

I also meet with Rachel and Jason's mom, Carol, to discuss the wedding plans. I tell them about my plan to surprise Jason with a trip to Vegas. Rachel is initially disappointed but then gets excited when I include her and Carol in the trip. Carol is just excited that her son is happy and agrees I should have whatever type of wedding I want to have. We decide to go in three months. That will at least give me a couple of months without paying rent, and I can save money.

Chapter 47

$\mathcal{I}$ put my magazine down and look over at Jason. He's busy typing something into my phone. We are about two hours into our flight to Vegas. Rachel and Jason's mom, Carol, are sitting three rows in front of us across the aisle. The last three months have flown by.

"Here," Jason says, handing me my phone. "I wrote up a list of things you should include in your vows to me."

"You're unbelievable," I say, rolling my eyes.

"What? I just want to help you out with what you should say. I think you'll agree with most of them," Jason says, smirking.

I sigh and read his list aloud. "'I promise to have, hold, and forever love you.' Well, of course I will. You don't need to write this out for me," I say, looking at him.

"Keep reading," Jason orders.

"'I promise to obey and do whatever you tell me to do without any lip.'" I sigh and roll my eyes again. "'I promise to learn how to cook at least one decent meal. I promise to walk around naked at home (whenever possible). I promise to serve plenty of beer and blow jobs to you when you are watching football on Sundays.' You are such a pig, you know that?" I say, leaning my head back on the seat and looking over at him.

"Hey, this is the stuff that makes for a happy marriage," Jason says, smiling.

I continue reading. "'And finally, since you can no longer have sex with other women, I promise to periodically have sex with other beautiful women and let you watch.'" I gasp. "Is that really what you want? I had no idea."

Jason is laughing. "No, that's not what I want. I'm too jealous to watch you with anyone else, male or female. But it provides a great visual, doesn't it?" He leans his head back in the seat and closes his eyes, smiling.

I gasp again. "Open your eyes." I poke him, but he keeps them shut, laughing. "Open them!"

"No way," Jason says, keeping his eyes closed.

"You got issues," I say, giving up.

"Oh, Lacey, it was all a joke," he says, reaching over and kissing me on the lips.

"So that isn't what you want?" I ask, looking at him in disbelief.

"No. You know how jealous I am. There is no way I could handle watching you with someone else," Jason says, smiling, still pleased with himself for irking me.

"All right. Because if there any oats you still need sowed, we need to discuss it before we get married."

"Oh, babe, you are so cute," Jason says, kissing me again. "And don't worry about my oats. They're sowed."

I keep staring at him while he is kissing me, debating whether I want to continue this conversation or not. I decide not.

"Here, read my list of vows to you," Jason says, opening another notepad screen on my phone. He slides down in his seat to get more comfortable and rests his head on my shoulder while I read the vows.

> Dear Lacey,
>> I promise always to adore and protect you.
>> I promise always to be your best friend.
>> I promise always to be honest and kind.
>> I promise always to have your back.
>> I promise to make you smile and laugh.
>> I promise never, ever to stop kissing you.
>> I promise never, ever to stop hugging you.
>> I promise never to hurt you.
>> I promise to beat up anyone who does hurt you.
>> I promise my arms will always make you feel safe.
>> I promise to make all your dreams come true.
>> I promise never, ever to stop loving you.

"Oh, Jay, you are so sweet," I say, wiping away tears. I lean over and kiss him on the mouth.

"Lacey, you are my world," Jason says, reaching over and putting his hand behind my neck. He pulls me back to him for another kiss. "Please don't ever doubt that."

I kiss him some more on the lips, nice, slow, tender kisses that I wish I could make last forever, or at least longer, but then we are interrupted by the flight attendant asking if we would like anything else to drink.

"I'll have a water, thank you," I say, blushing.

"Water, please," Jason says, unfazed.

He looks at my face turning pink and laughs. He takes our drinks and places them on the trays in front of us.

"She interrupted us on purpose, you know," Jason says, resting his head back on my shoulder and rubbing my thigh.

"Yeah, because she wanted to move along with the drink cart."

"She could have moved along without bothering us. She's been staring at you the whole flight," Jason says, taking a sip of his water.

"You're insane. You mean she's been staring at *you*," I say, resting my head on top of his.

"I'm not kidding you, Lacey. She's been eyeing you up," Jason says, smiling.

I nudge Jason off my shoulder and lean across him so I can look down the aisle where the flight attendant just walked. She is tall and thin with long straight brown hair. She is very pretty.

"Well, I could do worse, I guess," I say, sitting back down in my window seat.

"You're off the market, remember?" Jason asks laughing.

"Yes, but we can visualize, right?" I ask, leaning back in my seat, closing my eyes, and smiling.

"Lacey, the only one you should be visualizing is me," Jason says, lightly shaking my arm.

"How's it feel, Jay?" I ask, smiling but still keeping my eyes closed.

"You're a brat," Jason says, poking me.

"And you're full of shit. She was never looking at me," I say. "You're just imagining something to get your rocks off."

"You get my rocks off. I don't need to imagine anything." He kisses my neck. "How about if you meet me in the bathroom in two minutes, okay?"

"I will not. The bathrooms are way too small and disgustingly dirty." I crinkle my nose. "And besides the flight is almost over."

"Fine." Jason gets up to chat with his sister and mom.

"Excuse me, miss?" The pretty brunette flight attendant is bending down over Jason's empty seat. She smiles.

I'm startled at how pretty she really is. Her eyes are very dark brown, and her skin has a flawless, coffee-color glow to it.

"Uh, yes?" I ask.

"You look very familiar to me. Do you live in Vegas?" the flight attendant asks.

"Oh, no," I say, somewhat relieved at her question. "I live in New York."

"Have you been to Vegas before?" she asks.

"No. This will be my first time."

"Really? It's always interesting for first timers to experience it," she says, smiling at me. "I live in Vegas when I'm not flying, and I have the next few days off. I'd love to show you around if you would like."

"Okay," I say, taken aback.

I look at Jason, who is still talking with his sister and mom. Or at least pretending to be. He has no doubt noticed this woman talking with me and is probably listening in.

"He can tag along too," the flight attendant says with a wink, when she sees me looking in Jason's direction. She writes down her name and telephone number on a napkin. "My name is Jessica, by the way."

"Lacey," I say, wondering at what point should I tell her I don't need a tour guide.

"Here you are, Lacey," she says, handing me the napkin. "I hope to hear from you. I think we could have a lot of fun."

"Um, thanks, Jessica," I say, taking the napkin and smiling at her.

She walks in the opposite direction of where Jason is still kneeling and talking. When he sees the flight attendant walk away, he gets up and comes back to his seat.

"You heard?" I ask, already knowing he did.

"Yep," he says, grinning.

"Don't say it," I say to him, looking out the window.

"I told you," he says, still grinning at me. "When will you ever trust my judgment?"

"You're right. You are an expert at reading people," I say, still not believing he called that one. "I don't know how you do it."

"Well, if you don't work out, at least I got plan B," I say, winking at him and tucking the napkin in my purse.

Jason laughs. "You're stuck with me, honey. If I have to, I'll chase you all over the world and make it work."

The descent into Las Vegas airport is uneventful. As we are leaving the plane, Jessica touches my arm and says she hopes we can meet up later.

"Wow, she's got it bad for you, Lacey," Jason teases as we are waiting for our luggage. He wraps his arms around me as we are standing there. "I have to admit, babe, I'm in uncharted water here. I know how to protect you from other men but not quite sure how I should handle other women. I mean, if she was a man, I would have knocked her out. But I can't do that to a woman."

"Jay, don't be so dramatic. She was harmless. No big deal," I say, hugging him back.

"Who was harmless?" Carol asks.

"Lacey was hit on by another woman, Mom," Jason explains.

"I'm surprised you weren't all over that," Rachel teases him.

"Normally I would have encouraged it, but not with Lacey," Jason says.

I wish a hole would swallow me up.

"Oh dear. Where are your manners?" Carol asks her son. "I hope he doesn't always act this vulgar around you."

"He's normally very polite, Carol. I'm not sure what's gotten into him," I say, giving him a pinch when she looks away. "Behave."

We gather up our bags and head to our hotel. We are staying and getting married at the Bellagio. Jason and I are staying three nights and then moving on to the Bahamas. Carol and Rachel have decided to stay in Vegas for five nights and make a vacation out of it.

"I wish we were getting married tonight instead of tomorrow night," I say to Jason when we get to our room. I don't tell him it is because of how nervous I am and I want to get it over with so I can enjoy the rest of our time here.

"Then we'll change it to tonight," Jason says nonchalantly.

"No, let's keep it as scheduled," I say, after thinking about it for a few minutes. "Besides, I want to give you one last night to run."

"I'll marry you right now. You're the one I'm worried won't be here in the morning," Jason says.

"I'll be here tomorrow. But how about we focus on right now," I say, kissing him hard on the mouth and pushing him onto the bed.

I fall on top of him, hoping to release some of my nervous energy.

Chapter 48

We meet Carol and Rachel in the lobby of the Bellagio. The plan is to gamble, eat, and then catch a show. We pick a time and place to meet up for dinner. At first Jason is hesitant to let his mother go anywhere alone, but she soon reminds him she is no casino virgin and could probably teach him a thing or two about gambling.

"Okay, Mom. But have your cell phone on at all times and check it periodically since you don't always hear it," Jason says, clearly still not convinced he should let his mom go solo.

Carol rolls her eyes at him. "Get a grip, Jason. I'll be fine."

"You know how many times she hops a bus to the casinos around New York, Jason? She'll be fine," Rachel chimes in, defending their mother.

"Okay. But don't be late coming back here for dinner, or I will alert security to find you," Jason warns his mother. "And the same goes for you, Rachel. Check your phone, and don't be late."

"You can be so annoying," Carol says to her son.

I can't help but laugh, as I know exactly how she feels.

Carol and Rachel give waves as they escape.

"I'll also check my phone and will see you later," I say, giving him a quick kiss and walking away.

"Not so fast, Lacey." Jason grabs my hand.

"But I don't want to play table games. And you don't like slots," I say.

"I'll start off playing slots with you. How's that?" Jason asks.

"Fine. But I get to pick what games," I say, leading the way.

We sit down at two slots that look somewhat fun to play. After about five minutes, I can see Jason is bored out of his mind.

"Why don't you go play poker or something?" I ask.

"I'm fine," Jason says unconvincingly. He flags down a cocktail server and orders a whiskey. "You want anything?"

I shake my head no and cash out my machine. I stand next to him, leaning on his arm. Even though the air conditioning is cranking in the casino, his arm is warm. His skin is always warm. For some reason I have become so turned on just by touching his arm, even though we just made love less than an hour ago.

"How about we go back to the room and fuck our brains out before dinner?" I whisper in his ear.

Jason takes a swig of his drink, cashes out his machine, and takes my hand, leading us toward the elevator. Thankfully the elevator is empty when we get in, and I immediately kiss him and press myself up against him.

"Lacey, what has gotten into you?" Jason says, kissing me back.

"I don't know. I just need you right now," I say, holding back on my urge to stop the elevator. We ride up to our floor alone and luckily avoid any embarrassing scenes.

When we get to the room, I quickly undress to save time, so that he won't be slowed down with my clothes. And then I work on getting his pants off.

"What do you want, Lacey?" Jason asks in between kisses as I lead him over to the bed.

"I want you. Inside of me. Now," I say, pulling him on top of me in between my legs. "Make it hard and fast because I'm not going to last long," I whisper in his ear in between groans.

He happily obliges, thrusting himself inside of me until I crumble around him.

"Not that I'm complaining, but why are you so horny?" Jason asks as we lie next to each other, catching our breath.

"I'm always horny for you," I say, laughing. I roll over on top of him and kiss him again.

"Yeah, but you're different today. Faster. Christ, you were orgasmic in the elevator."

"I don't know. Maybe it's the desert air. Or the turbulence from the flight jiggled something. Or maybe I just have a lot of energy, thinking about tomorrow," I explain, kissing his neck. "Whatever the reason, I'm ready to go again."

"Oh, I feel so used," Jason complains still sprawled out on his back. "Can't we at least cuddle for a little bit before the next round?" he asks, trying not to laugh.

"No cuddling," I say, laughing and going down on him. "I'll give you three minutes to recover. And I'll even help you get started again."

Chapter 49

"Lacey, did you have any luck?" Carol asks me as we sit down to dinner.

"Oh, I got lucky a couple of times," I say, smiling at Jason's mother.

Jason is staring at me with a dopey, sexually exhausted smile on his face.

"Well, I'm glad someone did. I had a little luck in the beginning, and then it vanished."

"I tried my hand at roulette and broke even," Rachel adds. "How about you, Jason?"

"I was sucked dry," he says, not lying and making me laugh.

"Maybe after the show tonight we can walk down the strip and try different casinos? I was thinking..." Rachel starts rambling on, much to my relief.

I really don't feel like talking much, and I can see Jason isn't going to be much of a conversationalist during this dinner either. Thankfully, we don't have to wait long for the food to arrive.

"Oh my, Lacey, have you not eaten lately?" Carol says, looking at my plate that has been wiped clean.

"I was famished," I say, leaning back and wiping my mouth with my napkin. I look at Carol's plate, and she is about halfway through her meal. I guess I did inhale it.

"Lacey eats like a horse and, for some reason, doesn't gain any weight," Rachel explains to her mother.

"That's not true. I work out a lot," I say to Carol.

"Maybe when we get back to New York, we could work out together?" Rachel asks. "I need to lose some weight, and maybe if I get on your workout schedule, it will finally happen."

"Sure, that would be fun. We could meet a couple of times a week and go for a run," I say, wanting to help Rachel lose a few pounds. I think it would help her confidence tremendously.

The waiter comes over and fills each of our wineglasses, except of course for Jason, who is drinking whiskey.

"Okay, ladies," Jason says, eyeing his mother drinking another glass of wine. "We really need to wrap up this dinner if we are going to make this show on time."

After the show, we walk down the strip. We stop in at a few different casinos and then head back to the Bellagio. Jason decides he is going to play poker only after I promise him that Rachel and I will behave in the bar. I think he is comforted by Rachel being with me. Carol decides to hit the slot machines again.

"He really enjoys poker, doesn't he?" I ask Rachel.

"Yeah, our father taught him how to play. That was how they bonded. They would play cards, smoke cigars, and drink. Jason's pretty good at it too. He's good at reading people. He can sit at a table and know exactly how people are playing."

"He *is* good at reading people," I say, remembering the flight attendant.

"I am so glad you two are together," Rachel says, rubbing my arm. "He was so in love with you when you first started working together, but you were dating Tyler. He used to beg me to meet him out at bars because he knew you would show up if I was there."

"It's true," I say, laughing. "Whenever he texted me that you were there, I would head over to that bar to see you. I always thought you just liked hanging out with your big brother."

"Oh, please. Love my brother, but he kills my dating life. He invites me to cop bars and then forbids me to date a cop," Rachel says, shaking her head and laughing.

"Was he always so protective and controlling?" I ask.

"No. He got worse after our father died. Since he couldn't control our dad's health or death, it was almost as though he decided he would try to control everything and everyone else." Rachel takes a sip of her wine.

"Well, you're lucky to have a brother like him. He takes very good care of you and your mom. And now, me too," I add, smiling.

After about an hour, Carol comes wandering into the bar. "I'm beat, girls. I need to go to bed."

"Good night, Carol," I say.

"All right, Mom. I'll be up in a little while," Rachel says.

"You don't have to babysit me, Rachel. If you want to go, then go. I'll be okay," I say to Rachel.

"No, I'll hang out for another," Rachel says.

I pick up my phone and text Jason to get an idea as to how much longer he will be. He writes back that he has one more hand and then he's done.

"He's almost done," I say as we order another round.

"You know, Lacey, feel free to fix me up when we get home. I think it's been forever since I've had a real boyfriend."

"What about Brady?" I ask, referring to Brady Leary.

"We hang out here and there. Nothing serious."

"I'll see what I can do, Rachel. I'm just not sure I know anyone who's good enough for you," I say honestly.

"You sound like Jason now," Rachel says, rolling her eyes.

"It's true. Most of the guys I know aren't looking for a relationship, if you know what I mean. And you deserve more than that. But I'll think about who I know," I say when she looks dejected.

"What are you two talking about?" Jason comes up behind me and gives me a kiss on the cheek. He's smiling, so he must have done well at the poker table.

"We are talking about who we should fix Rachel up with." I take his hand and hold it in my lap.

"Not going to happen," Jason says.

"Oh, give me a break. There has to be some really nice guy you know who you would be comfortable letting her go out with," I tell him.

"They are few and far between."

"I'll work on it, Rachel." I grab her knee. "So how did you do at your game, Jason?"

"Wonderful. It's been a great day," he says, kissing me on the cheek again. "Are we staying here or going to bed?"

"I'm beat and need to go to bed." Rachel gets off her barstool.

"Me too," I say, standing up.

Back in our room, I kiss Jason again. I hate drinking whiskey, but I love the taste of it on his lips. It's intoxicating, as though I'm the one who had it to drink.

"Do you have any energy left for me tonight?" I ask in between kisses.

"Always," Jason says.

Chapter 50

"Jay, did you pack the rings?" I yell as I'm tearing apart our luggage. The wedding is in five hours, and I can't find the damn wedding rings. We had them fitted and picked them up from the jeweler a few days before we left.

"No, I didn't pack them. You said you did." Jason is lounging on the bed, flipping through the TV stations.

"Then why can't I find them? I think I told you to put them in your carry-on," I say, flipping his carry-on upside down and shaking the contents out of it. "Can you at least get off your ass and help me look for them?"

"Lacey, relax," Jason says, getting off the bed and trying to give me a hug.

"Not now," I say, nudging him away. "Just help me look, would you please?"

Jason rummages through the suitcases, looking in all the pockets. "They aren't here, honey."

"I can't believe I fucking forgot them," I say, sitting on the floor and putting my face in my hands.

"Lacey, it's no big deal. There's a jewelry store somewhere in this resort. I'll pick up replacements when you are getting your hair done," Jason says, kneeling next to me and putting his arm around me.

"What a waste," I say, standing up, and he gets up after me. My nerves are fried, and the last thing I want is to be consoled. "And then what do we do with the ones at home?"

"What does it matter, Lacey? Who cares about the rings? I don't plan on wearing mine anyway," Jason says, digging through another suitcase.

"*What?*" I scream at him.

"I shoot with my left hand. It will interfere with work," Jason says, looking at me and smirking.

"Don't give me that shit," I hiss at him. "You shoot with your right hand."

"Lacey, honey. I really need you to take a deep breath, okay?" Jason says, in his best soothing voice.

I glare at him.

"I will never take my ring off, I promise, okay? Now breathe. Please," Jason says, grabbing my hand.

"You're right. It doesn't matter. I just need to relax."

I walk over to the minibar and pull out a small bottle of wine. I twist it open and pour it into two glasses. I hand a glass to Jason and sit down on the bed. He sits down on the bed next to me and puts his arm around me.

"I'm sorry I snapped at you," I say. I take a sip of my wine and then rest my head on his shoulder. "I can't imagine the basket case I would be if we decided to have a traditional ceremony at home. Thank God we decided to come here and do it."

"Maybe Rachel should help you get ready, and I'll spend the day with my mother," Jason says. "Rachel has a more calming effect than my mother does."

It was Jason's decision not to bring any of his friends. He insisted they would only be trouble and a distraction and that the only people he cared to have at his wedding were his sister and mother. The weekend before we left, a group of his friends took him out on the town to celebrate his last weekend as a single man. I don't know what happened that night, but Jason insists nothing went on that would piss me off.

The plan today was for Carol to help me get ready and for Rachel to help Jason get ready.

"No, I need a mother today, and you need a friend. I'll be fine with your mom. She is surprisingly cool, you know?" I say.

"Of course she is. She's my mom." He kisses my forehead. There's a knock at the door. "Speak of the devil."

Jason gets up and lets his mother and Rachel in.

"I've come to take you away, Lacey," Carol says, barging in and taking my hand. "You two shouldn't have even slept in the same room last night. Don't you know you're not supposed to see each other before the wedding?"

"Whatever, Mom. I wasn't going to spend the night without her. And those traditions are so old anyway. Times have changed," Jason says, standing up. "You're lucky I'm letting you take her now. Maybe I'll just keep her here and dress her myself."

"Say good-bye, Jason. We'll see you later." Carol leads me out of the room.

I turn and wave to Jason, since she doesn't give me a chance to kiss him good-bye. Now I know where he gets his bossiness from. Rachel stays behind with Jason, so it's just Carol and me in the elevator.

We have appointments at the spa to get a massage and then have our nails, hair, and makeup done—a total bonding session between me and my future mother-in-law. It could be worse. I truly do like the woman. How could I not, when she gave me the greatest love of my life?

Renaldo did my hair before I left. I liked what he did the first time, and Laura insisted we go back there again before I left to get married. So the hair stylist at the spa doesn't really have much to do other than style it into a half updo for the wedding.

"You look beautiful, Lacey," Carol says as I slip into my wedding dress.

I had my wedding gear shipped to the hotel so I wouldn't have to deal with it on the plane. Rachel picked it up at the front desk when it arrived yesterday. The dress is a very simple white slip dress. It is shorter in the front, cut just above my shoes, and then longer in the back, touching the floor.

"I understand why Jason fell so hard for you," Carol says, giving me a once-over. "He's lucky to have you. And I'm lucky to be gaining another daughter."

"Oh, Carol, thank you for that." I give her a hug.

"Here, I want you to have something." Carol gets a few boxes out of her suitcase. She opens the box and pulls out pearl-drop earrings and a pearl necklace.

"These were my mother's. She gave them to me on my wedding day. And now I would like you to have them," Carol says as she helps me put the necklace on.

"Oh, Carol, I can't keep these. Please," I say, looking in the mirror and touching the necklace. "They are beautiful. But I don't want to step on Rachel's toes."

"I already told Rachel I was giving them to you, and she thought it was a wonderful idea." Carol hands me the earrings to put on.

"Thank you." I give her another hug. Tears are springing to my eyes.

"Lacey, don't cry. You'll ruin your makeup," she says, wiping away a tear.

"I know. It's just Jason and Rachel are so lucky to have you. I wish I had a mother like you," I say, getting weepy.

"Oh, dear, you're part of our family now." She rubs my arms.

I wipe my tears and fix my makeup.

"Are you ready, Lacey? It's almost time," Carol says, smiling at me.

"I'm ready." I do a last mirror check.

By the time we get to the chapel, I am ready to jump out of my dress from excitement and nerves. When I finally see Jason, I don't wait for the ceremony to start. I just run to him, wrap my arms around his neck, and kiss him. I hear Rachel giggling as the officiator is patiently waiting for us to stop.

"You look stunning," Jason says when we finally break.

I smile at him, and we turn toward the officiator to begin. The surprise during the ceremony comes when I go to put Jason's ring on his finger. He, of course, had bought replacements earlier in the day as promised. As I take his left hand, I see that he has gotten my name tattooed around his ring finger where his wedding ring should go. I laugh.

"See, I promised you I would never take it off," Jason says, smiling.

"You're too much," I say, kissing him again.

We are officially pronounced husband and wife and kiss some more.

Chapter 51

As we sit down to dinner after the ceremony, I'm looking more closely at Jason's hand. He has "Lacey" tattooed around his ring finger, once on the front and then on the back, separated by two hearts. Then on the inside, he has my name tattooed the length of his finger.

"I can't believe you did this," I say, looking at his finger.

Jason shrugs.

"We were just praying you didn't get cold feet," Rachel says, giggling.

"Rachel got one too," Jason says, outing his sister.

"It's just a little one." Rachel turns over her arm and shows us a yin-yang sunflower on her forearm. "My first."

"It was very painful. I almost had him stop midway but then realized how ridiculous that would look," Rachel says.

"Hey, I warned you, but you had to have one," Jason says.

"Maybe I'll get one later tonight," I say to Jason.

"Absolutely not," he says, shaking his head.

"Why not? I'll get a ring tattoo also."

"No."

"It was pretty awful, Lacey. I was surprised at how painful it was, and I have a pretty high tolerance for pain," Rachel says, taking her brother's side.

"Well, while you two were off being tortured, your mom and I had the most wonderful time at the spa. My massage was absolutely to die for," I say, rubbing it in.

"Yeah, I had an Asian girl who pushed knots out of me that I didn't know existed," Carol says. "She was tiny but had the strongest hands."

"What is the plan for tonight?" Rachel asks.

"Well, if you don't mind, I'm going to take my wife back to our room and spend some alone time with her."

Jason is looking at me and smiling. He takes a piece of my hair and twirls it with his fingers. I can't help but blush.

"My beautiful blushing bride," he adds, laughing.

Chapter 52

"Do you realize it's four in the morning?" I ask.

I am snuggling up to Jason in the bathtub, soaking in warm, sudsy water. After dinner we came back to the room, made love, made love, and made love. Now we are relaxing in a warm bath, sipping champagne from one of the bottles that Jason snagged from the bar.

"It wasn't too bad spending the day with my mom?" Jason asks, wrapping his right arm around me. He's careful not to let his left hand soak too long in the water to avoid any damage to his new tattoo.

"I had fun with your mom. You and Rachel are very lucky to have her," I say, taking the bath sponge and running it across his chest.

"You would have liked my dad too. He was a pretty cool guy." Jason sighs.

"You don't talk about him much. How come?" I ask, still sponging him up.

"It's still too painful. It happened eight years ago, but it feels like yesterday," Jason says, shrugging. "It's tough to talk about."

"Well, at least you have your memories. I don't really remember my dad. He was always working. I remember more of my mother since she didn't work and we were together all the time."

"Wasn't there anyone who was a constant in your life growing up?"

"No, not really," I say after thinking about it for a minute. "My living arrangements were constantly changing. There were some positive influences here and there. For the most part I always tried to be ready to move on."

"Which explains why you were so hesitant to give up your apartment?"

"Of course. That was a big step. For anyone," I point out.

"I suppose. It was an easy decision for me," Jason says.

"Well, I guess you are just better at making decisions than me," I say sarcastically.

"I'm glad you finally realized it. So that means I get to make all decisions then, right?" Jason asks. My alpha male.

"Wrong. But I'll at least let you think you make the decisions. I know how fragile your ego is," I say, smiling.

"Right. That's what most people say about me. I have self-esteem issues," Jason says, laughing.

"What's it like to be you?" I ask, nuzzling his neck. "To be so perfect and know it?"

"I'm far from perfect, Lacey. But I'm not going to wallow in my shortcomings either." He runs his hand down my back.

"Well, I think you're pretty perfect," I say, kissing his neck.

"I'll do my best to make you always think that," Jason says. He rests his head back on the tub and closes his eyes, obviously enjoying my kisses to his neck.

Jason's phone buzzes.

"Who can that be at this hour?" I ask, annoyed.

He reaches over the edge of the tub and picks up his cell that was lying on the bathroom floor. He smiles.

"Carrie had the kid. Chris has another son." Jason shows me a picture of a newborn that Chris just texted him.

"Aw, he's cute," I say. "Wow. Five kids. And he's your age. Doesn't that make you feel somewhat like an underachiever?"

"No, I figure I'll knock you up in a year."

"Oh, how you sweet-talk me. So that's your plan, huh? And why a year?" I ask, somewhat amused.

"Because I'm not ready to share you. I need you all to myself for some time," he says.

"And how many do you want?" I ask.

"As many as you want," Jason says, shrugging.

"You have no preference?" I ask. I find that hard to believe.

"No, not really. I'll give you whatever you want, Lacey. You should know that by now."

He pulls my hair so my head tilts back and plants a firm kiss on my lips. I can't help but smile as he's kissing me.

"I so love you," I whisper to him. I stroke his cheek with my hand and keep kissing him.

Epilogue

As it turns out, married life isn't much different than living with someone. Getting hitched in Las Vegas changed nothing between Jason and me. Our careers on the other hand, took a 180-degrees turn.

After Jason made lieutenant, he basically has been taken off the streets and put into an office. It's been a tough adjustment for him since he is more of a hands-on, street cop rather than an office paper pusher. He makes excuses here and there to get out of the office, but seventy percent of his time is now spent in the precinct, in his office.

NYPD's policy regarding married individuals is spouses cannot work in the same department with each other. As such, I've been waiting to find out what my future holds. Jason is staying put in the Major Crimes Unit since he is higher ranking and it would be more difficult to displace a lieutenant.

"Hey Burke, got a minute?" Captain Fuller approaches me while I'm at my desk. "I need to speak with you."

"Sure, Captain," I say and follow him into his office. He closes the door behind me. "First, let me just say you've been doing a great job since you began working for me a few years ago. You nabbed Rizzo when he was on his way out of the city, and if he had been able to get out of the city, we probably never would have seen him again. But you were able to bring him in without him knowing anything and without anyone getting hurt. And you also brought down someone in Internal Affairs which is something every cop in New York celebrated. And I just wanted to tell you that your work around here has been noticed by many."

"Anyway, I also wanted to let you know that Bill Chapmen is retiring."

"Finally, good for Bill Chapmen," I say. I don't know much about Bill Chapmen other than he's an older cop that has worked in Homicide most of his career. He's in the same precinct as Jason and me, a few floors up from us, so I have periodically run into him in the stairway. Other than the occasional "hello", our paths haven't crossed.

Captain Fuller smiles and continues, "Yeah, he has finally submitted his retirement papers. His last day is in two months. I'm letting you know that you're first in line for his position if you want it. If you don't want the job then let me know and we will fill it elsewhere. But you know the rules. Eventually you do have transfer into another unit. And this is definitely one of the more select positions."

A smile starts to spread across my face. Fuller is right. It is a great position and I am grateful for the opportunity. Most cops who become homicide detectives stay there until retired, so it's a difficult unit to transfer into because of the low turnover.

"Would I stay in this precinct?" I ask.

"Yes, you would be moved up to the third floor."

"Wow, thank you Captain. I'm definitely interested but need to think it over and discuss it with Jason. When do you need my answer?"

"How about two days? Let me know in two days either way. If you don't want it then it will get posted." Captain Fuller stands up and walks me to the door.

I practically skip back to my desk. I already know what my answer will be. And to not change locations is just icing on the cake.

"So, are we going to discuss it or what?" Jason asks me later that night as we are sitting in a sandwich shop near Times Square. We are at window seats eating dinner.

"Look, just tell me what you think I should do and that's what I'll do." Jason has been on the job longer and knows more people so if there are any downsides to this transfer he would know about it. And I figure that answer would make my control freak husband happy.

"Hmm, now if only you would say that tonight in bed," Jason says smirking and twisting my ponytail around his hand.

"Stop it. You're embarrassing me."

"You really are something. You have a no holds barred in the bedroom but then sitting here talking, you turn three shades of red." Jason is still smirking, looking at me like a lion eyes a gazelle.

I shrug my shoulders not really able to put into words the effect he has on me. A wedding ring didn't change that.

"Okay Laces, let's really discuss this," Jason untangles his hand from my hair and gives my neck a quick rub before sitting back and crossing his arms. "You and I can no longer work in the same unit so it's only a matter of time before it's not an option and you get told where to go. And if that happens, who knows the location you will be given."

"I know. It's pretty much a no brainer but I wanted to think about it in case there is a downfall I don't know about."

"The only downfall is you will get used to the smell of death," Jason says shrugging his shoulders. "It's something most cops get accustomed to anyway, you'll just get used to it faster."

"And of course, the biggest downfall is I won't be able to see as much of you during the day," I say, frowning. "No more joined at the hip."

"Don't count on it sweetheart. I'll still be keeping tabs on you, you're not ditching me that easily."

"You'll be busy, Jay. And I'll miss working with you but I also think we will be better off not being partners."

"Wow, and the truth comes out. Was I holding you back blondie?" Jason jokes.

"I didn't mean it like that. Like you said, I have terrible judgment sometimes and no fear that could get one of us killed one day."

"That's not quite true. You do have terrible judgment sometimes but you also have a knack for making things work out okay."

"I don't know. You and I are made from two very different molds. You gather information, I react to it. Like when we went to the Bronx. I would have just climbed over the wall at the pool and waited for someone to show up. But you talk to people and email sources to get more information before doing anything."

"I've just done it longer, that's all. And I know more people. I know not to exert my energy hanging around a pool all day when no one may show up."

"And it drives me crazy that you protect me more than yourself, whereas if you had any other partner you wouldn't act that way. You work twice as hard when you work with me to save my ass first and then yours." There I said it. No more sugarcoating.

"I can't change that. You will always come first." Jason takes my hand and kisses my palm.

"Right. But I also need you to save yourself. You're no good to me dead," I say.

"Transferring to Homicide is a very safe move for you. Much less dangerous. No more riding in backseats with Sal Rizzo so that makes me *very* happy. It will be a lot of talking and interviewing next of kin. You'll have to learn to be less reactionary and take more time to gather evidence." He smiles, leans over, and gives me a kiss on the cheek.

"I don't know Jay. I think you're wrong."

"About what?"

"I think you're wrong that working in Homicide will be less dangerous. I think my adventures have just begun," I say with a smirk on my face.

About The Author

A lifelong resident of the Syracuse, New York, area, A. M. Carroll lives with her husband, dog, and two horses. Nothing brings her more joy than spending time with family and friends.